The Retreat
A Kind of Lesbian Romance

by
Jane Retzig

The Retreat
A Kind of Lesbian Romance

First Published 2015

ISBN – 13:978-1518605161
ISBN – 10:1518605168

© Jane Retzig 2015

This novel is a work of fiction. Names, characters, places and incidents are either products of the author's imagination or are used fictitiously. Any other resemblance to actual events, locations or persons, living or dead, is entirely coincidental.

All rights reserved. Except for review, no part of this book may be reproduced in any form without permission in writing from the author.
janeretzig@gmail.com

For MDMK & TBD
With Love

Chapter One

Christmas Eve 2014

'Merry Christmas!' Natalie had seen Jo coming up the driveway. She'd felt her heart flip at the sight of her. And, flinging the door open before her oh-so-secret lover had even had chance to knock, she stood, back-lit and beautiful, smiling out into the darkness of a damp Christmas Eve tea-time with the warm, vinegary smell of baking mince pies wafting around her like some exotic perfume from the East. 'I'm just doing my Domestic Goddess routine in the kitchen,' she said, with the knowing twinkle Jo knew she reserved just for her.

On the doorstep, Jo blinked as the light from the hallway pooled around her. Her collar was turned up over the edges of her short, silver threaded, ash-blonde hair. And she was holding a pile of parcels that looked as if they could have been wrapped by a pack of not very tame gorillas.

'Merry Christmas sweetheart!' Jo had never quite got over her feeling of incredulity that someone like Natalie might actually be in love with someone like her. She felt it even more that night as she stepped into the house. The mirror in the hallway, catching her before she'd had chance to hoist her features into the natural face-lift of a smile, merely served to prove what she'd been thinking all day; that she was tired and, at forty five, just a little bit too old for all of this. In particular, she felt a whole lot too old for Natalie, who, both in and out of the mirror, was as gorgeously dark, sexy, and ridiculously bloody young looking as ever.

Trying to push her worries to one side, she kissed Natalie lightly and chastely on both cheeks, the parcels forming a convenient barrier between them. She was always cautious, in case the children were around, though the thrash metal coming from upstairs and clashing with 'A Fairytale of New York' from the radio in the kitchen suggested that Jacob, at least, was in his room, doing whatever fifteen year old boys do in the privacy of their bedrooms on the night before Christmas.

'Jake's upstairs wrapping his presents,' Natalie said, as if she'd read Jo's mind. She had an uncanny ability to do that, and it never failed to take Jo by surprise, comforting and unsettling her in almost equal degrees. 'And Alyssa's in the lounge,' she continued. 'I wouldn't go in there. She's listening to One Direction.' They both laughed indulgently at this, as if they'd never had crushes on pop stars when they were Alyssa's age.

Jo remembered that she had a message to pass on. 'Ed says he'll be home around seven thirty.'

'Okay.' Natalie shrugged. She didn't believe it. Particularly on Christmas Eve when he'd be in the pub, buying drinks for the few lads from work who weren't actually going to be driving that night, and, almost certainly, getting canned himself. She remembered the days when she would have cared about that. And the days when Jo could easily have been there with them all too, doing her best to keep up with the boys.

But the erstwhile hell raiser was surprisingly tame these days. She'd had a 'swift half'. Then she'd put a couple of 'entertainment' fifties behind the bar, made her excuses, and left.

'They think I've got boring in my old age,' she said wryly.

'Well, you've become a whole lot more interesting to *me!*' said Natalie.

Jo smiled at this, but Natalie could tell that something was wrong. She was trying to be light-hearted, but she looked tired and distant and her soft blue eyes were clouded, as they always were when she was hiding something. It wasn't the usual, 'hard day at the office' kind of tiredness. It was deeper than that. And it made her uneasy.

She was about to ask what was wrong when Alyssa decided to make an appearance.

'Hey, Auntie Jo!' Harry Styles and Co joined the cacophony in the hallway as Jacob's twin skittered out through the double doors from the lounge, accompanied by Dottie, the family's deranged five year old Cockapoo. Jo could just make out the chorus of 'Steal My Girl,' over the boys of the NYPD choir and something about bad boys, or bones, or some such thing, from upstairs.

Jo dropped her parcels and hugged Alyssa tightly before kneeling to tickle the dog, who had hurled herself onto her back in a tangle of black curls and was squiggling rapturously in anticipation of a tummy-rub from 'Auntie Jo'.

'Shall I put these under the tree?' Alyssa gave her present a surreptitious squeeze to see if she could guess its contents. Then, grinning cheekily at Jo. 'Did you decide to just screw 'em up in the wrapping paper then?'

Jo laughed. 'Well, you know me, all fingers and thumbs... The tree looks nice, did you and your mum decorate it?'

'We all did.'

'What? Even your dad?' Jo felt an unreasonable stab of jealousy at the thought.

'Nah!' Alyssa's voice dripped with adolescent scorn at the idea. 'Me and mum and Jake, *of course!*'

'Oh, right... well it's lovely!' Jo looked at the traditional Norway Spruce, dressed tastefully in silver and blue this year, with small white lights glittering like stars amidst its branches. She pictured Natalie, the perfect homemaker, with her perfect kids; Alyssa, blonde, and uncannily like her father, and Jake, an olive-skinned, though much skinnier, mini-me of his mum. She could even imagine the soundtrack - carols - probably from Kings, though they might have gone down-market and had 'Now That's What I Call Christmas' instead.

'Alyssa chose the colours,' said Natalie, directing a fond look at her daughter.

'Well... you did a *great* job sweetheart. Maybe I should get you to do mine next year.'

As she smiled at Alyssa, Jo was struck by just how precious this family was to her. In the old days, she'd always felt envious of exactly this kind of 'perfect family' with their 'perfect' family Christmases. She'd covered her envy with an inward desire to mock, or sneer. But even then, in her more honest moments, she'd known that she was simply longing for what she'd never had... a beautiful, clean, interested mum who cooked and cleaned and made the house smell nice and warm and cosy to come home to. She knew that the lure of all that had contributed to her falling in love with Nat. While Ed, Natalie's husband and Jo's best friend, had always, for some reason she'd never really understood, continued to keep himself on the outside of it, like a sulky kid who wouldn't come out of his room to play at the party.

She distracted herself by rubbing the dog, tickling her paws, teasing her with the tiny biscuits she always carried in her pockets for these special Dottie moments.

But the thought of Ed had drawn her back to what had happened at the office that morning and the knowledge that, sooner or later, she was going to have to tell Natalie about it and rip her 'perfect' world to shreds.

She felt a fresh spurt of anxiety as she stood up rather more creakily than she would have done in the past, leaving Dottie squirming for more. 'You're insatiable,' she said to the dog.

'She *is!* She's a total tart... especially for you!' Nat smiled into Jo's eyes while her daughter was distracted, perching the new presents on top of the pile already stacked under the tree. Jo knew she was still trying to encourage her into a lighter, maybe even, flirtatious, mood. Knowing Natalie well, she could see the anxiety building in her too, and she smiled to try to dispel it.

Alyssa stepped back from the parcels, with her head on one side. She looked even more like her father when she did that.

'Are you staying for tea?' she demanded. 'We've got mince pies.'

'No… Sorry love. There's a bit of a crisis at work.'

'There's *always* a crisis at work,' she pouted. 'But you *will* come to Midnight Mass with us later, at the Cathedral… right?'

'I'm not sure… It's a really busy night for us tonight. And some of the lads are off sick. I might even end up having to cover for them.' This was a lie. It was years since Jo had had to stand in for anyone at the chauffeuring branch of Ed's 'Classic Cars' company. As office manager, she'd got the whole thing running much too smoothly for that. She hated lying, though her years of living a double life with Nat had made her rather good at it. And now she found that she had to stop herself from wandering even further from the truth by hinting that 'Classic Cars' might have a special job to do for Santa – not because it wasn't true, but because she knew that Alyssa hadn't believed in any of that stuff since she was about ten. Sadly, Jo felt nostalgic for the days when she could have softened the let-down by presenting herself as one of Santa's Little Helpers for the night.

'You're as bad as Dad!' Alyssa's nose crinkled in disappointment. Just a few short years ago, she would have stuck out a petted lip, maybe even turned on the waterworks a bit, but she was much too 'grown up' to resort to such tactics now. 'Oh well... if you're not stopping, and we might not *even* see you later, I'd better go get Jake to say 'hello' before you go.'

She hurled herself up the stairs, two at a time, with Dottie yapping at her heels all the way.

Her mother sighed. 'She'll break her neck one of these days,' she said. 'Seriously though – I thought you *were* coming to the Cathedral?'

Jo heard the deflation in her voice. She looked away.

'It would have meant a lot to her. She's going to be singing the solo in 'Hallelujah'. The girl who was supposed to be doing it has gone down with laryngitis.'

Jo raised an eyebrow. 'Hallelujah, as in Leonard Cohen...? Isn't that a bit "Adult Advisory" for a school choir?' she asked.

Natalie thought of the song with its themes of adultery and betrayal, and wondered if she ought to feel guilty. She *had* done in the early days and she guessed that Jo still did. But somehow, their relationship had stopped feeling wrong to her a very long time ago. 'Well, it's practically a Christmas carol since the Alexandra Burke version. And let's face it. If you took out all the sex and violence, The Bible would be the size of 'TV Quick'.'

'Hey, Auntie Jo!' yelled Jacob from the landing.
'Hi Jake!'
'Thanks for my pressie!'
'You're welcome!'
'What is it?'
'That's for me to know and you to find out... But not before tomorrow morning.'
'Okay, I'll text you when I've opened it. Gotta go, sorry... I'm on the phone!'
'Okay Jake...'bye!'

'He'll be talking to his new girlfriend,' explained Natalie, with a little grimace. 'Her name's Tamzin. She's fifteen and looks like Taylor Swift. They terrify me. Thank goodness Alyssa's going through a holy phase at least... I just hope it lasts long enough for her to develop a bit of common sense to go with her hormones.'

They both stood, looking expectantly up the stairs, waiting for Alyssa to re-appear, but she seemed to have forgotten 'One Direction' and gone into her own room too. The dog, shut out, wandered back downstairs and went across to snuffle at the parcels. Natalie moved one of them out of her reach. 'Diabetic chocolates for Ed's gran,' she said. 'For some reason the daft dog still finds them irresistible.'

Jo nodded sympathetically, remembering the Christmas they'd found that out the hard way.

She wondered if this was a safe time to talk.

Nat could see that she was about to say something. She felt the familiar sense of dread that always tugged at her when she saw Jo struggling like this... The fear that their relationship had become too hard for her – that she was going to end it.

Jo decided to take the plunge. 'I think you should see this,' she said, reaching in her pocket and handing a crumpled Christmas card to Natalie.

It was fairly traditional - a picture of a robin on a snow-topped wall with a sprinkle of glitter lending a slight grittiness to its surface. It was the kind of card one of the mechanics might have given to Jo, usually with just a name scrawled inside, occasionally with an unintended greasy fingerprint, and sometimes, touchingly, with a clumsy message of thanks for some kindness during the year.

This was none of the above.

Nat opened it, and gasped.

The card was unsigned.

On the left hand side, someone had written in thick capitals in blue biro,

I KNOW ABOUT YOU AND NATALIE.

'*Shit!*' Natalie's voice, when she finally found it, sounded faint over the pounding in her ears. Her stomach felt like she was in a lift that had suddenly lurched downwards. 'Have you any idea who....?'

'... might have sent it?' Jo finished her sentence as she hesitated. 'No. Not the foggiest.'

'But there must be some clues... Where did you get it...? At home...? At the office...?'

Jo sighed. 'It was on my desk at the office, but I don't know when it arrived, or whether it was hand delivered, or came in the post.... *I know... I know...*' she raised her hands. She was notoriously untidy, and she could see what Nat was thinking. That her desk always looked like it had been freshly ransacked by burglars. Nat had always been bemused that Jo could be such an efficient manager when she lived and worked in such apparent chaos. It had been something she'd been critical of in the early days. But now she more often smiled indulgently and teased her about it.

There was no evidence of that smile now.

Jo struggled on. 'We always get *loads* of cards and I've just been opening them and putting them in a pile for when I could find some string to hang them from. Then I found the string a couple of days ago but I couldn't find the drawing pins. And we've been so busy, I only got round to tracking *those* down this morning.'

'Don't you even *read* them when they arrive?'

Jo's shoulders sagged despondently. 'Not always… no. Not if the phone's ringing or I've got one of the lads wanting something. You know what it's like in there. It's hell on wheels, especially in the run-up to Christmas. I guess it must have arrived a few days ago though. It was near the bottom of the pile.'

Picturing herself at her desk that morning, Jo remembered the mixed feelings of shame, exposure and something akin to terror that had flooded through her as she read the card. They must have shown on her face, because, Ed, not normally known for his sensitivity, had looked up from ordering Jensen Interceptor spares on his computer and asked if she was alright.

Jo saw those same feelings crashing over Natalie now as she slumped against the banister of the open plan staircase. She'd gone pale.

Jo wondered, anxiously, if she was going to cry.

'You should have called me,' she said.

'I couldn't, Ed was there… And anyway, I didn't want to worry you.'

'So you kept this to yourself all day? God, Jo, when will you learn that you don't have to manage everything on your own?'

'I'm sorry.'

'What are we going to do?'

'I don't know.' Jo had thought of little else since that morning. She struggled to breathe. 'I think maybe we have to stop seeing each other.'

Now, damn it, Natalie *was* crying. 'I can't,' she was saying. 'Oh God, I can't. How could I be without you now?'

Jo wanted nothing more than to take her in her arms. Not being able to do those natural things had always been hard. It felt unbearable now. She glanced anxiously up the stairs to make sure the kids couldn't hear. 'I think we might have to.'

'But I *can't!*'

It frightened Jo when she talked like that. 'But you have all this….' she tried to sound reasonable. 'Ed loves you….You have two beautiful, well-adjusted kids…' *The material comforts too,* she thought. *The things that mattered when you didn't have them.* 'You've got this lovely house… nice car….. great holidays…'

'I hate holidays. I hate being without you!'

'… good food on the table…' Jo ploughed on. God knows, she knew only too well what it was like to be without all that.

'It isn't enough.'

'Well, it would be more than enough for most people. This would be heaven for most people.'

'Well, I'm not most people, and it's not enough for me. It never *was.* You know that.'

They stared helplessly at each other in the hallway.

And from the kitchen came the sharp, insidious smell of mince pies burning.

-0-0-0-

Having told Alyssa that she had to work, Jo felt honour bound to go back to the office. But by 10pm, she was tired and feeling slightly uneasy, alone in the portacabin that served as the nerve-centre of 'Edward Mason Classic Cars', the company Ed's dad had created for him as a 21st Birthday present way back in 1990.

Back in the old days, Ed and Jo had pretty much comprised the entire company. Two best friends 'daft as brushes', Ed in the garage, Jo in the office, and both of them doing the chauffeuring work in the Rolls Royce Silver Cloud and the creamy white Bentley Continental Ed had bought at auction and lovingly restored during his college days. Back then, everything had seemed like fun. The uniforms - traditional grey - shirt and tie for both of them, and a peeked cap with the company badge on it. Ed trying to get the oil from under his finger nails before a big job. Jo succumbing to gender stereotyping and making sure their shirts were ironed. Weddings, graduation ceremonies, romantic drives along the coastline... people spilling champagne and canapés and getting up to all sorts in the back.

It was a much bigger company now – nationwide. And financially, the situation was still the same. Ed owned it. And Jo worked for him. That had always been the deal. It had been enshrined by Ed's father who, after all, had put up the money, and didn't want Ed in partnership with somebody as totally 'wrong side of the tracks' as Jo.

Jo turned off her computer and looked around. The small, rather sad-looking, artificial Christmas tree winked at her from the corner and reminded her of the much smarter tree at Natalie's. And the cards, strung now, like washing, on two eight foot lines across the wall, dragged her mind back to the message on the card in her pocket. She wondered if she should tear it up and throw it away, but something made her feel that she should keep it, even though she felt contaminated by its presence so close to her.

Sighing, she turned off the tree lights and glanced at her watch, figuring that some of the lads would probably still be in the pub. Reluctant to go home to an empty house, she reached for her coat and headed out into the damp night air in the direction of 'The Tapsters Arms'.

-0-0-0-

Ed's big black Range Rover was still in the car park when she got there. And Bill Jones, the oldest and most reliable of their drivers, was just coming out of the pub.

He grinned apologetically at Jo when he saw her. 'I'm just off home now,' he said. 'If I'm not back by ten thirty, "Her Indoors" will have me guts for garters.'

'You can't kid a kidder Bill!... Bet you're on a promise!'

She laughed affectionately as he squirmed. Fiona, Bill's gentle and very laid-back wife was a good friend of hers, and one of the very few people she trusted to cover for her at the office when she was on holiday or having a rare weekend off. Fiona's rottweiler image was useful then. It kept the lads on their toes when she was away. But Jo knew full well that her alleged scariness was a convenient excuse for Bill to get home for the cuddles, cocoa and early night he'd probably been looking forward to all day.

Bill unlocked his car, an ancient, but lovingly maintained, grey Volvo.

'Party's only just getting started in there,' he added, with a little grimace. 'They've got Vodka Red Bulls lined up now.'

'Did Ed get a lift home?' Jo gestured in the direction of the Range Rover.

'Nah,' he shrugged. 'Still in there… drunk as a lord!'

Jo could see that he wasn't saying what he was thinking – that Ed was an idiot who didn't realise what a lucky b****d he was.

She was careful not to let her own feelings show too.

'Oh well,' she said. 'I hope you and Fiona have a wonderful Christmas.'

'You too lass…. hope you're not going to be working all through it. You deserve a break.'

'Thanks Bill.' Touched by his concern, she waved as he reversed. She knew from the on-line bookings that he, at least, was off till Boxing Day, cosy at home with his wife and slippers.

She started to walk towards the pub, then stopped, struggled with herself for a moment, and turned back to her own car. If Ed couldn't be bothered to be with his own wife and kids on the most family-orientated night of the year, then she damn-well could.

She pulled out of the car park and headed for town.

-0-0-0-

The Cathedral was a hidden gem in a tired and generally depressed city. Gradually morphing over the centuries from its low key Norman beginnings, it was tucked away in a forgotten quarter of town where, in the late 19th century, German textile merchants had built grand offices to capitalise on the booming wool trade. The area had seen 'green shoots' of development again recently, with some of the more architecturally impressive of the Victorian buildings renovated and turned into new office units and flats. There were signs of a burgeoning service industry too. A "Cappuccino and Wrap" bar, "Muscles" gym, and 'Ultrawox', a trendy restaurant with a Chinese/Thai fusion buffet. They'd sprung up in excited anticipation of the hoped-for influx of new office workers and residents. But the recovery had only just begun, and as Jo pulled into the windswept and eerie car park, she was flooded with memories of how rundown it had been when she was in her teens - a scholarship girl at the Grammar School (single-sex then, but merged with the boys now), twenty minutes' walk away over the dual carriageway that shushed quietly along the top of the hill.

The school had always had a special relationship with the cathedral. Staunchly 'C of E', they held their 'Founders' Day', 'Remembrance' and 'Carol' services there each year. And the school choir regularly performed concerts with the Cathedral choristers. As a kid, she'd often been herded with her maroon-clad schoolmates through the urine scented underpass; past the sad, sun-starved municipal bedding plants, graffitied walls and occasional flasher emboldened at the thought of school girls; down through the precipitous streets and boarded up buildings rustling with rubbish; into the cool, time-warped sanctuary of the Cathedral.

Jo had always thought it was a beautiful place, with its stark stone walls and worn floor and scent of candlewax and cut flowers and wood. She'd loved the pre-

Raphaelite stained glass sweeping upwards and, on sunny days, casting rainbows over the pews. She'd felt sad at the regimental flags by the big brass plaque commemorating 'Our Glorious Dead' while a trumpeter played the 'Last Post'. She'd always been keenly aware, with her elder brother enlisted in the army, that one day the name Liam Cooper could be engraved there too. And, like all the kids, she'd looked forward to, and enjoyed the carols on the last day of school that signified, finally, that the waiting was over, and the Christmas holidays had begun.

Jo had never been religious in any way. She'd seen far too much of the legacy of her mother's guilt-ridden Catholic upbringing for that. She barely knew the side of her family who owned rag and bone carts and went to Mass and played Three Card Brag with the priest, though most of them lived only a few streets away on the other side of the estate where she'd grown up. They hated her father, bad boy Barry Cooper, the handsome 'prodder' who'd swept her mum off her seventeen year old feet and knocked her up in a back alley behind the Mecca Ballroom, while the other kids were inside smooching to 'It's Now or Never'. Jo wasn't daft. She knew that her mum's parents had wanted to give Liam to the nuns for adoption. That she'd taken a dizzying hormone-fuelled leap from frying pan into fire when she rejected all of that and married Barry in a church not one of them would set foot in. And that she'd probably regretted it ever since. Jo's mum lost her family that day. And the fear of eternal damnation had eaten away at her health and happiness ever since.

So Jo wasn't about to succumb to religious temptation in a hurry. And by the time she was in sixth form, she'd acquired a sophisticated older girlfriend and a sex life that the church would most definitely not have approved of. She had a slight, secret contempt for the kids who prayed and crossed themselves in all the right places while she was passing on notes with jokes like 'Jesus Saves – put him in goal', or giggling when the organist, who played in a rock band in his spare time, sneaked a few bars of 'Burning of the Midnight Lamp' into the intro to the school anthem at a particularly turgid Founders Day service.

It felt strange now for Jo to re-enter that long ago teenage space in a much more repentant frame of mind, and find it very much as she'd left it – almost as if it had been waiting for her. It was still candle-lit, as it had been on her last carol service of sixth form. There were no rows of maroon, of course – and no noticeable giggles. But the space was still full of people in damp woollen coats giving off the same dull wet-sheep kind of smell, with scarves and hats, and coughs and low, murmuring voices that sounded like the drone of some Tibetan chant over a meandering festive fugue with not the slightest hint of Hendrix.

For a moment, as she stared down the long sweep of the central aisle, towards the altar, with its golden cross, she felt the same dizzying feeling she had experienced when she'd read the accusation on the Christmas card. A sense of panic swept through her, making her want to turn and run. But then she spotted Natalie with Jacob, scrunched down in the pew in his beanie, shoulders hunched up towards his ears as he played some game on his phone, and she remembered why she had decided to come.

As she squeezed in to join them, Natalie's initial look of surprise lifted into a brilliant smile of gratitude and love.

And later, as Alyssa's perfect voice soured in an ascent of Hallelujahs, and tears ran down her mother's cheeks, Jo's troubled heart was soothed by the warmth of her lover's hand creeping over hers under cover of their coats in the still, cool, half-light of the church.

-0-0-0-

On the way home, Natalie was comforted by the sight of Jo's car just behind them, turning finally with a little flash of her headlights, on the last left before the bigger houses, security cameras and electric gates of her own street.

There was no sign of Ed's SUV on the driveway, so she guessed that he'd at least had the good sense to get a lift or a taxi. But she knew he was home because he'd (probably accidentally) switched off the outside lights as he'd gone in. And, in the kitchen, the fridge door was open, the kettle still warm, a smear of milk and water on the worktop where he'd made a cup of tea before splashing most of it on the stairs on his way up to bed.

Alyssa, who'd been flushed and exhilarated till then, looked anxious at the sight of it.

Jake was unreadable.

'Okay,' said their mother, in the crisp, overly jolly tone she always reverted to at times like this. 'Does anyone want supper?'

They shrugged their shoulders, subdued. And she knew they were fearful of a row.

'I'm off to bed,' said Jake.

'Me too,' said his sister. But she held onto her mum just a little bit longer than usual when she kissed her goodnight.

-0-0-0-

Ed was lying on his back in bed snoring. His shirt and trousers were inside-out on the floor. He had his arm round Dottie, who was curled up on the pillow beside him, breathing dog's breath into his face. She lifted her head and wagged the end of her tail as Natalie came into the room but showed no other sign of moving.

The room smelt of alcohol and the kebab Ed had brought home with him. The greasy remains were on the bedside table. Natalie bundled them into their wrapper and took them downstairs to the bin.

Then, wearily, she climbed back upstairs to the guest bedroom, where she so often slept these days.

Under the covers, like a kid reading by torchlight, she texted, 'God, I love you.'

Her phone flashed silently and almost immediately with a message back from Jo.

'God I love you too,' it said.

And tears sprang into her eyes again as she thought of the card and the threat of the words inside it.

Chapter Two

Boxing Day 2014

'I'll just take Dottie out for her walk.'

To Natalie's relief, none of the family offered to come with her; Jacob being pre-occupied with his X Box, Alyssa busy on Facebook, and Ed still flat-out, snoring in bed after the effort of spending the whole of Christmas Day at home, with his family.

Five years ago, when Jake and Alyssa had nagged incessantly for a puppy, swearing that they would look after it, Natalie had said 'No,' knowing that the responsibility would fall on her. She'd been furious with Ed for just turning up one evening with the tiny bundle of wriggling energy, soon to be known as Dottie, under his arm. He'd bought her, along with a tiny red collar and lead and a tin of cheap dog food that upset her stomach, from 'some bloke at the pub'. It was the kind of thing Ed did from time to time. A crazy, spontaneous, short-sighted gesture that undermined her and curried favour with the kids.

So she always felt that there was some karmic justice in the fact that the dog furnished her with an excuse to escape from the house on a regular basis, creating ideal cover for her clandestine visits to Jo, who she yearned for constantly, as if a part of herself were missing.

Today, after the dreadful revelation of Christmas Eve, the pull towards Jo was even stronger than usual. Ever since she'd seen the card, Natalie had felt a heaviness in her chest that wouldn't lift. It had stayed with her all through Christmas Day. All through the stuffing of the turkey and the peeling of the sprouts, and the last minute rush to get everything on the table, still hot and edible. It undermined the pretence at jollity with the in-laws, the crackers and paper hats and charades. It was still there after several glasses of champagne, the Christmas 'Soaps', and the festive episodes of 'Call the Midwife' and 'Downton Abbey' that everyone had insisted they wanted to watch, and snored all the way through.

It pressed on her now, making it hard to breathe, as she shut the door quietly, leaving the house with Dottie, low to the ground, tail whirling, panting and straining at the leash in her excitement to be off.

It was good to be out in the fresh air.

The road outside felt deserted. It was as if the whole world had fallen into a Christmas coma and wouldn't reawaken till after the New Year. And the birds, emboldened by the lack of human traffic, were singing as if spring had already arrived, high in the bare branches of the trees, against a light grey sky.

It said a lot about the impact of the anonymous card that Natalie found herself checking behind her several times on the ten minutes' walk from her rather large house to Jo's very much smaller one, tucked away, thankfully, in a space most of Nat's neighbours were unlikely to frequent, just down the road, in a small seventies cluster, behind the Co-op and the post office.

She struggled to find the words for how she felt. She was frightened, of course, but she also felt violated. She wondered how much their accuser had spied on them when they were absorbed in each other and careless of who might be watching. She wished she could put that out of her mind, but she couldn't. It was as if her love for Jo, which had always felt so pure in the privacy of her own heart, had suddenly been dragged out onto the streets, shaking in terror and humiliation, for any passing stranger to see and judge and spit upon.

She glanced around furtively again when she reached the bottom of Jo's street, ready to just keep walking if anybody was obviously on the snoop. For a moment, she thought she saw a curtain twitching at the house opposite. Jo had told her that the elderly lady who lived there was a bit eccentric and more than a little nosey. She was unlikely to know Ed though. So, while she may see Natalie as a girlfriend of Jo's, there was little risk of her reading any more into it than that.

Taking a deep breath, Nat held her head high and walked up the short driveway to her lover's door.

-0-0-0-

Jo was in her dressing gown. Her hair was still damp and spiky from a late shower. She'd just been rubbing it dry with the towel she'd draped round her neck like a scarf as she came to answer the door. Natalie leaned in to kiss her on the cheek, like any friend, visiting.

She smelt of shampoo, with a hint of rosemary.

'You shouldn't be here,' she said, stepping aside, nonetheless, to let her in.

'Well, you shouldn't have been at the cathedral, but you came.'

Nat released Dottie, who ran to rub herself on the silk rug in the hallway before disappearing into the lounge to see if there was any chocolate to be found.

'It's okay,' said Jo. 'There's no food in there.... And you *really* shouldn't be here.'

'I know, but I need to talk to you…. Can I wash my hands please? I've just put Dottie's poo bags in your wheelie bin.'

'You say the sexiest things!'

'I know. And I'm only just getting warmed up.'

They were flirting. They couldn't help themselves. Jo forced herself to put a lid on it. 'Would you like a coffee or something?' she asked in that more official tone Natalie had already come to hate. 'I've just made some.'

'Well, in that case….' She followed Jo into the kitchen and washed her hands under the cold tap. It always took forever for Jo's water to warm up anyway. 'How was your Christmas?'

'Oh, you know… the usual. Everybody drunk and maudlin by three… All screaming at each other by five…. Tears and sick before bedtime.' She didn't fill in the gaps; the bruises on her mother's arm that may have been just from bumping into things like she said; the turkey not even in the oven when she arrived at twelve; her father trying to tap her for cash, as always. 'How was yours?'

'Okay, you know. Jacob was over the moon with his 'Young Libertine' T-shirt. How did you manage to get it signed by the band?'

'One of the drivers at work knows the drummer. Nice guy apparently. I'm glad he liked it.'

'*Liked* it?... He loves it. It's on Facebook already… Thirty Likes!' She reached for the mug as Jo handed it to her, wrapping her fingers around it for comfort, though she wasn't particularly cold. It smelt good. Jo's coffee was always strong and rich – Italian blend. 'I've been thinking,' she said.

'Sounds ominous.'

'No… it isn't!' She wanted to say, *Don't fob me off like this Jo. You have no right to make this decision alone.* But she couldn't. Instead, in a mild tone that belied the turmoil underneath, she asked, 'Can we go upstairs?'

'Uh-huh!' Jo shook her head.

'Not to do anything. I promise. It's just… I want to hold you. Is that so wrong?'

It *felt* wrong to Jo, and always had. It wasn't even so much the idea of Natalie being unfaithful to Ed. She didn't actually blame her for that. No, it was more the fact that *she* was being unfaithful to Ed. The treacherous best friend, sneaking around behind his back, playing fast and loose with his wife. Wasn't that the ultimate in betrayal? She thought so. She felt ashamed whenever she thought of it. So for a lot of the time she tried not to. Most of the time, even, she'd managed to be quite successful in that. Not since the card though. There was something about being accused like that that made the whole thing very hard to shove back in the 'don't go there' drawer.

But Jo never could say no to Natalie, so she said 'Okay,' and stepped back to follow Natalie up the stairs. And she knew it *would* be to do something. It always was.

-0-0-0-

The bed was still unmade. It felt clean and crumpled and familiar and safe.

Natalie snuggled into Jo's arms, feeling her tension melting as it always did when she could feel her lover's firm, warm body against her own.

The coffee, abandoned, cooled on the bedside table.

'Look… I really *have* been thinking…' Just in case this was the last time, she tried to memorise the pale blue walls; the TV in the corner where Jo occasionally watched 'Xena Warrior Princess' DVDs and repeats of 'Everybody Loves Raymond'; the framed photograph of the four of them on a day trip to Alton Towers for the kids' tenth Birthday; the latest Cari Hunter paperback on the bedside table…. 'I think we need to go public,' she said.

She felt Jo tense beside her. 'Are you crazy?'

'People would be shocked initially, I know. But they'd get over it. The kids adore you. Ed would be upset, but he'd move on. And I think, in a way, he might even be relieved. Let's face it… There must be at least five women at the tennis club who'd be scratching each other's eyes out to console him.'

Jo pulled away from her. She reached out for her own coffee and took a gulp. Natalie knew she was strengthening herself against her. 'No,' she said. 'Ed would be devastated and that would make him mean and vindictive. And the kids would never forgive me for splitting up the family. They'd become surly and resentful and start doing badly at school and take drugs and drive too fast just to spite us. And we'd feel so *fucking* guilty and torn about it all that we'd start believing all the awful things they said about us and start arguing, and forget why we ever loved each other in the first place.'

'God, sweetheart! Where the hell are you getting all *that* from? It really doesn't *have* to be like that.'

'Of course it does… It always *is*…. Have you never read 'Anna Karenina'?'

'We're living in 21st century Britain, not Tsarist Russia. It's different now.'

'See! We're arguing already!'

'You are *so* stubborn Jo…. Please… just promise me you'll think about it.'

Jo sighed and shook her head.

Natalie felt her stomach lurch. 'Please,' she said.

'I just don't see…'

'Shush….' Nat touched her fingers to her lips to stop her talking. She felt her eyes filling with tears. 'Please….'

'Okay. But the answer's still going to be the same.'

Fear filled Natalie then, tearing at the breath in her chest, making her throat feel cold, like when you've run too fast, too far. She pulled Jo towards her.

'If the answer's going to be the same,' she said, surprised at the hoarseness in her voice. 'You'd better make love to me right now. You owe me that much if you're going to condemn me to spending the rest of my life without you.'

-0-0-0-

It was rushed, as it so often had to be. It was also fierce and lost and full of grief. But while they were still entwined in each other, while they breathed the same air, sliding in each other's wetness, while they cried out in each other's arms, it gave them the temporary illusion that nothing really had changed.

After Natalie had gone, Jo sank down onto the stairs and buried her head in her hands. She felt so bereft she wanted to wail her pain out into the empty air. She dug her fingers against her eyelids to stop the tears from coming.

She didn't notice the clicking of claws on the oak flooring at first.

Or the wet nose snuffling at her ankles.

Then she did.

'Shit!' She leapt to her feet, just as the doorbell rang.

'Forgot the frigging dog!' said Nat, standing in the doorway.

They collapsed into hysterical laughter as Dottie joined in and yapped herself silly around their feet.

-0-0-0-

At 8pm it started to snow. Jo watched it from her window, settling first as slush on the wet pavements and roads, then slowly blanketing and muffling the estate.

She thought of Natalie, at home with Ed and the kids, settling into their evening in front of the fire, curtains drawn, cosy.

And she remembered Natalie's body against hers, opening for her, arching against her... the little cry she'd made, biting her lip as she came softly, like the snow falling now.

What kind of a person does that with their best friend's wife?

Her laptop was open on the table in front of her. She'd been doing the business accounts, like the 'sad fuck' she was, with nothing better to do on Boxing Day.

'Who am I really?' she typed into Google, suddenly, on a whim.

It had been a rhetorical question. So she was surprised at how many results flashed up on the screen. Life coaching organisations, Yahoo questions, song lyrics. One entry caught her eye, hallway down the second page:

BRANDON HOUSE
Personal Retreats in the Heart of North Yorkshire
Are you feeling lost, alone, ashamed, or guilty?
Maybe you're wondering
  Who am I really?

How did I get here?
How can I find a way forward?

There was something about the way the words spoke to her that seemed spookily co-incidental, even for a dyed-in-the-wool sceptic like Jo. And she reckoned if someone had decided to echo her feelings quite so specifically, their answer must, at least, be worth considering. Feeling nervous all of a sudden, she leaned forward on her chair, and read on…

-0-0-0-

Sister Ulrika's footsteps echoed down the stone passageway to the office. She usually checked for voice and e-mail first thing in the morning and then again, at night just before Compline, the final service of the day. Through the window, in the light by the entrance to the chapel, she could see the snow, still falling on the garden in flakes the size of 50 pence pieces, hard and fast, creating white woolly caps on the statues of the saints and on the head of the tiny stone sparrow perched on the finger of St Francis.

It had been a busy Christmas with twenty guests swelling the numbers at the centre over the actual Christmas break, though the party of sixteen from Our Lady of Sorrows were due to leave after breakfast the next morning, hopefully spiritually nourished, creating a temporary lull before the next influx over New Year.

Most people booked their time at the centre, especially over the 'festive season' a long way in advance. Many of them were lonely - retired priests of one denomination or another; older, single people who couldn't face being 'charity cases' in other people's homes; or those who were newly struggling with divorce or bereavement. They booked early because places were limited and they didn't want to be disappointed. So the last thing Ulrika expected on a snowy Boxing Day evening was an enquiry from a potential new retreatant. Especially one who had so little idea about how things worked that they were hoping to arrive tomorrow.

'Dear Sir or Madam,' said the email. *'Do you have any spaces? I could come tomorrow and stay for a few days. I've got something I need to sort out. Yours faithfully, Joanne Cooper.'*

Ulrika guessed that, at such short notice and this time of year, an enquiry like that must have been prompted by a fairly major crisis. And something about the starkness of it tugged at her heart.

Sitting at the computer, her soft-lined face illuminated by the desk lamp, she replied:

'Dear Joanne, If the weather does not prevent you, you are very welcome to join us tomorrow. I am attaching a booking form. Yours sincerely, Ulrika.'

-0-0-0-

Sister Ulrika always prayed for visitors to the centre in the days prior to their arrival.

So that night she added Jo's name to her list.

Ever since she came to this place, in the autumn of 1998, her room had been her sanctuary. In childhood, she always had to share with her older sisters, three of them, top and tailing in an ancient double bed that had once belonged to her great grandparents. At the convent of the Blessed Virgin, where she had taken her vows, her room had been tiny, like a prison cell, with a cobwebby window six feet up on the bare wall and nothing to distract her from her thoughts. But here, in the daytime, there was a proper window, with a view over the gardens and the fells. The mattress on the single bed was only slightly lumpy. And the 1930's wardrobe, of dark, varnished wood with matching drawers, reminded her of the bedroom furniture in her parents' room at home, where sometimes, when she was still small and the other children had gone to school, she had been allowed to play with the tortoiseshell hairbrush and hand mirror that lay lovingly dusted on the crocheted mat on her mother's dressing table.

In the old days, before the arthritis had rendered it impossible, Ulrika had always knelt to pray. Now she sat, at her desk, head bowed, reading glasses forgotten and still perched on the end of her nose. On the wall above her hung a crucifix - Christ's broken body sagging on the cross. To her right, on a small bookcase from MFI that had seen better days, were some of her favourite books: Revelations of Divine Love, The Cloud of Unknowing, The Interior Castle, and The Dark Night of the Soul. There were plenty of other books if she needed them in the library, but she liked to keep these close, familiar and thumbed, like friends to turn to at the close of day.

Sometimes, working through the people she must pray for, the names became automatic, a kind of rote, disconnected from the flesh and blood people who belonged to them, as her mind drifted off onto other things. But she found herself tugged back when she came to Joanne's name – feeling again the anguish she had sensed in the short, almost casual email. And as she mentally commended this new guest to the protection of the Almighty, she prayed, not only for her safety on her journey tomorrow through the snow, but also for the well-being of the people Jo might love, and for their safe passage through the dangers of the days ahead.

-0-0-0-

If Jo had known that she was being prayed for, she would probably have decided not to go. As it was, misled by the rather vague wording of the website with its emphasis on its beautiful Dales location, home cooking, single rooms, and personal and group meditation instruction, she'd already made the completely false assumption that the Retreat Centre was Buddhist; and Ulrika, perhaps because of some sub-conscious link between the name and the snow falling outside… an icy Swedish blonde.

And so, she was in a state of ignorance about quite what she'd signed up for as she texted Ed to ask if it would be okay for her to take a long weekend of unscheduled leave.

She didn't think there'd be a problem taking the time off. She'd already contacted Fiona, who was perfectly happy to cover the office for her, particularly as Bill was going to be working. Over the years, Jo had got the business running like clockwork anyway. And most of the drivers were perfectly capable of just getting on and looking after themselves for a day or two, regardless of whether 'The Boss' was keeping a beady eye on them or not.

Ed's reply came back almost by return, suggesting that, as usual, he was giving rather more attention to his iPhone than he should have been on a Boxing Day evening with his family.

His message, short, as always, simply said 'No probs.'

Relieved, Jo applied herself to the much harder job of explaining herself to Nat.

She'd typed and deleted her message several times before she wrote: 'Sweetheart, I'm going away for a few days. Some sort of retreat thing. I don't think there'll be any mobile reception. Sorry....' She hesitated before typing 'Please don't ever doubt how much I love you'. She always feared that one day Ed might see one of these texts. But she knew she wouldn't be able to go without sending it. And she knew how carefully Natalie guarded her phone.

-0-0-0-

Natalie always kept her mobile on 'silent', but Ed saw it flash as the text came through. He noticed that she flushed slightly and bit her lip as she saw the name on the screen. And he knew who it was from.

'Who's that?' he asked.

The pain in her eyes seared through him as he watched her reading the message.

'Just Jo,' she said. 'She says she hopes that her being away won't cause too much extra work for you.'

She hit delete before he could come and see the message for himself.

-0-0-0-

'It's still snowing.' It was 11pm and Ed was standing by the bedroom window in his T-shirt and pyjama bottoms. They were new – royal blue – a Christmas present from the kids. His reflection, hazy and slightly soft-focused in the double-glazed window told him he'd need to lose a few pounds after Christmas. Otherwise, he told himself, he was still in 'good nick' for his age, despite his lifestyle, and regardless of whether or not his wife ever seemed to notice anymore.

She was already in bed, reading. He noticed, resentfully, that it was the book Jo had bought her for Christmas, an illustrated Folio edition of 'Wuthering Heights'. The light from the bedside lamp poured over her like liquid gold, adding a silky glow to her skin. One strap of her camisole had slipped down over her shoulder as she read. It made the soft material bunch away a little from her left breast, and added a touch of eroticism that made his breath rasp in his throat. Despite himself, he wanted to touch her, in awe of the beauty that had always made him weak.

'What's going on with Jo?' he asked, checking for any tell-tale sign of tension in his voice and deciding that it sounded innocent enough. He thought, with some bitterness, that he had become rather good at hiding his feelings over the past few weeks.

Natalie stiffened and lost her place in her book. She told herself she needed to stop being so jumpy. 'How should *I* know?' She was aiming for nonchalance and succeeded only in sounding a bit stroppy and defensive.

'I thought you two were thick as thieves these days.'

'Not really,' Nat tried to inject a lighter tone into this. 'You know how she is. She's probably met some woman over Christmas and taken her off on a jaunt.' Despite her best efforts, her voice trembled, imagining that, someday, this may be exactly what she would have to endure.

Ed's eyes narrowed as he heard how expertly she lied to him.

He knew how vulnerable she was now that he'd managed to scare Jo out of the picture.

And he felt himself hardening at the thought of that.

Chapter Three

Saturday 27th December 2014

The next morning dawned icy and still dusted with snow. The grey-scale sky slowly turned pink and baby blue as Jo de-iced her car. It was a silver Astra, nice and sensible and family oriented, as befitted her status as unofficial second taxi driver for Ed and Natalie's kids.

Unofficial dog-transporter too, she thought, looking at the muddy dog hammock fastened in the back. Baulking at the idea of having to move it, she put her walking boots into the passenger footwell, and shoved her bag onto the front seat, with the seat belt around it to stop it falling off.

Halfway out of the drive, and grateful for the heated steering wheel, she paused to let the paper boy slither past on his bike. He was a sweet kid - a bit Harry Potter-ish and flushed by his exertions in the cold. His shoulder drooped and his bike listed under the uneven weight of his huge orange fluorescent delivery bag.

He nearly skidded into a lamp post as he looked up at her and waved.

Jo waved back sympathetically. She knew he came from the estate where she'd grown up and where her parents still lived. His mother had, in fact, been a good friend of hers at primary school. But then she'd got the scholarship and become a 'Grammar Bug', and none of the kids at home wanted to be her friend anymore. Sometimes Jo wondered how different her life might have been if her teacher hadn't entered her for that scholarship exam. It had probably seemed like the best thing to do with a kid from the estate who, even at the age of ten, was adamant that she wanted to be 'an entrepreneur like Richard Branson'. And it had certainly opened doors for her that might otherwise have taken a lot more bashing to get through. But it had turned her into an outsider, both at home, and at school, where her second hand uniform, druggy brother, and dodgy postcode had ensured that most of the kids didn't really want to have very much to do with her. Jo had cared deeply about this at the time, though she was fairly phlegmatic about it now. Sometimes, she'd even been known to joke that it had saved them having to reject her when she came out as gay.

Ironically, this lad went to the Grammar School too. Nat taught him. He'd sent her into paroxysms of paranoia by spotting her leaving Jo's place with Dottie early one morning during the school holidays a couple of years ago, and calling out 'Hello Mrs Mason' loud enough for the whole neighbourhood to hear as he sped past. Jo doubted very much that it would ever cross his mind to wonder why his English teacher was paying visits to the local lesbian at that time in the morning. But she *did* wonder how his mother had made her peace with the idea of her son's defection to the realm of the grammar bugs.

Having delayed herself for a few more seconds, she half hoped that she might see Natalie turning the corner at the bottom of the road with the dog.

She didn't.

And she told herself it was probably for the best.

-0-0-0-

The snow became much deeper as she headed out of town and into the National Park. In the fields flanking the road, sheep ripped at the few sparse uncovered blades of grass. A flock of pure white doves swooped in formation over the wind-blown ridges of Braxton Moor. And the line of slush running down the middle of the road was scoured in places by skid marks.

She played the radio, wondering why 'Blank Space' always conjured up for her a darkly erotic image of a chorus-line of hip grinding Kit Kat Club dancers in smeared lipstick and Grayson Perry dresses. She was sometimes glad that people couldn't see the weird stuff that went on in her head. She sang along to keep her spirits up and then had to stop singing to concentrate as she pulled into a snow-banked layby to allow the Hopper bus to pass. She wondered, as she waited there for the driver to ease his way slowly past her, just *how* much Jake's new girlfriend looked like Taylor Swift.

Then, unexpectedly and maybe because it was Christmas, there was the Alexandra Burke version of Hallelujah, with the reminder of Alyssa and Natalie and Jake in the Cathedral, and the coldness and the brokenness of it all crashed over her in waves that felt like they might drown her.

After that she turned the radio off because she didn't want to listen to music anymore.

-0-0-0-

'The Retreat' was a dark and slightly gothic looking mansion, hemmed in by brooding black and white fells and swathed in low, heavy, yellowish clouds. The entrance, through an archway that came upon her suddenly, to the right, wouldn't have been out of place in a Hammer horror film.

But that was nothing compared to the shock of the nuns.

The first was in the car park hoisting boxes out of the boot of an elderly Cortina. Jo told herself she must be a fellow retreatant... and an admirably open minded one at that. But the snow-topped statues in the garden looked distinctly Catholic... as did the bright-eyed sister in a thick grey woolly jumper, grey skirt and wellies, who was bearing down on her now.

She tapped gently on the window of the car and Jo wondered if it was obvious that she'd been contemplating doing a runner. Reluctantly, she wound it down.

'You must be Joanne,' said the nun, with some certainty. 'I'm Ulrika. We've exchanged emails. Come on in, we have coffee and cake for 'elevenses', and it will be very welcome, I'm sure, after your journey. We can get your bags later when I've given you the guided tour.'

Jo baulked at the idea. 'Look, actually... I'm not sure...' She was at eye-level with the nun's crucifix now. More Hammer Horror images flashed through her mind.

'But you've just driven...' Ulrika pictured Jo's journey, much of it on country roads that must have been treacherous. '...well over an hour to get here.'

'Yes, but to be honest... I didn't realise... I mean... I'm not Catholic....' Again, she remembered her mother and the awful, energy draining depression that haunted her. Jo still blamed the Catholic Church for that, though, to be fair, four kids and a miserable marriage couldn't have helped much either. 'In fact, I'm not actually religious at all,' she added, hearing an unexpected quaver of apology in her voice that *sounded* so much like her mum it scared her.

Sister Ulrika seemed strangely unfazed by her denial, and determined not to let Jo escape.

'That's fine,' she said firmly. 'Most of the people here aren't very religious either. Come on, it's ginger cake today. And we've got a lovely fire burning in the common room. It's very cosy.'

-0-0-0-

And it was. But then, at eleven thirty, there was a session of meditation. And *that* wasn't cosy at all.

There were six of them, including Sister Ulrika. They met in the library. It had built-in oak cupboards along two walls, with bookshelves above stretching up to the ceiling. The books had titles like 'Contemplations on the Martyrdom of the Lesser Saints' and 'Ecclesiastical Latin for Modern Times'. They looked like no-one had read them since they put them there.

A third wall had a large mullioned window looking out over the snow-covered garden and fells, and the fourth held a fireplace set with dusty logs and no fire, and a huge oil painting of 'The Betrayal in the Garden' in various shades of gravy-browning. This wall also held the door, three inches thick with woodworm holes and an un-oiled creak. Instinctively, Jo positioned herself opposite it. She still hadn't unpacked the car, but she was wondering whether to go out and get an extra jumper. An ancient radiator was wheezing under the window, but it was still very cold and there was a distinct smell of damp on the air. Jo noticed that two of the women, both eightyish with permed grey hair, Damart jumpers and fleecy slippers, had brought thick woollen shawls to put round their shoulders. Clearly they'd been here before.

The other two retreatants were both men. One, a handsome young priest with silky black hair and matinee-idol jaw, sat with his hands clasped on his lap as if in a permanent state of self-conscious prayer. The other was very tall, angular and scruffy with long uncombed grey hair and a scraggly beard. He reminded Jo of the elderly recluse on the estate when she was growing up. He'd been a sad character who held conversations with himself and pushed an old pram full of rubbish he'd picked up out of the gutter. Liam had nicknamed him 'Catweazle' after a character in one of his favourite TV programmes when he was a kid. The TV Catweazle was a time travelling magician. Jo had been too young to remember it, but Liam still made jokes from the show about 'Telling Bones' and 'Electrickery'. His kids had reached the age where they'd heard them so many times they rolled their eyes and said 'Oh Dad!' every time he did it.

Anyway, this guy was a dead ringer for Catweazle. He grinned at her across the circle and wiped his nose on the frayed cuff of his thick hand knitted grey jersey. Then he winked. Jo wasn't sure whether it was deliberate, or if he just had something in his eye. She didn't get chance to find out. An air of expectant stillness had descended on the group.

'So...' said Ulrika cheerily. 'I'll just begin the hour by leading you in a short relaxation exercise...'

-0-0-0-

It was the longest hour Jo had ever known. Though it felt marginally shorter than the one she had to endure *after* lunch. Some people used mantras, Ulrika explained, as she talked them from relaxation into meditation.

'God is Good,' was, apparently, the favourite of many, with 'God' on the in breath... 'Is' in the pause... and 'Good' on the out.

The same applied to 'Peace Be Still'.

And 'Rest in God.'

Jo resisted the temptation to adopt 'Give me Strength.' and tried to get into the spirit of things, with a neutral 'In – Pause – Out,' but she found that she kept drifting - into worries about the anonymous message, thoughts of work, and how they'd all be coping without her, distant memories of school, then off to sleep, and from there into images of Natalie, in her arms, naked. Nat's warm skin touching hers, lips seeking hers…. The mantra becoming, 'I love you'… 'I *want* you'… until she woke, with a start, and looked guiltily across the room to see Sister Ulrika staring at her as if she knew exactly how aroused she had become in her dreams.

-0-0-0-

At four thirty, it was time for 'Personal Direction'

Apart from the small lamp casting a dim yellow-ochre puddle of light up the wall and over the corner of the desk, the room was dark. Jo still felt sleepy. She wondered if the other-worldly pace of the place was starting to catch up with her.

'Your room is comfortable, I trust?'

Actually, it was cold, the mattress felt like it might have been previously owned by Anne Lister, and there was a faint background whiff of sawdust and ammonia that Jo had always associated with the presence of mice.

She figured, maybe, all retreat centres were a bit like that. 'Yes, thank you,' she said.

'Good!' Ulrika smiled. 'Well, I'm here to help you direct your time if you would like me to. So, please just use me anyway you'd like.'

'Thank you.' Jo anxiously remembered Nat saying something similar to her the night she'd first declared her love. She shuffled in her seat at the thought of it. Then, 'Okay,' she said, trying to remember what on earth she'd hoped to achieve by running off and throwing herself at the mercy of the inhabitants of this strange and slightly creepy set-up in the first place.

Sister Ulrika, at least, had a reassuring feel about her. She seemed kind and down to earth. Jo didn't think she would judge her, despite the 'uniform' that suggested otherwise.

She decided it was probably best to just dive straight in.

'I'm having an affair with my best friend's wife,' she said. 'And I need to fathom out what I'm going to do about it.'

'Okay,' Sister Ulrika didn't bat an eyelid. 'Do you feel alright talking about it?'

'I think I'm going to have to.' Jo wondered if that sounded rude. After all, she'd come to sort this thing out, hadn't she? 'It's just... I'm not very good at talking,' she said. 'And I don't know where to start.'

Ulrika eyed her astutely. She could see the natural reticence in her new retreatant. She had all the tell-tale signs of someone who was always busy looking after everybody else and never, actually, the centre of her own world at all. She knew that Jo was deeply uncomfortable in this environment too and wondered if she'd bullied her into staying. She mulled over Jo's opening gambit in her mind. The words *affair*, *best friend*, and *wife*, flitted through her thoughts as she searched for a question that might be helpful.

'How long has this... affair... been going on?'

'Eight years.' Jo looked ashamed.

Ulrika didn't bat an eyelid. 'That's a long time!'

'You're not kidding!'

This sounded so heartfelt, Ulrika knew she was dealing with a long, slow burning kind of pain. 'So what's brought things to a head now?' she asked.

'Someone knows... I received an anonymous note on Christmas Eve.'

Ulrika was surprised to feel a sudden chill of fear. She told herself she must be picking it up from Jo. 'You don't know who sent it?'

'No.'

Fear shuddered through Ulrika again, and she found herself struggling to thrust memories of her own from her mind. Memories of love and the dangers it held... She put her feet firmly on the ground and folded her hands on her lap. Then she noticed that her fingers were gripping each other rather more tightly than usual and found that she had to consciously ease them apart as she composed herself.

'Do you love her?' she asked. She'd noticed that Jo hadn't said 'I'm *in love* with my best friend's wife,' and it felt important to know whether this was 'just' sex... or obligation... or something deeper.

There was a long pause.

Finally, Jo nodded, 'I love them both,' she said. Then exhaustion hit her, and she covered her eyes to try to hide the fact that she was crying.

Chapter Four

It was summer 1985, the first day of the school holidays, and a perfect opportunity for Jo's mother to take an unofficial break from work.

After a couple of sleeping tablets the night before, her deep, chesty snores, like a grizzly bear in the early stages of hibernation, suggested that there wouldn't be much movement before lunchtime.

'Has she been at the 'Moggies' again?' Jo's four-years-younger brother Andy was standing behind her on the olive green, wood-chipped landing. He was shorter than the rest of the family, and he was a comfort eater. He was wearing stained, beige pyjamas inherited from his brother Cliff. The stains came from Cliff, not Andy, who was generally quite fastidious. The sleeves came down beyond his fingertips, and the buttons strained over his tummy.

At twelve, Andy was the only one of the lads still living at home.

Liam (24) had enlisted in the army straight from school. He was a decent bloke, but this was before he married his girlfriend Angie and settled down, so he was drunk and with his mates most of the time when he was on leave.

Cliff (20) was in prison for a string of felonies including possession of a Class A drug and dealing in a Class B, plus burglary, and assault of the police officer who arrested him when his trousers snagged on the smashed window of the house he was robbing and slowed down his generally well-honed capacity for 'legging it'.

The judge had been unsympathetic to Cliff's defence that he was withdrawing from heroin and frantic about the damage the police officer might be doing to his testicles as he hauled him off the broken glass. Even with exemplary behaviour, he was unlikely to be awarded his 'Get out of jail free' card much before his 25th birthday.

Andy was dreading it already. He knew that Jo would be long gone by then, and he'd already started his escape fund. He was building it up steadily one job at a time. He cleaned people's windows and mowed their lawns, shovelled snow in winter and leaves in autumn, and helped out at car boot sales on Sundays. He was never short of jobs. Unlike Jo, he'd gone to the same secondary school as all his mates, so he'd managed to keep 'in' with everybody on the estate. He was the acceptable face of the Cooper family. People actually *liked* him.

'What about the Masons' place?' he asked anxiously.

This was the house their mother was supposed to be cleaning.

'I'll do it.'

'Don't they want you in at work?'

'Yeah – but not until tonight.' Jo had landed a job at the local Co-op for the holidays. As the new girl, they'd given her all the shifts nobody else wanted, but they were tempting her with the possibility of regular weekend work if they liked her, so she certainly wasn't complaining.

'Well, I'll come help you with the Masons.' Andy turned to go back into his room to get dressed and Jo's heart swelled with love for him. She knew (because their mother told them with monotonous regularity) that his arrival had been the final straw for her. He crept through life being helpful, as if he hoped that someday he might be able to make amends for the 'mistake' of his conception. Looking at him there, all bed-headed and bleary eyed, Jo would have liked to hug him. But he wasn't into any of that 'soppy stuff' anymore, so she did the next best thing and granted him his liberty instead.

'It's okay love. You go out with your mates. I don't mind doing it.'

She could see how much he wanted to take her offer and run as far away from this grim and grubby place as possible, out into the fresh air and the countryside. Hope and honour warred for a moment on his chubby young face.

'Are you sure?'

'Yeah.'

'Well I'll do it next time.'

'Okay.' She wouldn't let him, they both knew that.

-0-0-0-

Jo didn't mind doing 'The Mason's Place' anyway. She'd been 'covering' for her mum's holiday absences since she was twelve, and unlike a lot of the posh houses she'd had to clean, the Masons' house was always spotless. The work wasn't hard and you didn't feel like you needed a sandblaster or industrial strength cleaners to get rid of any encrusted grime in the sinks or toilets. The floors never actually needed scrubbing to get mud or grease or horse or dog poo off them. And in the winter, the owners didn't turn the heating off the minute they went out, so, even on very cold days, you could never see your breath on the air or have to keep your rubber gloves on all the time to try and stop the skin on your fingers cracking. The Masons never 'forgot' to pay either, which was a big bonus for Jo's family back then. The money was always there, in cash, with a friendly little note saying what needed to be done and signed 'With kind regards'.

Jo knew the owners, Mr and Mrs Mason, by repute. A lot of people on the estate worked for them at their garage or at their big carpet factory on the edge of the moors. Mr Mason was strict and miserable and it didn't do to get on the wrong side of him. But Mrs Mason was a whole lot younger and prettier and nicer than her husband. She was the old man's second wife, a long-term comfort to him after he lost his first to leukemia in his early thirties. She was also mother to his son-and-heir Edward, and had had the good sense to refuse to raise him in her husband's former matrimonial home, a gloomy Victorian pile full of memories of her saintly predecessor.

Consequently, the current Mason residence was light and bright, detached (of course) and situated behind the church, looking over fields that seemed to stretch for miles. There was a basketball hoop mounted on the side wall of the house, and a trampoline in the garden. There were shiny worktops in the kitchen, an automatic washing machine, and an 'en-suite' bathroom off the master bedroom. Jo liked all that stuff. She wanted to have a place like that herself someday. She had no intention of ending up like her mum, with four kids, an absentee husband, and depression that hung over everything like a cloud of toxic waste.

Sometimes, when the cleaning was done, and always with a wary ear for any of the family making an unexpected appearance, Jo liked to imagine that she actually lived at the Mason House. She indulged herself in little treats then, making herself a cup of black Gold Blend coffee, which she sipped in the conservatory, looking out over the garden and the fields, with a Rich Tea biscuit if the tin looked full enough to take one without it being missed.

Up till now, the house had always been deserted when she arrived, so she felt slightly anxious that day when she found the door not double locked, as it usually was, but just on the Yale. Her 'stand-ins' for her mother weren't exactly official, and it was possible that Mrs Mason might not approve of an un-vetted sixteen year old having the run of her house, particularly bearing in mind the chequered criminal history of her brother Cliff.

'Mrs Mason!' She stood in the hallway and called softly. If the lady of the house made an appearance, she'd just have to tell her that she'd come to say her mum wasn't well and wouldn't be able to come. But there was no reply, so she decided that they'd just forgotten to double-lock the door, pocketed the money to give to her mum, and checked the note to see if anything special needed to be cleaned today.

-0-0-0-

Meanwhile, Edward, home from his expensive private school in the Midlands, was blissfully unaware that Monday was cleaning day - his mother having forgotten to remind him the night before. And, thinking he was home alone, he was happily soaping himself under the shower while belting out an excruciating rendition of Barry White's 'What Am I Gonna Do With You'.

It was a well soundproofed house. Jo didn't hear a thing until she flung open the bathroom door and went trotting in.

Both sixteen year olds screamed.

But Ed screamed the loudest.

With three brothers and a dad with no sense of decorum, Jo was inured to the sight before her, even erect and soapy as it was. Ed, however, was an only child. He attended an all boys' school. And he'd just discovered that his favourite 'caught in the shower by the cleaning maid' fantasy was actually horribly, excruciatingly, bloody embarrassing in real life – particularly when you factored in the Barry White.

'BLOODY HELL!!!!' they yelped in unison.

And Jo discretely reversed out of the bathroom, taking her Domestos, Ajax, and non-scratch bathroom cleaning sponge with her.

-0-0-0-

Fifteen minutes later, Ed found her vacuuming his parent's bedroom. She was still grinning to herself as she silenced the vacuum and clicked the handle into an upright position. 'You must be Edward,' she said, offering her hand for him to shake.

She'd heard some of the girls on the estate, talking about the Mason's 'snoggable' lad and how he must be 'worth a mint'. Now he was dry, she could see that he *was* good looking, with floppy blond hair and blue eyes. Thankfully, he was also dressed, in a sweatshirt and jeans... pretty much the same as hers, except his sweatshirt said 'Petershaw House Rugger Squad' on it, while hers was a plain grey charity shop number that had originally come from C&A.

He took her hand and gave it a hearty pump.

'That's right,' he said. 'Edward Mason... Ed to my mates. But who the hell are you? Last time I saw her, our cleaner was some shaky old bird who smelt of fags and black coffee.'

It was Jo's turn to be embarrassed then. 'Yes,' she said. 'That's my mum.'

'Oh bugger! That was really tactless of me wasn't it? You must think I'm a right knob now.'

She'd already decided that he was a bit of knob anyway. 'It's okay. I liked the singing by the way.'

'Oh… yeah… I was just fooling around, you know.'

'Yeah,' she gave a little smirk, just to put him down a bit, in a girl-boy kind of a way. 'I noticed!'

He wished she hadn't, but she didn't seem too fazed, so he wondered if she might be flirting with him. 'How come you've taken over from your mum then?' he asked.

'I haven't. She's just poorly today.'

'Oh… I'm sorry. I hope she feels better soon.' He was keen to keep the conversation going.

He didn't often meet nice girls.

There were the ones who were sometimes shipped over from the local girls' school to put him through the humiliation of ballroom dancing classes. His two left feet, chronic blushing, and lack of any discernible sense of rhythm, were minor problems there in comparison to his tendency to get over-excited the minute anyone of the opposite sex came within six feet of him.

Then there were the same girls at the End of Term Dances - bussed across in perfumed, made-up, high-heeled mobs to snigger and deliver precision-engineered put-downs to any lad who gathered up the courage to talk to them. Ed had noticed that some of the chaps at school seemed to find this bizarre behaviour both tantalizing and erotic. Those were the lads who could give as good as they got and ended up sneaking out and 'getting some' on the railway embankment before the end of the evening. But Ed saw what happened to his braver comrades on the way to that prize, and knew he wasn't quick enough to dodge the bullets. So he never risked it, even though he sometimes noticed that he was being watched coyly through mascaraed eyelashes, and his mates often told him that some girl or other was 'hot for him' and ribbed him about his 'lack of balls'.

It wasn't much better at home. All his cousins were either boys or ancient. There was no 'girl next door'. And the lasses at the factory were an ordeal for him, 'common-as-muck' in their polyester overalls and hair tied back so it wouldn't snag in the machinery, giggling behind their hands when he couldn't avoid going in to see his mum or dad. Mortifyingly, he found that *they* made him blush too, especially when they made loud comments about his bum or worse.

So, nice girls were rare in Ed's world. But he thought this one was cute, with her cheeky, slightly lop-sided grin, and unruly 'Desperately Seeking Susan' haircut that looked like she must have done it herself with nail scissors.

'Thanks.' She smiled politely and tried to get past him. She felt uncomfortable trapped in a bedroom with a strange lad blocking the doorway.

He let her past. But he didn't want to let her go. 'Can I help you at all?' he asked.

'Don't be daft!'

'I'm not. If I help we can get it done in half the time and then we can sit and have a cup of tea or something and talk.'

Jo eyed him warily. She wasn't sure whether he was quite nice really or just some spoiled brat who thought he could have anything he wanted.

'I'm not some kind perve or anything,' he said, in a rare moment of sensitivity. Then, grinning sheepishly… 'Well, apart from the Barry White, that is.'

She decided to take his word for it.

'Okay,' she gave in. 'I've nearly finished anyway. Why don't you put the kettle on and we can go and sit out in the garden for a bit.'

-0-0-0-

'A bit' stretched easily into two hours. Ed was surprised at how comfortable he felt in Jo's company, and he found himself opening up in ways he never had with anyone before. He told her how much he hated school where his nickname was 'Thick Ed', and how he wished he could just be a mechanic in his dad's garage. Then he confessed how shy he was with girls. And how badly he felt he let his father down by being clumsy and tongue-tied, and 'not much good for anything but messing around with cars'.

Jo warmed to him as he talked, and told him about her family too. How her parents were struggling to keep her at school so she could go to college and achieve the stuff *they* never had. And how her dream was to set up her own business, make loads of money, and help them all out. Drowsy in the sun, lulled by the hot, warm scent of the rose bushes around them, she found that she didn't particularly want to leave. She knew she had to though. They didn't have a phone at home, and if her mum woke up disorientated, she could easily have an attack of guilt and trail all the way here when she didn't need to.

'Okay,' she said. 'I'd better be getting back.... see if mum's decided to surface.'

'Can I just show you something first?'

'Depends what it is.' She remembered the shower, and wondered if he'd lulled her into a false sense of security.

'In the garage.'

Oh-oh… this was where he turned into a weirdo!
'I dunno…'
'It's a car… *my* car, to be exact.'
'Well, in that case….' Jo loved cars and had already decided that when she was older, and she'd done her business studies course and made her first million, she was going to own a Jag.
'It's gonna be a classic someday.'
'Even better!'
She followed him across the garden to an ivy covered red brick garage that she'd assumed was the house next door. She was expecting something pretty spectacular. But the car looked like it might have been pulled off the top of the pile in a breaker's yard. One wing was missing and the bonnet was up. Engine parts trailed across the concrete floor like some grisly automotive mass murder scene. It was a mess.
'Ford Anglia 105E, 1963,' he said, in the entranced tone of someone who is head over heels in love. 'Glacier Blue… Dad bought her for me at the auctions. Isn't she gorgeous?'
Jo stared at the car in amazement. It looked a bit like the one her own dad had scrapped when she was eight. Gorgeous wasn't quite the word she'd use to describe it. 'It's… very old…' she said.
'Yeah! I'm doing her up. Isn't she beautiful?!…. D'you wanna sit in the driver's seat?'
She eased herself gingerly onto the seat, ran her hands around the wheel and gazed at the dash, wondering what on earth anybody could say about a wreck like that.
Ed jumped in beside her. They sat, side by side, gazing out through the windscreen. He wondered if it would be

too forward to try to kiss her. Then he thought it might be.

But he felt he needed something to bring her back. An offer she couldn't refuse...

'Hey... I'm thinking,' he said. 'How about you come into business with me when we leave school? You know... like a classic car garage... I could fix them up... And we could do chauffeuring... or something like that? I've got the skills and you've got the brains. You could be my manager.... deal with all the paperwork... and the money and that...What do you think?'

Jo looked at him with her head on one side. She thought he was full of BS. But she liked him.

'I think we'll need a posher car if we're going to do chauffeuring,' she said.

-0-0-0-

'Of course,' Jo added to Ulrika, smiling ruefully at her lack of prescience. 'I wasn't to know that J.K Rowling would give Ron Weasley a pale blue flying Anglia in the Harry Potter books. That car's one of our biggest earners now. All we have to do is stick a ginger wig and cape on one of the lads and it goes down a bomb at kids' parties. Ed's never let me live that one down!' She laughed. 'Typical of Ed. He's a walking disaster area in a lot of ways, but my dad always said he could fall in bucket of shit... oh, sorry!...' she glanced quickly at Ulrika and noticed with some relief that she was smiling... 'and come out smelling of roses,' she finished, hastily.

'I can see that you *are* very fond of him,' said Ulrika. Then, after some hesitation, 'Were you lovers back then?'

Jo wondered if nuns were supposed to ask about stuff like that.

'We were just kids,' she said.

'I know.'

'No, we weren't lovers.' Jo shrugged, remembering that idyllic summer, lying in the long feathery grass in the field behind Ed's house, breathing the scent of camomile as she drifted, hands behind her head, gazing sleepily at the patches of blue sky, making pictures out of the clouds. She remembered the taste of Coke from the can they'd shared, sweet and metallic on his breath as he suddenly did what he'd been longing to do for weeks and leaned over to kiss her. Guiltily, she remembered how she'd jumped away from him, saying **'Bloody hell, Ed!'** And the look of hurt that flashed over his face, quickly masked by a strained new version of the 'idiot' smile he'd perfected over the years. 'I'm sorry,' he stammered. 'I thought…'

'Well, you can think again!'

The truth was that Jo had recently started 'seeing' someone – Veronica, a much older woman who worked at the local TV station and who thought (or pretended she thought) that Jo was nineteen, and at college. Nowadays, Jo would probably define such a relationship as abusive. She'd have been horrified if Alyssa, or Jake, for that matter, fell into the clutches of somebody like Veronica. But back then she'd been fairly clear that it was really just a means to an end.

She'd met 'Ronnie' at the Lavender Bar, a place she'd read about in a copy of Gay Times she nicked from W.H.Smith's in her one and only venture into shoplifting. Too embarrassed to actually *buy* the magazine, she'd sneaked it down from the top shelf when no one was looking, and smuggled it out in a carrier bag containing a Cosmopolitan she'd paid for but didn't want. Then she'd legged it down the street, panting in terror and expecting the store detective to shout after her at any moment, denouncing her to the world as a Lesbian and a Thief. She'd prayed that if only she could get away with it, just this once, she would never, ever, do anything like that again. And she hadn't.

It had taken her another two months before she'd actually dared to visit the bar.

It was a grubby downstairs dive, located in a backstreet just behind the meat and veg market. This location provided a source of endless amusement for Mal, one of Ronnie's friends, who never seemed to tire of screaming *'Hey handsome, fancy to go round the corner for a bit of meat and veg!'* at every halfway 'straight acting' guy who dared to venture into the place. Mal was somewhere in the region of seventy, five foot nothing, and camp as Christmas. He never seemed to get many 'takers' for his offers.

The bar had aspirations to be 'classy' but it didn't quite make it. It smelled of beer and burgers and stale chip fat, and there was a mildly adhesive feel to the carpet as you walked across it. It was friendly though, and the bar man didn't ask any questions about how old Jo was when she asked for a lager and lime, a drink she'd barely had chance to sip, before Ronnie spotted her and headed across the sticky carpet like a cruise missile locked on target.

'I haven't seen *you* in here before.'

'No, it's my first time.'

'*Is* it now?' The woman was a predator of course. But back then she'd seemed sophisticated and pretty damn sexy as she'd swept Jo head to foot and back with those cool grey eyes. 'Fancy to join us?'

She gestured in the direction of her friends; a couple of very butch looking older women in checked shirts and jeans, a tall, auburn haired beauty who turned out to be a drag queen – and Mal. They were seated at a table at the far end of the room next to a small stage stacked with disco equipment that wouldn't really get going until after 9 o'clock. They all waved cheerily as Jo looked across at them.

The barman raised an eyebrow. 'She's just a kid,' he said, quietly to Veronica.

'Really?' she flashed back. 'Well *you* just served her alcohol, *didn't* you?'

He shrugged, flushing slightly as he turned away.

Later, Ronnie had given Jo a lift home. She had a red and black soft-top Ford Capri that Ed would have loved. She pulled into a quiet spot near the park entrance, unbuttoned Jo's pants and slipped her hand inside.

'I shouldn't have done that,' she said in that silky voice when she'd finished.

But 'should' and 'shouldn't' weren't really words that had ever made much difference to Veronica.

Now, two weeks and several long, hot afternoons at Ronnie's place later, Jo saw that tight, self-lacerating look on Ed's face, and feeling instantly remorseful, knew that the only way to make amends for unwittingly 'leading him on' was to make herself every bit as vulnerable as he had been.

'I'm gay,' she said. 'I've got a girlfriend. I thought you knew.'

There was a long silence. She knew he was gathering up his wounded pride, and she had no idea if it would be followed by a blast of homophobia. So she waited anxiously for his reply.

Finally it came... 'Bloody 'ell,' he said, with his easier, more relaxed grin returning. 'That's a *right* bloody turn on, that is! Have you got a picture of her? Don't suppose there's any chance of watching sometime is there?'

And he squealed like a girl as she picked up the Coke can and poured its warm and sticky dregs over his head.

-0-0-0-

'So you were friends from that summer?' asked Ulrika.

'Well, there was quite a long gap where we didn't really see much of each other. Nowadays, I suppose we'd have been 'Friends' on Facebook. But then... my family didn't have a phone. And Ed's school just had a payphone in a corridor. It wasn't exactly private. And we wouldn't have had anything much to say to each other anyway. We never talked much. We just *did* stuff together... messed around with the car, played computer games... He had a basketball hoop and a pool table.... I think we both thought we'd get back together in the next holidays, but then we just never did. His parents started sending him to 'cramming' schools, trying to get him into University. And when he wasn't banging his head against *that* particular brick wall, he was off on some school trip or other, or working at the garage or the factory. I suppose we should have known really. I reckon Ed's dad had got wind of us getting close and he'd decided to keep his precious son well occupied and away from me. So, we didn't see all that much of each other for about three years. But then one night I was out with a group of mates in a bar in town and I felt a tap on my shoulder and heard this familiar voice saying my name. I turned round and there he was... and somehow, we just seemed to pick up where we'd left off.'

Memories of that evening flooded back as she spoke of it. 'The Only Way Is Up' on the jukebox, shifting, with a sudden change of tempo into 'Didn't We Almost Have it All', a song that had always been able to reduce her to tears, even before she really knew what heartbreak was. Smoke was hanging in the air like fog, and Ed looked older, bulked out, in a fawn, shoulder-padded eighties suit that wouldn't have been out of place in a flash-back from an early episode of 'Friends'. His hair was big and gelled, and his vacuous girlfriend (the latest in a long line) had glared at Jo and clearly thought she was someone to be jealous of. Struggling back through the years, she remembered that this girl's name was Sheryl, and she was blonde, with a pout and called Ed 'Baby'. Apart from the expansive cleavage, it was hard to understand what he might have seen in her. But then, judging from the magazines she'd once found accidentally in a carrier bag behind the driver's seat of his Anglia, he always *had* been fond of a nice pair of Double D's.

'So, when did Ed's wife-to-be come on the scene?'

'Gosh!' Jo leaned back in her seat and closed her eyes, rolling back the years. 'That was a few years later,' she said. 'Nineteen Ninety Six....' She remembered, because The Spice Girls were on a different jukebox now – 'Wannabe', mingling with the bar-noise at the Tennis Club as she conjured herself back through time.

-0-0-0-

It was the sixth anniversary of 'Classic Cars' and they were celebrating.

Ed, Jo, Bill Jones, and Jo's brother Andy, were perched on high stools at the bar.

Bill was cradling his 'half a mild in a straight glass' as if his life depended on it. He'd been the first driver they'd employed when the business got too big for them to do all the driving themselves. Andy had joined them straight from college. Ashad and Mo, who didn't drink and had already made their excuses and gone home, worked in the garage, but occasionally did driving jobs when the others weren't available. And Jo was, as promised, Operations Manager – full time now she didn't have to don her chauffeur's uniform anymore. She'd grown up a lot since her first fateful meeting with Ed. Her hair was shorter, spikier, and actually cut by a hairdresser. Her clothes, a smart linen jacket and cream pants, were from 'Next'. And she'd eyed her Russell and Bromley boots in the shop window for weeks before she'd managed to save up enough cash to splash out on them. She knew she looked good. Even so, she felt uncomfortable. This was Ed's home turf. Not hers, or Bill's... and certainly not Andy's.

Anyway, Ed was the boss and this was where he'd wanted to come.

He was teaching Jo and Andy how to drink Tequila shots. It was one of the few things he'd learnt at school that he actually enjoyed. Needless to say, it hadn't been on the official curriculum.

'One, two, three - Salt – Tequila – lime – eeurgh!' he demonstrated.

Bill screwed up his nose and took a defiant sip of his 'mild'. He didn't understand why anyone would want to drink 'foreign muck' like that. At thirty seven, he was a lot older than the other three, and he felt daft in this snooty place, perched on the uncomfortable bar stool like some silly 'yuppy'. He was sweating a bit, with his tie pulled down and top button undone. His shirt kept coming untucked from the grey Marks and Sparks trousers drooping under the early middle-aged spread from Mrs J's excellent home cooking. And, with Ed clearly set to make a night of it, he wished he'd been quick enough to escape earlier, like Ash and Mo had done. Jo noticed him covertly looking at his watch, and guessed he was calculating how much longer he needed to stay before he could make his excuses and bolt without looking rude.

She half wished she could do the same. She'd been investing a lot of time recently in one of the barmaids at 'Rainbow's End', a new gay place in town. And she figured if she went down there tonight she might be able to edge things up a notch. She was also trying to fathom out if there actually *was* a grub in the Tequila bottle, though Chris, the bar man, had been too quick as he was pouring the shots, and she hadn't been able to see. She wasn't sure she fancied to drink anything with dead things in it. Andy looked dubious too. But Ed, half-cut as usual, shoved the salt pot towards them.

'Come on you ***pussies***!' he said. '*Your* turn.'

'Oh, what the hell!' she took a deep breath and went for it. She often suspended her better judgment where Ed was concerned.

She was pretty sozzled by the time Nat walked into the bar. And if she hadn't already been way past thinking of dropping in at 'The Rainbow', her first sight of this striking new arrival would certainly have driven the idea out of her head.

Nat was gorgeous, by anyone's standards. Early twenties, tall and with amazing long legs, she had a red, white and blue look going on that night. White skinny jeans, a deep red V neck top, and navy blue jacket. Her hair was raven-black and glossy. She wore it slightly longer then than now, rippling down beyond her shoulders. She was tanned without any trace of orange. And she was looking, apparently captivated, in Jo's direction.

Jo, thinking all her birthdays had come at once, smiled brilliantly back through an alcohol-induced haze of stupidity.

The newcomer smiled even more brightly.

Then, 'Jesus!' she heard Ed gasp, behind her. 'I think I'm in love!'

And it was only then that it dawned on Jo that the beautiful newcomer was smiling at *him* – not *her.*

She was with Greg Widdicombe. He'd walked into the room behind her and was now leaning into her to take her jacket, stepping back like a magician making a smug flourish as he revealed his new acquisition's smooth golden arms and nicely sculpted cleavage to the world.

'*Fuck!*' said Ed, admitting defeat before he'd even started. 'Might 'a known she'd be with Widders.' He knocked back a shot of the Tequila without lime and slouched despondently over the bar, gesturing to Chris to 'fill 'em up'

In terms of eligibility, Greg and Ed were probably just about on a par, though Greg was undeniably more ruthless. He was traditionally tall, dark and handsome. He was a great tennis player, and - since his father's death - owner of a real ale brewery in Tadcaster. His step-mother was still contesting the will about *that* one, but she was unlikely to win, even though she'd been running the place ever since Greg's father had the first of his increasingly debilitating strokes. It didn't matter a jot to Greg that the poor woman had managed to snatch the business from the jaws of the receiver, or that his father would probably have changed his will to make sure she got it if he'd been well enough to do so. People didn't win where Greg was concerned. He was used to getting what he wanted. Everybody knew that. And he had a reputation as a serial womaniser. Jo had never seen him without some stunning bit of eye candy on his arm.

But this one didn't seem like his usual type. She wasn't all over him. And she was *definitely* interested in Ed. Jo couldn't help but notice her reluctance in dragging her eyes back to her escort, and the glances, more covert now, fluttering in their direction from time to time as Greg held court with his friends, laughing loudly, talking a lot, and obviously trying very hard to impress his date. She was being polite with him, but she seemed, despite all his best efforts, to be distinctly underwhelmed by his company.

By 9pm, Bill had had more than enough. 'Best be getting home,' he grunted, heaving himself off his bar stool. 'See how Mrs J's getting on.'

Jo knew his cocoa was beckoning. 'And I'd better go to the Little Girls' Room,' she said, jumping down too, then staggering slightly as her feet hit the floor and her legs almost buckled under her. 'God, that lime's lethal!' she quipped. The room spun slowly, like one of those old fashioned fairground carousels with painted horses.

'I'll get some more in then, shall I?' asked Ed.

'Think I might have had enough.'

Ed turned to Andy. 'Just you and me then, eh mate?'

'And don't be getting my little bro plastered,' she shot back over her shoulder.

Andy cast her a grateful look. He wanted to go home too and had been wondering if he could cadge a lift with Bill.

This place was *way* too posh for him. He thought the Tequila tasted like the petrol he'd got in his mouth once when he'd been daft enough to try siphoning some from his car to help a mate who'd run out. And the salt and lime were making him feel sick. But Ed seemed 'set in' for the night, and, where drinking was concerned, Ed had selective deafness about the word 'no'.

The minute Jo's back was turned, he ordered another round.

Andy's heart sank.

Greg's entourage were sitting by the jukebox, which, ironically, was playing 'This Ain't A Love Song.'

They stopped talking when she came over to their table, but she knew that the music would make it hard for them to hear what she was about to say. She put her hand on the back of Natalie's chair and leaned in to talk quietly to her. Despite herself, she felt her pulse rising as her lips hovered close to this beautiful woman's ear. She smelt faint, unfamiliar perfume and felt the whisper of hair against her cheek. There was something exciting about the woman's refusal to shrug away. It was as if she were daring herself not to move, even though every muscle in her had tensed at their closeness.

Jo knew that up till then, she'd been invisible, but she was very much on the radar now - and not necessarily in a good way. From Nat's immediate unease, she sensed that Greg may have already identified her as 'That lesbian gopher of Ed's', a description she'd heard on several occasions here where people talked about her deliberately loudly to make her feel unwelcome. As far as insults went, it didn't particularly bother her. It was one of their more polite ones, and at least it had the virtue of being true.

Around the table, people sipped their drinks and played with beer mats as they pretended not to look.

'At the risk of sounding like we're in the school playground,' Jo murmured... and she could hear the soft slur of Tequila in her voice...

A look of mild anxiety flashed over Natalie's perfectly made-up features.

Jo found that she couldn't resist pausing a moment to let the anxiety really take hold. Then she felt bad about taking pleasure in that.

'My mate fancies you.'

'Oh!' Relief replaced the anxiety. 'Which one?' Nat brushed her hair back with her hand, and her eyes swivelled up to the bar.

Jo glanced up with her, still holding onto the back of the chair to steady herself. Their cheeks were as close as if they were dancing.

It was pretty obvious it wasn't going to be Andy, sweating and sitting chubbily on his barstool, looking slightly green around the gills.

'The one you've been ogling all night,' she said.

Natalie looked affronted. 'I haven't ...' She didn't get chance to finish her denial. A shadow had already fallen over them. Jo looked up sideways into Greg's chest. He was clad in a black short sleeved Ralph Lauren shirt. The tiny embroidered polo player swam hazily in and out of focus at the edge of her vision. He smelt, rather strongly, of Aramis. Behind him, the jukebox winked and slid smoothly into 'Boombastic'.

Jo slowly pushed herself up so that she was, at least, on a level with Greg's chin. Then, while she had the boyfriend distracted, she back-handed a 'Classic Cars' business card to Natalie.

Gratifyingly, she felt it slide from between her fingers.

'Is this person bothering you?' Greg asked his date. He was too busy eye-balling Jo to notice the card. He reminded her of a boxer trying to psyche his opponent out before the big fight. Just in time, she remembered not to laugh.

'No, not at all.'

'I was just going anyway,' said Jo.

'That sounds like a good idea. Maybe you'd be happier at the Working Men's Club.'

Jo knew this was aimed at her background *and* her sexuality.

A faint, malicious snigger ran round the table. But Nat didn't join in. Out of the corner of her eye, Jo noticed that she was slipping the card into her shoulder bag under cover of taking out a tissue.

'Maybe I would,' she shrugged, heading for the 'Ladies' – mission accomplished. 'At least there, I wouldn't have to put up with dickheads like you.'

-0-0-0-

It took a week for Natalie to follow through on the card.

Jo had almost given up on her by then, but her desk faced out of the window of the Classic Cars portacabin, so she was the first to see her walking hesitantly onto the garage forecourt. She was deep in concentration and checking directions written on a scrap of paper. Her pale grey pants suit hinted at having come straight from work. And she looked every bit as stunning as she had when Jo first set eyes on her.

'We have lift-off!' Jo murmured.

Andy came across to look. He'd been eating a Big Mac and fries before heading off on his 6pm hen night pick-up in the stretch limo. He hated hen nights.... Hated being teased and chatted up and groped by the girls.... Hated the drunken lads who invariably joined them in the back of the car.... And, more than all of that put together - he hated the mopping up afterwards. Andy wasn't really assertive enough to cope with large concentrations of women and booze. But Bill hated it even more than he did. And Ed was at some VIP foreign trade envoy bash at the Town Hall. So, even though he would have actually quite enjoyed the attention, and probably found himself a girlfriend into the bargain, he wasn't available tonight, and Andy was lumbered with it.

Glad of the distraction, he crumpled his McDonald's bag into the bin and joined his sister at her desk, following her gaze over the petrol pumps, round the Ford Escort complete with little girl in Brownie uniform and mum filling up... to the stunner making a bee-line for their cabin.

He whistled appreciatively. 'I don't know how Ed does it,' he said.

'It's that 'Little Boy Lost' look of his,' said Jo. 'They fall for it every time.'

She wished, secretly, that she could cultivate that kind of a look herself. It seemed to work wonders with women.

Natalie was nervous. An entry bell chimed as she opened the door, stepped inside and looked around. The place smelt of burger. She wondered if she should have knocked. 'Hi!' she said tentatively.

'Hi!' This was Jo and Andy in unison. They looked guilty. As if she'd walked in on them doing something they shouldn't have been doing. She wondered if they'd been skiving a bit while the boss was away.

Andy looked at his watch.

'Well,' he said. 'My 'naughty nurses' await me…. Once more into the breach!'

'Or close the wall up with our English dead,' added Natalie, smiling.

'Sorry?'

'Henry the Fifth?' She felt herself losing ground, wondering if she'd sounded like she was showing off.

'No… just a hen night,' Andy stammered, blushing and bolting for the door.

Jo noticed that he'd abandoned his tea in his confusion.

'Please excuse my brother,' she said. 'He doesn't meet many women… Well, not sober ones anyway….. I'm afraid Ed's out on a job.'

'Oh…' Natalie did well at not looking disappointed. 'Well, I'm sure you'll be able to help me anyway.'

Jo smiled, amused. She wondered if Nat had actually gone to the trouble of arranging some kind of event to justify her visit.

'Would you like a drink?' she asked.

'Thank you. That would be nice. Tea… milk… no sugar.'

'The fridge is broken. We've only got powdered milk.'

She noticed Natalie wince at the idea.

'That'll be fine,' she said, gamely.

She watched Jo surreptitiously as her back was turned, making the tea. And just as she had the previous week at the tennis club, she thought she looked nice… tall and smart and capable. She knew Jo was gay from Greg's less than flattering comments about her. Not, as Jo had imagined, the one about being Ed's lesbian gopher, though one of Greg's friends had used *that* one. But insultingly, a comment about getting the wrong reputation if she wasn't careful who she mixed with, that had served to confirm her growing impression that her date was the kind of narrow-minded homophobic snob she wouldn't go out with again, even if some awful cataclysm suddenly made him the only remaining man in the world.

'It's a bit horrible with powdered milk,' Jo confessed as she brought back a mug of the stuff.

'Yes, I *thought* it might be.' Natalie peered at the hot, brown liquid.

Then she looked up and smiled at Jo. The smile went all the way into her eyes. Jo caught herself feeling pleased about that. She distracted herself back to the tea.

'I've got some Plain Chocolate Hob Nobs to help take the taste away.'

'Okay!' Nat thought Jo had nice eyes too. They were a gentle shade of powder blue, like a summer sky. There was something compelling about them. She pushed that thought away as she took the mug.

'I'm sorry about the way Greg behaved last week,' she said. 'He was very rude.'

'It's okay, I'm used to it.'

'Well you shouldn't be. It's nineteen ninety six, not the middle ages…. There's no excuse for that kind of thing anymore.' She took a sip of her tea. It *was* awful. 'Actually, my best friend, Ruth, is gay. She came out while we were at uni.' This tumbled out more quickly than Nat had intended. She wondered afterwards if it was because she had found herself warming to Jo too much and wanted to turn the spotlight onto someone else. It didn't work at all. Instead, it just left her feeling even more horribly exposed as her mind flashed to all the complications of her relationship with Ruth.

And it alienated Jo. *Oh Gawd*, she thought... *Here we go... 'Some of my best friends are gay...'*

Natalie didn't notice Jo's hackles rising. She was too busy thinking that she might, in fact, be perfect for Ruth, who'd never had a great deal of luck with women.

Jo, thankfully, was unaware that she was being sized-up in this way. 'Were you at University locally?' she asked politely.

'No... Norwich.... I'm from King's Lynn originally. I moved here after I graduated. I hadn't really planned on moving so far away from home, but it was quite hard to get a job. I'm teaching English and Drama at the Grammar School.'

Well, thought Jo - *that explains Henry the Fifth.* 'That's my old school,' she said.

'Oh?' Natalie smiled, genuinely interested. 'I bet a lot of your old teachers are still there.'

'Well, it's a long time since I was there, and I imagine there were a lot of changes when they amalgamated the girls and boys schools. But, yes, I guess so. It's unlikely that anyone else would want them!' Jo grinned.

Natalie wasn't sure whether she was joking or not. She laughed anyway. 'I don't really know many people around here yet,' she said. Her eyes clouded briefly as she pictured her khaki bedsit with its desk and portable TV and mouldy bathroom, and landlady upstairs who drank a lot and played 'The Power of Love' very loudly in the middle of the night. The staff at the school were moderately friendly, but at the end of the day they all headed home to their own families, or their own routines, while she had only the smell of cabbage or frying onions from upstairs, and marking and preparation for the next day's lessons to look forward to. Greg had seemed like he might offer some relief from the dreariness of all that when he'd engaged her in conversation by the 'Ready Meals' fridge in Waitrose. She had no way of knowing that was one of his favourite pick-up spots. And of course, it was only when she got to know him that she could see she'd just been grasping at straws.

Jo heard the loneliness in her voice. She almost said, 'Well you know *me* now.' But she didn't. Some spirit of self-preservation told her she was in danger of falling for this woman. And she really didn't need that when Nat so clearly fancied Ed.

So she just said, 'That's hard!' as she opened the Hob Nobs and offered one to Nat. And when her next words came, they sounded cooler than she meant them to… 'Anyway, did you *really* want to book a car or is that just an excuse for seeing the boss?'

-0-0-0-

'It seems there was some kind of attraction between the two of you right from the start?'

Jo knew what Ulrika was doing. She was signalling that she was open-minded and wouldn't be shocked by what was to come.

She shrugged. 'Yeah, maybe… Certainly on *my* side…. Maybe on Nat's too…. She claims so now, though I think she's just rewriting history. And there's no way it would ever have crossed her mind to do anything about it back then. She was well and truly signed up for the straight team. Anyway, it's all a bit academic, because then I messed it all up… *big time!*'

'What happened?' asked Ulrika.

'It's a long story,' said Jo.

-0-0-0-

Double dates can be a minefield. Though this one had seemed like a good idea at the time.

It was the beginning of November, a chilly night, with damp brown leaves on the ground, and just a touch of mist hanging in the air.

Ed had hatched the idea of providing chauffeur services for 'Tandoori Nights', the local high-end Indian restaurant. The Singh family, who owned the restaurant, served great food and had a massive banqueting suite upstairs that was very popular for weddings. Ed had often been dazzled by the spectacle when he was in there with one girlfriend or another, watching as the bride and groom and hoards of wedding guests, exuberant and shimmering, were drummed up the stairs. He figured there must be a whole new untapped market there. Particularly as the new 'Classic Cars' stretch limo, which he'd just bought at auction, had once enjoyed the very great honour of ferrying major Bollywood stars to their film premieres in London. Ed had the signed photos to prove it. And Ajit, the ambitious young heir to the Singh curry empire, was desperate to have those photos in his wedding brochure.

He'd offered Ed a candlelit dinner for four to seal the deal.

But it wasn't really ideal timing as far as Jo was concerned.

She was finally going out with Lucy, the 'Rainbow's End' barmaid, though she was starting to wish she wasn't. Jo liked her women uncomplicated. And Lucy came with major complications. Jealousy for starters... followed closely by paranoia. Two massive green-eyed monsters that had crept into bed with them the first night they slept together, never to be entirely exorcised since.

Jo had been a sitting target that first morning. Emerging blearily from the heavy, contented sleep that always followed a night of passion for her, she'd been gratified and disarmed by the sight of Lucy putting coffee mugs on the bedside table and unwrapping herself from her dressing gown to join her under the covers. The feel of skin against cool skin had set her tingling in a good way, making her wonder if there might be time for making love again before they got up. But the deranged questioning about some woman she didn't even remember at the bar the night before had acted as a very effective passion killer.

Jo was fairly empathic in general. And she 'got it' – she really did. Lucy's last girlfriend had been a notorious philanderer, and it had left scars. Lucy was a nice kid. She wasn't particularly bright, but she was petite and pretty, and she could be kind when she wasn't 'off on one'. She was also, always, deeply repentant once her jealous rages had passed.

Jo certainly didn't want to hurt her, but she'd been through it all a few too many times now and she'd reached the stage where she'd had enough and was gently trying to edge her way out of the relationship. The more Jo edged, of course, the more twitchy Lucy became. After all – just because you're paranoid, it doesn't mean they're not out to dump you.

So Jo felt anxious when she picked Lucy up that night. Particularly when she saw her swigging Rescue Remedy straight from the bottle the minute she'd belted herself into the passenger seat. They'd got off to an okay start. Lucy'd had a bit of a Patti Smith look going on, with a black pants suit, white shirt, white pumps. She looked sexy and Jo had told her so. But the Rescue Remedy was never a good sign.

'Aren't you supposed to dilute that?' she asked.

Lucy didn't answer. '*This Natalie?*' she demanded as she put the remedy back in her bag. 'What's she like?' She had the edge to her voice that Jo had come to fear - a kind of croakiness that was always a sure indicator of her jealousy rattling its cage.

'She's okay...' Jo put the car in gear and braced herself. 'Bit posh. Bit boring. She's a teacher. Nothing special.'

'Do you fancy her?'

'Nah... not my type.'

'Are you sure? Because you *look* like you fancy her when you talk about her.'

Jo wasn't sure how to answer this. She felt fairly confident that she couldn't have actually spoken about Natalie much, because she'd learnt to keep well away from the topic of any woman under the age of ninety when she was with Lucy. Nonetheless, the accusation was difficult for Jo to deny and she knew that anything she said on the subject was likely to sound shifty and evasive. She'd fallen into a kind of generalized shiftiness around Lucy anyway - a tense sort of 'damned if you do/damned if you don't' type of feeling that dogged her most of the time, whether she actually had anything to feel guilty about or not. It intensified now as Lucy's jealousy homed in, for once, on a genuine target.

'She's okay,' she said again, knowing that Natalie would expose her for a liar the minute she walked into the restaurant. 'But she's not a patch on you.'

'Oh?' Lucy sounded slightly mollified.

Then Jo spoilt it. 'And anyway,' she said. 'She's going out with Ed.' It was one of those moments when anxiety makes you blunder into saying too much. She realised her mistake immediately and could have ripped out her careless, stupid tongue.

'I see!' said Lucy, ominously. 'So basically, the only reason you "don't" fancy her is because she's straight and wouldn't fancy *you* even if you were the last human being on the planet.'

'No… I mean I have to be nice to her because she's my best friend's girlfriend.' Jo knew this was mere damage limitation, because, just for once, Lucy was right. She guessed it had been bound to happen sooner or later.

Lucy knew it too, and she shuddered ominously as she clamped herself into that nasty, menacing, hyper-charged silence that Jo had come to dread.

-0-0-0-

Of course, Natalie was stunning as ever when she arrived, looking flushed and gorgeous and totally loved-up on Ed's arm.

'Not your type, eh?' hissed Lucy, into Jo's ear.

It flashed through Jo's mind that they were probably late because they hadn't been able to drag themselves out of bed, or the shower, or wherever else they'd been all over each other before they set off.

But she couldn't help melting as Ed's girlfriend kissed her, continental-style, on both cheeks, saying 'Jo!' as if she were her best buddy.

'And this must be Lucy?' Nat turned her innocently knock-out smile towards Jo's glowering partner. 'It's so lovely to meet you!'

She treated Lucy to her own shower of kisses.

Any less psychotic lesbian would have been won over instantly. And for a moment Jo felt hopeful. Then she saw the sulky expression deepen on Lucy's face and knew she was in for a very rocky night.

'Has Jo told you that she acted as match-maker for me and Ed?' Natalie asked, reaching for his arm and pulling him softly into her. He looked like the cat who'd got the cream, lucky devil. Jo could have slapped him.

'No,' said Lucy. 'She's very secretive, I'm afraid.'

Natalie sat, oblivious to the atmosphere, in the red velvet covered seat Ed had pulled back for her. 'Well, you must ask her to tell you,' she said. 'It really was quite funny.'

She seemed to be mistaking Lucy's surly expression for shyness, and Jo, remembering the loneliness she'd felt from her that first day, could see that she was making superhuman efforts to engage both of them in conversation, probably in the pure, innocent hope of making a couple of friends in her new home town.

The awful futility of it made her want to cry.

Ed wasn't much use either. Jo had confided in him about her 'Lucy problem', but he'd just been laddish about it and made a lot of jokes about 'Fatal Attraction' and locking up the local bunnies. And now, seeing his girlfriend struggling, all he did was raise a bemused eyebrow at Jo and mutter 'You poor sod!' on his way to exchange greetings with the elder Mr Singh, who had suddenly made an appearance beside his grandson at the reception desk.

Jo's hopes raised again briefly when he returned. He could be charming and witty and disarming when he wanted to be. If he'd really made an effort, he just might have been able to deflect Lucy from her trajectory. But the starters were arriving, and it soon became clear that any attention he could spare from his food was going to be focused fairly exclusively on getting plastered, as usual.

Jo abandoned hope and surrendered herself to her fate.

It was Saturday, so the place was packed. The sound of contentedly raised voices was almost drowning out the soundtrack from 'Rangeela', and Jo, who actually wasn't all that wild about curry, had snuffled her way uncomfortably through her starter and could feel herself getting more and more sweaty and uncomfortable with every blisteringly hot tandoori that sizzled past her.

Bleakly, she wished that she'd had the sense to come by taxi, as Nat and Ed obviously had. But it's easy to be wise after the event, and she was lumbered with the car now, so she didn't even have the option of getting wasted on Cobra like the other three.

Somewhere along the evening, 'Rangeela' became 'Dilwale Dulhania Le Jayenge'. On reception, Ajit sang along and waved across the room at them, like a handsome young Shah Rukh Khan. Jo could see he was fantasizing about that stretch limo and all the extra wedding parties it would bring.

Then the main course arrived. And, Natalie's general sweetness, enthusiasm and desperation to engage someone - anyone - in conversation just served to highlight the contrast between Ed's girlfriend and her own.

Eventually, over a barely touched korma, and despairing of the others, Jo succumbed to the only person at the table who seemed to want to be bothered with talking to her. 'It's strange, imagining you teaching at my old school,' she said. 'Is Wiggy... sorry Mr Wigston, still there?'

'Absolutely!'

'Does he still have that dusty old cloak?'

'He *does!* It makes him look like a bat, flitting through the corridors.'

Jo grinned. 'He used to clean the board with it,' she said. 'I guess it's all white boards and marker pens now.'

'Yes....' Nat smiled ruefully. 'My first day, the kids switched the white board markers for ordinary ones. I had to spend my entire lunch break trying to rub the writing off.'

'Coke's good for that, apparently,' said Jo.

'So I was told – *after* the event.'

'You should have given 'em all a damn good thrashing!' Jo raised a provocative eyebrow, letting Nat know she was teasing, and enjoying, just for a brief, foolish moment, the surge of chemistry she'd felt on their previous two meetings.

'Sadly, we're not allowed to thrash the little darlings anymore. Apparently it contravenes their human rights!' Nat, smiled back with just a hint – probably unconscious – of flirtation, while Ed worked his way through a Lamb Dopiaza with extra chillies, and Lucy nibbled churlishly at a very red Chicken Tikka, with a tomato and onion salad on the side.

It hadn't been wise to leave her out of the conversation, and she signalled her displeasure by suddenly blowing her nose so aggressively it jolted Jo back into reality. She sighed and pushed her barely touched plate away.

'Hey!' Ed had been quite content in his own little world, enjoying the faint tracing of Nat's thumb over his thigh. But the sight of potentially wasted food made him sit up and take notice. 'Did you not enjoy that?' he asked.

'No... it was nice.' She knew it was just a matter of taste with these things. 'I'm just not very hungry.' Lucy was spoiling her appetite anyway, with her brooding silence and nose blowing.

'Well giz it 'ere then. S'a shame to waste it.'

Pissed as a rat! thought Jo, wondering how he managed it without throwing up.

She handed him her plate.

'Did *you* go to the Grammar School too?' Nat asked Lucy, getting a bit desperate by now.

Lucy spluttered. 'Do I *look* like I went to the frigging lah de dah Grammar School?'

This was unmistakably rude. Even to Nat, who hadn't realised until then that this particular native wasn't all that friendly. She looked down at her meal, hurt, and Jo felt murderous towards Ed for not helping.

'I think I need a fag,' she declared. She'd started smoking when she was going out with Veronica, continued all through college, and given it up when she didn't have to hang around outside chilly nightclubs in the hen-party limo anymore. But recently, due to Lucy-related stress, she'd started again. She shoved her chair back. She'd never liked lighting up when other people were eating – even before the smoking ban. Right now, she figured she needed some fresh air anyway.

'Could you order me a kulfi if they come round with the desert menu?' she asked Ed. She hoped it might cool her down a bit.

He nodded as he mopped at his plate with a chapatti, oblivious to the fact that his girlfriend, beside him, was upset.

'You coming?' Jo demanded of her own partner, with a sharp jolt of her head in the direction of the door.

Lucy trailed after her like a whipped dog, knowing, full well, that she'd gone too far. The air hit them, cold and dank as they stepped out of the over-heated restaurant and into the drop off area at the front of the building.

Jo was seething, but she held off until a gaggle of thirty-somethings had climbed into their taxi. She inhaled smoke deep into her lungs as she waited, feeling the nicotine locking itself into her brain, giving her a false sense of courage.

'That was really rude!' she said finally, when they were alone.

Lucy knew she was in the wrong. She didn't need to be told. It made her feel defensive and bad about herself and close to tears. 'You lied to me,' she said, swerving the accusation and tossing one of her own. 'You told me she was like the back end of a bus.'

'I never *did!*'

'*And* you told me she was boring. If she's so bloody boring, how come you were hanging onto her every word like that?'

'I was being polite.'

'Don't try and worm your way out of it. You'd practically got your tongue down her cleavage.'

Jo sighed. 'I was just being polite,' she said again. 'Which is more than anyone could ever say about *you*.'

Lucy felt ashamed. And she hated feeling like that. So she attacked even more viciously.

'Don't give me that!' she hissed. 'You fancy the knickers off her. And she was all over *you* too.'

'**She was not!** She kissed *you* when she arrived as well. She's just a bit over the top that's all. That's how all those posh birds are... All air kisses and *'Absolutely bloody fabulous darlings!'*... It doesn't actually *mean* anything.'

'She couldn't keep her eyes off you!'

'Well, she was sitting opposite me. And anyway, she's practically been tossing Ed off under the table all night.'

'Yeah… and don't you just wish it was *you*!'

This was how she was. Whatever you said, she had an answer for it.

Jo slumped - exasperated now and beyond caring. She tossed her cigarette, half-smoked, into the gutter and ground at it with her foot. 'Don't be so bloody stupid!' she said.

'Oh, stupid, am I? You're telling me you don't fancy her then are you?' She was drunk, of course and she was practically shouting. Ed had kept buying drinks for her and she'd kept drinking them. Jo knew she should have stopped him. Drinking always made Lucy worse.

And then, suddenly, some survival instinct kicked in. It had been a long time coming. But now it flashed into Jo's head in neon lights, screaming ***'Run!'*** She wondered afterwards if it had been the cigarette, reminding her of her mother's agitated chain smoking by the window on the nights her dad was late home from the pub, or from work, or from the football. Back then, she'd believed her mum's accusations - overheard through the walls and floorboards – waking them in the night when they were in bed. They'd all believed it - the screaming about this 'floozy' and that 'fancy woman'. And they'd unanimously seen their distant, bad-tempered and occasionally heavy-fisted father as a bastard. People always love their mums best don't they? Especially when their dads just create an atmosphere when they come home? Jo still remembered the early days. The familiar comfort of her mother's nicotine stained fingers with their smell of tar and onions. And the smoky kisses when she tucked her up in bed. She remembered how all that stopped when Andy arrived and the Nitrazepam kicked in and her mother became convinced that her dad was having an affair ('again', as Liam explained, because this definitely wasn't the first time). But now she wondered; What if he'd never actually been a womaniser at all? What if he *had* just been at work, or the pub, or the football with his mates?

The sign expanded its message. *'Run now,'* it said, *'while you still have the strength.'*

And she snapped. 'Of course I fancy Nat,' she said. 'She's gorgeous. I fancy loads of women. Of course I do. That's just normal. I'd never do anything about it. And it's never stopped me being in a relationship before. But if you can't handle that, I think we should just call it a day.'

Lucy's face crumpled. She looked stunned, like she'd just accidentally driven herself into a brick wall. 'What do you mean?' she stammered.

'I mean I can't cope with this. You're a lovely lass, and I really thought we might have been able to have something special... But I'm obviously not capable of making you feel secure. So it's never going to work... is it?'

Lucy looked bewildered now. Her fists clenched and unclenched at her sides as if she might be about to punch something. Jo tensed herself, ready to duck.

'Don't say that,' Lucy wailed. 'I can't bear it. I love you!'

'No – you don't... If you loved me you wouldn't treat me like this. And you certainly wouldn't be rude to my friends.'

'But I *do* Jo... I *do* love you and I thought you loved *me.*'

She burst into tears as a private hire white Toyota drew up in front of them. The couple in the back were middle aged – the man in an open necked shirt and jacket – the woman in a navy blue winter coat with a pale pink top beneath it. The man leaned forward to pay the driver as his wife stared through the window at Lucy sobbing and Jo beside her, embarrassed now, trying to get her hysterical girlfriend to quieten down.

Her efforts were completely counterproductive.

'I thought you loved me,' wailed Lucy.

'Sssshhh!' Jo tried to calm her, reaching out to lay a restraining hand on her arm.

Lucy tossed it aside.

'I can't believe you're doing this to me,' she wailed, very loudly. 'You just used me for sex.'

'I never did!'

Mortified, Jo saw the look of horror on the faces of the middle-aged couple as they got out of the taxi. The man's arm went protectively round his wife, shielding her from this unexpected display of lesbianism. In Victorian times the horses would have been well and truly frightened by now.

Then suddenly Lucy dragged herself away and ran round to the driver's side of the cab.

'Can you take me to Midland Street?' she gasped, through her tears.

The driver glared at Jo... vile seductress that she was...

'No problem love,' he said, protectively. 'Hop in!'

He revved the engine as she climbed into the back of the cab, then reversed in a puff of exhaust smoke and screeching tyres. He sounded like some Hollywood hero who'd just snatched the heroine from the clutches of the bad guys.

Jo stared after his blinking right indicator as he pulled out of the car park and onto the main road. She couldn't believe it had been so easy in the end. But she felt bad about it. She didn't like that she'd had to hurt Lucy. And she hated knowing how it must have looked to the strangers who'd witnessed it. She didn't want to have to go back into the restaurant with their accusing eyes on her. And she didn't want to have to admit to Nat and Ed that, in the course of one cigarette, she'd managed to lose her girlfriend.

Maybe if she smoked another?

But it was only delaying the inevitable. She was still dazed as she went back inside.

Ed had ordered her a pistachio kulfi. It was pale green and half melted, with a tiny paper parasol on a cocktail stick that quivered as it sank slowly beneath the rim of its silver dish.

Natalie was just returning to the table. She'd been to the 'Ladies'. She seemed to be avoiding looking at Jo.

'Lucy had to go home,' Jo said, trying to strike the right balance of concern. 'She wasn't feeling very well.'

'How come you didn't take her in the car then?' This sounded unexpectedly harsh, coming from Natalie.

But it was a good question. Jo glanced across at her, wrong-footed, trying to read where the anger was coming from.

'She didn't want to break up the evening,' she said, realising she was now exposed, either as a heartless girlfriend or a liar. She prodded at the liquefying kulfi with her spoon. She didn't actually want it anymore. 'Reckon I need a straw for this,' she said, glumly.

Ed grinned. 'Come on mate... Tell the truth and shame the devil! You finally *dumped* her, didn't you?'

The polite lie hadn't worked very well. Jo threw herself at the mercy of the truth. She shrugged. 'More the other way round actually.'

'Good move mate – how'd you swing *that* one?' Ed laughed and knocked back the double brandy he'd ordered with his coffee.

Nat scowled at him. She didn't seem to want to get involved in this conversation.

'I think maybe we should go home too,' she said.

Ed looked crestfallen. 'Why love? Are you feeling okay? You don't need to get upset about Lucy. She was a *right* cow. Jo's been trying to ditch her for weeks. Look, the night's still young and we can all relax now. Let's get some more drinks, eh? It's on the house!'

Nat was not going to be mollified. 'Don't you think you've had enough?' Her eyes flashed at him. She was very upset. Close to tears. There was no doubt about that.

And Jo could see that the evening was over, even if Ed was still bargaining.

'Okay… look… I'll drive you both home!' She was keen to make amends for wrecking the night. She began to struggle to her feet.

Ed, confused at the suddenness of it all, looked as if he was about to accept.

But Nat pre-empted him. 'No,' she said, very firmly. 'We wouldn't want to take you out of your way. *Would* we, Ed?'

-0-0-0-

On her way out of the restaurant a few minutes later, Jo stopped off at the 'Ladies'.

It was a smart affair with a crinolined woman in silhouette on the door, and, inside, pink marble sinks and matching toilet seats. She had to wait to get into the end cubicle, but she'd already guessed what she would find. And there it was - the air grill - set into the wall about a foot above her head. Miserably, over the delicately piped music, she heard the murmur of Nat and Ed's voices, talking outside as they waited for their taxi.

Their words were perfectly audible, even though they weren't half-shouting, as Lucy had been.

And it sounded like they were in the embryonic phase of a row.

'Your friends all hate me,' Natalie was saying.

'Don't be daft!' Ed must have tried to put his arm round her, or kiss her, or find some clumsy Ed-like way of getting back to the warm, fuzzy feeling they'd had at the start of the evening.

'Don't think you can get round me like that!' she hissed.

And despairingly, Jo rubbed her hands through her hair, shaking her head as she wondered just how *much* of her conversation with Lucy, Natalie had heard.

Chapter Five

It was pretty much all of it. She'd spoken to Jo about it since. How she cried that night, holding herself very still after Ed had fallen asleep, slightly miffed that he wasn't getting any sex, and leaving her alone with her distress without ever really trying to get to the bottom of it.

She could never have told him how she felt anyway. It was too shameful to be described as 'boring', 'posh' and 'over the top', all things that, on a bad day, she suspected the people of this staunchly northern, still living somewhere back in the 1950's, town thought about her anyway.

But it was a shame, because Ed would have laughed it off and he may have been able to persuade her to laugh it off too. He knew exactly what the problem was with Lucy. It wasn't like he wouldn't have said the same things himself if he'd been in Jo's shoes that night. And he wouldn't have meant them anymore than Jo had.

But Natalie was too embarrassed to tell him, so she believed what she'd heard.

And it cast a shadow over her relationship with Jo for the next three years.

-0-0-0-

Nat thought about that shadow now as she dropped the kids off – Alyssa at the small block of flats where her best friend Roxanne lived with her mum and brother. And Jake, ten minutes later, at Tamzin, his girlfriend's place - bigger and much smarter, with a mum and a dad, and a Porsche in the driveway.

'Mind you behave yourself,' she cautioned him. It wasn't something she ever felt she had to say to Alyssa, but Jake had been a crazy, hyperactive kind of kid, always escaping out of windows and getting into scrapes at school, and she didn't trust him not to land himself in trouble now, particularly with Tamzin's parents out for the evening and his hormones raging.

'I *always* behave myself,' he protested, pulling his overnight bag out of the car, looking, for all the world, like a younger, raven-haired version of Shaggy from Scooby Doo.

Despite herself, Nat couldn't help but smile at that. Of her two children, she knew Jake would find life easiest. He had none of Alyssa's complexity. He cared little what anyone thought of him. And he'd had girls falling for him ever since he started nursery school. Natalie sometimes wondered if Jo had secretly taught him some of her chat-up lines. Certainly, his father's influence had been minimal, though he could have passed on a few handy hints of his own if only he could have been bothered.

Tamzin was the latest in a long string of 'girlfriends' for Jake. But he seemed to be more than usually smitten this time. Nat saw it in the way he reached for her hand as she ran towards him, long legs skinny in her teenage girl outfit of woolly tights, shorts and Doc Martens. Her feet skidded on the salted driveway. The sleeves of her huge knitted sweater were pulled down way below the tips of her fingers. Her breath made clouds upon the air. She was sparkling with excitement, but she remembered to call 'Hello Mrs Mason' through the car window when she caught sight of her, reminding Nat that this girl, unlike Jake, who went to the altogether more practical local academy - was a class-mate of Alyssa's at the Grammar

School. *More* complications if the relationship with Jo became public knowledge, she thought ruefully, as she waved and returned the girl's greeting.

'Hi Tamzin. Did you have a nice Christmas?'

'Lovely, thank you,' she snuggled cosily into Jake's side. 'How was yours?'

'Very nice, thank you,' she lied.

Nat could see that they were in love.

And she felt moved and horribly lonely all at the same time, as she watched them loping up the driveway, deep in conversation, jostling against each other affectionately as they walked.

-0-0-0-

Ed had already started drinking when she got back. He stood in the kitchen in the stained grey marl sweatshirt and jog pants that Natalie had tried on many occasions, to throw away. He had a 'Famous Grouse' bottle in one hand and a heavy lead crystal whisky glass in the other. He waved the bottle ironically in her direction as she came in, offering her a drink he knew she wouldn't accept.

'No thanks,' she said stiffly and headed for the house bathroom to get ready.

In the old days, she never would have locked the door. She would have wanted Ed to wander in while she bathed. She'd have hinted for him to join her in the shower, or sit on the side of the bath and talk to her, maybe touch her through the bubbles in candlelight while she was warm and drowsy and relaxed. They used to do that all the time when they were still in love. And there had been a long time after the children had come along - after the early days when she was too tired to feel like doing anything like that at all - when she'd have welcomed it still. But then, suddenly, one day, she'd found that she didn't want it anymore. And as she lay there tonight, thinking guiltily that she wasn't sure she actually *liked* the aromatherapy bath foam Jake had bought her for Christmas, she wondered when that switch-off day had been. It was long before the first time with Jo. She was sure of that, though maybe the love, so long denied, had already been there. But one evening, when the kids were at Ed's parents, and they'd had the house to themselves, and she thought those sweet old memories might call him to her, she had found herself locking the door. And it was automatic now... that need to stop Ed intruding on her space.

So it was shocking, and a little bit frightening to hear him trying to come in to her that night. To hear the door rattling as the handle flexed. He soon gave up. And he didn't knock, or call through the door to her. So it was easy to pretend that she hadn't heard.

Anxiously, she sank down beneath the surface of the water and tried to tell herself that Jo would be home soon, and then, somehow, they might find a way for everything to be back to normal.

Though in her heart, she knew that nothing, ever, would be the same again.

-0-0-0-

Ed waited for Natalie to emerge.

He knew she'd be completely dressed, made-up, and ready to get in the taxi the minute the driver arrived. 'Fully packaged', he thought grimly, remembering the happier days when she still loved him and would emerge naked and still damp from the shower, misty in the steam, completely unselfconscious, to dress in front of him. He remembered watching, sometimes secretly... and sometimes, deliberately, erotically, marvelling at the fullness of her, delaying her by pulling her towards him and unpeeling some item she had only just put on.

He'd loved those moments. The underwear that went with the different dresses... The pants, high leg, lacy, silk or cotton, soft under his rough fingers... The bras, white – nude – black – strapless, up-thrust, sexy or demure – cupping her perfectly full breasts, hiding them from the other men who would be looking and wanting to go where he knew he would be going later.... where he might, if he was quick and lucky, and they weren't too last minute, get to go now.... And the tights, or better, the stockings or hold-ups, rolled over those perfect legs, making them shimmer as she walked. A whole sensual brew of erotic arts, sealed with a dab of perfume at her throat and wrists. There for him to breathe in as he stood close to fasten a necklace or bracelet.

She kept all that from him now, like a punishment.

Sometimes he thought he might even be able to forgive her if she didn't do that.

But she *did*, and she emerged, as predicted, fully dressed. He saw that she'd even struggled alone into the gold and diamond chain he'd bought her for Christmas, wearing it dutifully, but independently, as if to emphasise just how much of a no-go area she was for him now.

He told himself that he hated her then. Though that was, in every way, a lie.

'You locked me out,' he said when she joined him in the bedroom.

He was straightening his tie in the mirror. He didn't turn round.

'Sorry sweetheart. It's so automatic these days... Not wanting to traumatise the kids!'

'I don't just mean tonight,' he said.

-0-0-0-

Nat had bought a new dress for the evening. It was soft and sheer and silver grey. She'd modelled it for Jo when she came back from shopping one Saturday in November. Jo had drawn her into her arms as 'Halo' came on the radio. They'd kissed and joked about this being their perfect wedding song. Then she'd buried her face in Jo's shoulder to hide the tears that had pooled at the idea that they'd never be able to dance together in public like that.

She smoothed her hands over the dress, feeling the warmth of her body beneath the soft jersey material. She wished she didn't have to wear it now. She wanted to preserve the memories it held for her.

Ed poured himself another whisky.

And a shudder of grief ran through her.

-0-0-0-

Ed's drinking had only very faintly worried her at first. She'd told herself that he was no different from her friends when she'd been in the Sixth Form at school, or at University. It had been normal back then, getting drunk at the weekends, having fun.

In retrospect, of course, the warning signs had been there right from the start....

Within a week of their first date he'd fallen asleep and failed to meet her at the cinema. They'd had a row about that. She'd wondered about him then. But he'd soon won her over with that woeful, puppy-dog look of his, and she'd sacrificed her better judgement to the deep, almost compulsive need she felt towards him.

The lonely nights had started early too. Those nights when he'd gone from 'life and soul of the party' to 'passed out on the sofa'. There were only a few of them at the start, when he'd wanted to be sober enough to have sex when they got home. But they'd grown more frequent as the years went by, particularly when she agreed to live with him and became more available.

She remembered finding the boxes of empty bottles in the cupboard under the stairs when she moved in. She'd felt embarrassed enough about those to lie to an elderly lady at the Bottle Bank. 'Party!' she'd grimaced, apologetically, as she stepped back to allow the old dear to post her single 'Mather's Black Beer' bottle into the 'Green' container. But she told herself that he just wasn't great at recycling. And after she joked with him about it, the 'empties' never mounted up under the stairs again – They moved, as she discovered, when it was already too late, into the garage… and the car boot… and the loft.

Then there were the 'accidents' - the times he mistook the wardrobe for the en-suite. He never seemed to want to hear how much that upset and disgusted her.

But it's amazing what you can explain away when you really don't want to see it.

And for a while, at first, Natalie went through a phase of drinking more heavily too.

She couldn't deny that she had a wonderful time when she let her hair down and 'had a few'. She'd had to be so careful all her life. It was good to feel relaxed and mellow for a change.

She didn't worry about Ed making a fool of himself when she was tipsy too. His friends seemed so much more interesting and the jokes actually funny. And the sex? That was great – wild and uninhibited and open in a way she was much too self-conscious to be when she was sober.

Ed was drunk when he proposed to her.

'Marry me!' he said, upending an empty champagne bottle in the ice bucket and clicking his fingers to the waiter for another.

There was something in his head about wanting this moment to last forever.

And he figured that she'd say 'Yes'.

All her friends were getting married, and he was a good catch.

She loved him too, and she told him often enough. But he never quite managed to bring himself to believe in that.

-0-0-0-

Ruth, Nat's best friend, had been cautious when she heard the news. She'd met Ed by then, and she'd already sent Nat a copy of 'Women Who Love Too Much' in a not very hopeful attempt at making her see sense. Ruth's father was a drinker, so she knew the signs.

'Are you sure this is a good idea?' she asked. Over the years, she'd seem Nat fall for more than her fair share of 'lame ducks'.

'I love him.'

'That's a pretty daft reason for marrying an alcoholic.'

'He's not an alcoholic.'

'Have it your own way!'

Nat could almost hear Ruth's shrug on the other end of the phone. It just made her all the more desperate to defend Ed. 'He's just shy that's all. And he drinks to feel more confident. It's no wonder he struggles. He's obviously dyslexic – and goodness knows how that awful school he went to never picked it up.'

'Yeah, yeah...' Ruth wasn't one to mince her words. 'So you're helping him restore the battered fragments of his self-esteem are you?... Bonking him back to health?'

Natalie had smiled at this, despite herself. 'Well, he *is* happy with me,' she said.

'So happy he's prepared to face the world sober?'

'He's not *that* bad. He's only a social drinker.'

'Yeah, he's a very sociable guy! No sign of him heading for AA in the near future then?'

'No. he doesn't believe in them.... And anyway, he doesn't need them. He could cut down anytime he likes.'

Ruth huffed. 'Mmm, if only I had a quid for every time I've heard *that* one,' she said dismissively. 'Well, I'll tell you, Ed might have zero self-esteem, but *you* don't, and I don't think you've got what it takes to keep forgiving him when he keeps letting you down... unlike my stupid doormat of a mother who falls for it every time with Dad... But hey... I'm only your best buddy, so what do *I* know? Maybe by the time you're forty you'll have developed a taste for Country and Western music and wide-eyed emotional masochism.... So marry the guy if you must. And when it all goes pear-shaped, I might just not be able to resist saying 'I told you so.'... I can't say fairer than that, can I?'

At some level, Natalie feared that she was right. But she was in love. And love is blind.

'No,' she conceded, reluctantly. 'I guess not. But I really do wish you could be happy for me, just this once.'

Chapter Six

'Are you sure Natalie's safe?' Ulrika asked cautiously. She always felt wary about introducing fear where there may be no reason, but as Jo had talked, she'd continued to feel that cold, prickling sense of dread.

Jo laughed, slightly nervous suddenly. 'With Ed...? God, yes! He's a complete pussycat.... Wouldn't hurt a fly!'

Ulrika remembered seeing the retreat centre cats playing with flies. They seemed quite ruthless to her.

She was wondering whether to share the image when, faintly, a bell tolled.

They both jumped. And Jo remembered from the laminated timetable on the back of her door, that Vespers (whatever *that* might be) was at 6.30pm. It seemed rude to look at her watch, but it must be about that time now.

'I'm sorry, I must go,' said Sister Ulrika. She eased herself painfully to her feet.

Jo stood too. 'Thank you,' she said. 'I've appreciated you listening.'

'I feel that we've barely scratched the surface... There's a sheet outside the door with my availability. Please just put a cross on there if you would like to see me again tomorrow. You needn't put your name on. I'll be here anyway. And don't forget, dinner is at 7.30pm and, of course, you're welcome to join us for any of the Offices. You could come with me now if you'd like...' she waited, looking encouragingly, but without much hope, into Jo's eyes. The gentle blue of them jolted her, as it had earlier, and she looked away... from Jo and from the memory of her own impossible longing, all those years ago, before she ran away from all of that and back into the cool sanctuary of her 'calling'.

'Well, like I said earlier...' Jo was saying, with one of her deceptively indifferent shrugs.

Ulrika forced herself to hear her. *I'm not religious.* She'd said that clearly enough, hadn't she?

'That's fine. I understand. The important thing is that you use this time exactly as *you* need to.'

She stepped back to let the younger woman out of the room, then she turned out the lamp and padded down the stone flagged corridor in the direction of the chapel.

-0-0-0-

A wave of loneliness swept through Jo as she heard Sister Ulrika's footsteps fading away. Through the window she could see the still, snowy statue of St Francis, illuminated by the light from inside the building and the wall lamp at the door of the chapel. Beyond him, the garden and fells were black against a cloud-heavy, paler grey sky. She wasn't used to being inactive, and she wondered what on earth she would do for the next hour. Part of her was tempted to just leave a note for Ulrika, jump in the car and head home. She was painfully aware that, never having really confided anything to anyone in her life before, she'd just splurged out some of her deepest secrets to a total stranger. It had left her feeling vulnerable and sad and a bit afraid. She wanted to run home to Natalie, where she could just hide from herself again and feel loved and safe.

The idea that she may have permanently lost that safe haven gnawed away at her too, reminding her of what her life had been like before she'd had the comfort of Natalie in it.

And like an addict, bargaining for 'just one more', she went up to her dingy, cold, smelly bedroom, took her mobile phone out of her bag, and started a slow, methodical search for any slight glimmer of reception anywhere around the house.

By 7.25, she'd almost given up. She'd prowled practically every corner of the place... upstairs, downstairs, the library, meeting rooms, ladies shower block and loos. She'd been outside in the frozen night, holding the phone up to the stars, to north, south, east and west... And all the time, there was nothing, not even a single bar of hope.

Miserably, she headed in the direction of the dinner bell that tolled suddenly like the start of a John Donne poem.

-0-0-0-

Supper was a strange affair. 'Elevenses', and lunch – cheese sandwiches in curled white bread, on a large plate and covered with cling film - had been served in the big cosy common room by the fire. But supper was in the refectory - a huge, echoing, high-ceilinged, stone-walled hall with massive, scrubbed wooden tables that could have easily accommodated fifty or sixty people. There were five nuns, in various stages of decrepitude – one, in a wheelchair, clunking furiously at a set of rosary beads. And the retreatants were all there too. They sat in silence, watching the kitchen staff shuffle in with a creaking stainless steel trolley and lay out a couple of huge pans of stew and dumplings (one vegetarian), a bowl of trifle for pudding, and a loaf of sliced bread with margarine and jam, that reminded her so strongly of childhood tea-times at home with her brothers that she could have wept.

'Catweazle' seemed to have taken a fancy to Jo. He'd seated himself opposite her when he came shuffling in. He was wearing a grubby duffle coat and scarf and showed no sign of taking them off to eat. He was rubbing his hands together, whether out of cold, or in excited anticipation of the food, Jo wasn't sure.

Either way, the tension seemed to be mounting...

Until, as if answering some unseen signal, a chair shrieked backwards on the stone floor. And they were off... creating a cacophony of squeaking and clattering, clanging and crashing that just seemed all the louder somehow because of the 'silence'.

Jo was still feeling dejected about the phone signal situation and not very hungry, so she waited until the scrummage around the food had died down before getting herself a small bowl of the vegetable stew that looked slightly less greasy than the meat version. She stood politely behind her chair while Sister Ulrika, who must have been at least ten years younger than the youngest of the rest of the nuns, said grace.

When they finally sat to eat, Jo found that the food was surprisingly good; steaming hot, fragrant and herb-rich. And the dumplings, *very* distantly related to the slimy affairs her mother used to make, were nicely crunchy with fluffy insides.

She'd finished her bowl and was wondering about 'seconds' when she looked up to see Catweazle pushing a note across the table at her.

It said 'SMALL CHAPEL'.

She looked across at him quizzically.

He lifted his hand to his right ear with thumb up and little finger down in the universal gesture for 'Phone.'....

or 'Telling Bone', as his TV namesake would have called it.

She wondered if he was an angel in disguise.

'Thank you!' Flooded with gratitude, she reached out in a spontaneous gesture, touching his leathery, knot-veined hand with hers. And as she smiled into his eyes, she noticed that they were moist and rheumy and so pale that hardly any of their original blue was left in them at all.

-0-0-0-

The small chapel was like the kind of multi-purpose prayer room you might find in a hospital or airport.

It was painted the colour of hessian sacking, and had six red plastic chairs.

The table at the front had a flower arrangement in seasonal shades of red, silver and green.

Two small red artificial votive candles glowed on either side of it, flicking shadows like flames, up onto the walls where, to the right, an abstract tapestry hung. It was, maybe four foot by six, geometric and embroidered in rich primary colours. It reminded Jo of the John Piper baptistry window at Coventry Cathedral. She'd been there once, many years ago on one of the rare school trips her parents had managed to fund. She'd thought it was one of the most beautiful things she'd ever seen.

Entering quietly, Jo sat and took her phone out of the pocket of the thick, cable knit fisherman's jersey she'd packed, 'just in case it was cold'. The reception bars on the left hand side of the screen crept up to two. She kissed the cold glass, she was so relieved.

Then she huddled down in the seat, the jersey sleeves as far down her hands as she could get them and still compose… 'My heart's breaking without you. I miss you so much. God I love you!'

She hit 'Send' and prayed, watching the 'Out tray' symbol finally disappear from the bottom of the screen. Then she closed her eyes and waited.

Chapter Seven

Like all adulteresses, Natalie always checked her mobile when she went to the 'Ladies' - even when she thought that her lover was out of range and unlikely to be able to get a message to her.

The text brought tears to her eyes (of relief and loneliness in just about equal measure), and she typed hastily in reply, perched on one of the maroon velvet covered buffets by the make-up mirrors, nodding to a friend who came in and disappeared into one of the toilet cubicles, knowing that she daren't be away from Ed for too long.

'Come home then, you idiot. I'm going crazy here without you.'

From the cubicle came the sound of tinkling followed by the distinctive grating sound of toilet roll being teased out of the dispenser that never quite worked properly.

She added two hearts and a very long row of kisses, and hit 'Send' - just as Andrea Banks walked in.

'Ed's sent me to find you.' She smiled apologetically. 'Actually, I think it's just a ruse to get me out of the way so he can talk business with Robert.' If she'd noticed how guilty her friend looked when she came in, she pretended not to. 'So, are you texting the kids? Or have you got a secret lover?' This was meant as a joke. Andrea didn't know how Nat put up with Ed sometimes, but she'd certainly never seen her as the kind of woman who would 'play away'.

Natalie pretended to look disappointed, and deleted the incriminating texts under cover of switching off the phone. She wondered if she'd actually been away from the table for longer than she'd realised. 'If only!' she laughed. 'Though I've missed my chance now with George Clooney... But yes, it's "just" the kids... Daft, isn't it - texting to say 'nite-nite' to them at their age? They'll probably be teased mercilessly by their friends.' She put her phone back into her handbag and wondered if she would be punished for lying about the children like that.

But Andrea laughed, so she knew she'd carried it off okay. 'Well, I'm ashamed to say I still do it with mine, even now Martin and Gemma are at uni... God alone knows what *their* friends make of *that*.'

Natalie smiled. Andrea was her idea of an ideal mum and had always been something of a role model for her. Her own mother, 'Stephanie', was self-absorbed and childlike, and even at sixty five, something of a nightmare. She'd had a very public and highly lucrative divorce from Nat's father when Nat was just three years old, and had behaved like a let-loose teenager ever since. With a procession of unsuitable and often dangerously lecherous men at home, Nat had soon learned to spend as much time out of the house as possible (usually in the soothing quiet of the public library) and since she'd left home to go to university, she'd rarely returned. Sometimes she wished she'd had a better relationship with her mother. But at least, it had been easier for her than for her brother, Ralph. 'Stephanie' had always adored *him* and was frequently to be seen on his arm, loving it when new acquaintances assumed this handsome younger man was her partner rather than her son.

Andrea, in contrast, was cuddly and not overly made-up. She preferred sensible shoes and clothes, and scruffy, family-friendly cars. She never seemed bothered if she, her house, or her garden got messy. She was never on a diet or away at health farms. The idea of boob jobs, tummy tucks and liposuction horrified her. And she cared about her children as individuals, tolerating their 'off' days, and loving them no matter what... her daughter, as well as her two sons.

Robert, Andrea's husband, was a great dad too. But then, Natalie didn't even want to get *started* on what she'd encountered in the father department...

In the old days, before Ed's drinking began to make such things too risky, the two couples had sometimes been round to each other's houses for dinner parties. Once they'd even rented a huge villa with a pool in Majorca and taken all the kids on a two-family holiday. But then there had been the times when Ed became drunk and loud, and argumentative, or just a bit too vulgar in his jokes, or too openly, embarrassingly critical of Natalie, and, as if by mutual unspoken agreement, the invitations had stopped and they had gone back to meeting on more public occasions, at the Rotary or Tennis Clubs, where it was easier to get up and go, or talk to someone else when the going got tough.

Tonight, they were sharing a table and Nat had been glad of the quiet feeling of safety she had when she was with them. But she wasn't happy about Ed sending Andrea to look for her. It didn't bode well for the rest of the evening.

'Is Ed okay?' Andrea asked, as if she'd read Natalie's mind. She fluffed at her bobbed grey hair in the mirror. Their reflections, side by side, looked back at each other. Andrea noticed that Nat had dark rings under her eyes.

Natalie was startled by the question. 'As far as I know,' she said. 'Why?'

'I just wondered. I thought he looked stressed…. You too, if I'm honest.'

Natalie could see that Andrea was genuinely concerned, and genuinely *fond* of them both. She would have liked to confide in her. But she couldn't.

'We're fine,' she said, brusquely. 'Just tired, I think. You know what Christmas is like. It's all a bit crazy really. All that rushing around for just one day…. It's silly!'

-0-0-0-

'I think Ed's finally lost the plot,' said Robert to Andrea.

He was in the passenger seat. He'd enjoyed wine with his meal and a few fine brandies afterwards, so Andrea was driving. They'd just dropped Ed and Natalie home before turning in the direction of their own house. Andrea hoped that their youngest son Stephen (always rather more of a handful than his older brother and sister) wouldn't have burned it down, flooded it or had the police called out before they got back. She told herself it was pointless worrying about it now.

'His drinking's certainly getting worse.' She dragged her thoughts back to Ed.

'Yeah… I think it's addled his brain…. He thinks Natalie's having an affair.'

Andrea's heart sank. 'How ridiculous!' she said. But she remembered the phone, and the way Natalie had seemed to want to hide it. 'Who on earth does he think it is?' She'd already started to run through the list of possible suspects in her mind.

'Well, this is really gonna make you laugh!'

'Try me!' She stared ahead, slowing for a left turn at the roundabout on the edge of town.

'Jo!' said Robert triumphantly.

'Joe Eldwick?' Andrea glanced sideways at her husband. She was surprised. Joe was the new coach at the tennis club and Alyssa had been having lessons there recently. He may even be Nat's type, a bit like Ed when he was younger - blond haired, blue eyed, and good looking in a six-packed but gentle kind of way. He was certainly attractive. A lot of the local cougars had been sniffing him out. But at twenty eight, Andrea figured he'd be way too young to interest Natalie. She'd also heard on good authority that he was gay, though something stopped her sharing that particular piece of information with her husband.

'Nah... *Much* dafter than that!' said Robert, with a little flourish. '*Ed's* Jo... Jo Cooper... I *mean*... can you imagine it?... Natalie having a relationship with *Jo*?'

Andrea could tell that this was a rhetorical question, and she knew she was supposed to join in with Robert's derision at the whole crazy, impossible idea of it, but she found that – yes – actually, she *could* imagine it.... That she had, in fact, seen evidence that could have pointed to it if only she'd known what she was looking for.

Realising suddenly that Natalie may be in need of her protection, she forced herself to laugh along with Robert. 'Oh come on!' she said. 'He can't really think that... What exactly did he say?'

Robert spluttered. She could tell he was slightly tipsy. It always made him as giggly as a schoolgirl... 'I was trying to get him to ease up a bit on the Jack Daniels. And he said... pardon my French... "You'd be getting bladdered too mate, if you'd just found out that your best friend's poking your wife"… And I said "Don't be daft, Ed. Bill's as happily married as I am," and *he* said, "Not friggin' Bill, you tosser… *Jo!*" And I was just speechless… I mean…. The guy's lost it…. Gorgeous woman like that, what the hell would she be doing messing around with someone like Jo?'

Andrea wondered if she should be worried that her husband had just referred to Natalie as 'gorgeous'.

She decided against it.

But she *did* wonder about Natalie and Jo. She'd noticed over the years that Jo had an eye for 'gorgeous women', and quite a talent for 'pulling' them too. She was wondering whether she should text Nat to warn her. But then she turned into their drive and nearly ran into the back of the police car that was parked there. And the thought fled, temporarily, from her mind.

Chapter Eight

When they got home, Ed wanted sex. He'd hoped it might bring them together, but it was turning out to be lacklustre, missionary position stuff that only served to remind him of how far they'd drifted apart. Pushing into her, against a resistance she couldn't hide and probably hoped he wouldn't feel, he wondered why she was even bothering to go along with it. Resentfully, he told himself it was just to keep him sweet. He knew he'd been prone to sulking when he 'wasn't getting any'. So she probably did it for an easy life. Or maybe out of guilt. Or because she'd taken wedding vows with him and figured that it was part of the deal, even though she was breaking those vows in every other which way with Jo.

'You could at least *pretend* that you're enjoying it,' he said bitterly.

She realised too late that this time she'd forgotten to act. She began to move under him, stroking his back… gripping his backside, the way he liked it…starting to kiss him… though he noticed that she still avoided kissing him on the mouth. 'Sorry darling, I was just…'

'Just thinking about something else?' he said. 'The shopping list maybe, or the kids… eh… is *that* what it is?'

She shook her head and started to protest, but he knew that she'd been thinking about Jo.

He searched for her mouth with his, but still she moved away from him, catching his face, kissing his forehead, his cheek, moving down to his shoulder.

Unbidden, he felt his pent up anger surge. His whole body stiffened with it. He felt hard and cold and powerful suddenly.

When she tried to turn her face away again, he forced his mouth onto hers and shoved his tongue in, hard as he wanted, enjoying that she couldn't breathe and was struggling to pull herself away from him. He put his hand under her head so she couldn't push back into the pillow. It felt satisfying that he could do what he liked with her. *Serves you right,* he thought. *Serves you **both** right!*

'Ed... no.... stop...' she gasped, tearing herself free for a moment.

In the faint light of the bedside lamp, she saw him smile.

Then he unleashed himself fully into her, knowing that he could do whatever the hell he liked to her now and she couldn't stop him.

He knew he was hurting her. And in that moment, he was glad.

-0-0-0-

Sister Ulrika stopped and switched out the light in the small chapel as she made her way softly along the corridor. It was late, and she had been settling Sister Benedicta for the night. When the half-blind ninety year old had initially become bed-bound, she'd been crabby and uncooperative and Ulrika had come to dread their regular evening tussles with bathing and nightclothes and bedtime reading.

But then she'd realised that 'I'm getting low in my spirits,' meant that the elderly nun's whisky decanter needed replenishing. And the 'historical novels' she preferred at bedtime weren't quite Walter Scott or Jean Plaidy.

The pair of them had been firm friends ever since.

Turning into her small room now, Ulrika was still smiling at Benedicta's latest bedtime favourite, a rather lurid bodice ripper that made her grateful for the advent of the e-reader. But then she remembered Jo, and the impossible choice she was facing, and her smile faded, as she allowed herself to think of Florrie, her own forbidden love.

-0-0-0-

Florrie was tactless and feisty, but her eyes, almost the same shade as Jo's, were kind. Her slightly muddy blonde hair was cut into a short 'swinging sixties' bob. And her Gorbals accent was so strong the other sisters would call on Ulrika for translations. 'Ulrika understands Florrie,' they used to say, shaking their heads and adding, 'Heaven help her!'

Florrie used language that could make a Glasgow docker blush, and her sentences shrank to half their original size when all the swearwords were taken out. Ulrika still smiled when she thought of some of her more colourful phrases. But the foul mouth was just a part of Florrie's bravado - a 'don't mess with me' image that she presented to the world. She didn't swear so much when they were alone together. In fact, she was often quiet, sitting peacefully, as if, with Ulrika, she didn't feel that she had anything to prove.

There was a sense of melancholy in remembering those days... The stolen times spent sipping scalding tea next to the range in Florrie's kitchen, the air suffused with the smell of freshly washed nappies and underwear, drying on the clothes pulley above them. The deliciously forbidden sound of Elvis and The Beatles and Cilla Black booming from the red and white Dansette record player that made all too frequent trips to the pawn shop. Those rare precious moments when they found a way to be together, sitting quietly, or laughing till the tears streamed down their cheeks.

Florrie had a merchant seaman husband and a growing family. She used to joke that the family grew more every time her husband came home on leave. But there was something in her eyes that suggested that it wasn't really as funny as she made it out to be. She was four months gone with her third child when Ulrika arrived in Glasgow. And she was nursing the fifth when she left. She 'minded' her sisters' children too. The 'wee 'uns' scampered through her cosy kitchen and ran like feral creatures through the soot blackened Glasgow streets, skipping and playing conkers and hopscotch, chalking patterns onto wooden whipping tops. They were carefree in their grey knitted hand-me-downs, snot-nosed, dirty-kneed and never home before tea-time.

Their love had taken them both by surprise. But it changed everything. It was 1964. Florrie was married. And Ulrika was a nun. She did the 'right' thing. But she remembered the small anguished gasp that issued from Florrie's throat when she told her that she was leaving. And nothing could have prepared her for the grief that seared through her, almost taking her legs from under her as she walked away, forcing herself not to look back.

Thirty five years later, Sister Bernadette from the Glasgow mission had come to the centre on an extended retreat. They'd fallen into reminiscing over coffee.

'Do you remember Florrie Sweeney?' asked the rotund and elderly sister as she tucked into a second slice of chocolate cake. 'Such a character… Dreadful language!'

Even after all those years, Ulrika's heart had flown into her mouth at the mention of Florrie's name. She wondered if a day had passed when she hadn't thought of her. 'I do,' she'd said. 'How *is* she?'

'Oh,' replied Bernadette, sadly. 'She died... I'm sorry. I thought you must have heard. You were always so close. But maybe you were in Africa at the time... The sixth pregnancy was too much for her. We'd warned her, of course. But you know how these women are.'

-0-0-0-

If I could have my life again, thought Ulrika. *Would I have made the same choice?*

She didn't know.

On the bookshelf her eyes were drawn to her well-thumbed copy of 'The Dark Night of the Soul'. She knew the words by heart...

On a dark night, kindled in love with yearnings,
I went forth without being observed
In darkness and secure
In the happy night
In secret when none saw me.
Nor I beheld aught, without light or guide, save that which burned in my heart...

She knew that people looked at her and saw only the 'uniform'. They thought she understood nothing of passion. She was glad she could be invisible like that.

Shaking slightly, she sat down at her desk and faced the cross. The past was gone and no amount of remorse could change it. Bowing her head, she prayed for Jo and Natalie and Ed, and for Florrie's blessed, immortal soul. And then, with tears in her eyes, she offered herself up to the Blessed Virgin.

Holy Mary, Mother of God,

Pray for us sinners,
Now and at the hour of our death.
Amen.

-0-0-0-

There wasn't much to do at the centre after dinner. Some of the retreatants had taken themselves to the common room, where there were a lot of religious books, a filter coffee machine and, surprisingly, a small drinks table with an Honesty Box.

Jo suspected that if she started drinking she might not stop. So, after she had sent her text and cried over Nat's reply, she braved a chilly shower, and headed to her room for an early night.

Sleep, of course, evaded her. The talk with Ulrika had begun to stir memories she'd been keeping at bay for years. And now, without the distraction of overwork, the never ending demands of Jacob and Alyssa, and her furtive, heart breaking and guilty liaisons with their mother, those memories were starting to claw their way with horrifying insistence, to the surface. There were some things she *really* didn't want to think about, though she knew that she had to if she ever wanted to feel better. They were pushing through the ground beneath her now. Little flashes – fragments of images, gasps of sound, smells and touch – Fears that fluttered like a breath over her skin, making the hairs stand to attention. They pulled her out of what had passed for a comfort zone, and into a world where everything could be stolen from you in an instant.

As the main chapel clock tolled midnight, she gave up trying to sleep, pulled the light on and wrapped the thin continental quilt around her shoulders. The radiator that had been lukewarm during the day was ice-cold now. The dimness of the energy saving bulb dangling from the ceiling was almost smothered by its pale green shade.

She drew back the curtains so that she could see outside to the stars. Then, with a sudden sense of purpose, she sat at the desk, pulled a notepad and pen out of her bag, and like a detective on a cold case, she began to write, starting from the date she met Ed to the present, filling in the events, page by separate page, tearing them out and blu-tacking them to the wall above the desk, around the crucifix that hung there.

-0-0-0-

When Ed finally fell asleep, snoring whisky fumes into her face, Natalie dared to take stock of her situation. Her husband seemed to be 'out for the count' now, but he was still on top of her, a dead weight, flaccid and wet against her, his hand still tangled in her hair. She held her breath as she slowly eased herself away from him and crept, shivering, across the landing to the bathroom. She would have loved to have a bath or a shower. She was sticky, and sore and bruised, and she could feel his saliva dry on her cheek and the edge of her mouth. But she daren't risk waking him, so she rinsed herself as best she could with water from the washbasin tap and tried to scrub the feeling away with a towel that she tossed, disgusted into the dirty laundry afterwards.

In the spare room, there was some brief reassurance in the coolness of the sheets, and some safety in the confined feel of the single bed. But then she remembered the rattling of the door handle in the bathroom earlier, and the way he had hurt her just now, and she couldn't get away from the fact that she had asked him to stop, and he hadn't.

Under the covers, she typed hopelessly into her phone.

'PLEASE come home Jo. I think Ed knows. I'm scared. I love you!'

Then she pressed 'Delete'.

She knew that Jo would race to her defence if she asked her to. But she wanted to be chosen freely, or not at all.

-0-0-0-

At the retreat centre, Jo had finished filling in the events she had described to Ulrika and had moved on to Natalie and Ed's wedding. She was getting closer all the time to the things she didn't want to think about. She kept writing, quickly, trying not to analyse anything too much, knowing that if she was ever going to keep those memories from running away from her, she would have to creep up on them very cautiously indeed.

And so, still within some bounds of safety, she brought herself to the night of Ed's 'stag do'.

It was mid-July, a week before the wedding, and he had every intention of getting hammered.

He'd invited a whole crowd of his rugby buddies from school, plus a couple of cousins, all of the lads from work… and Jo.

Jo *really* hadn't wanted to go. 'It should be lads only,' she'd said, over a coffee at the office. 'That's why it's called a *stag* do.'

'No, it's *me* that's the stag,' Ed argued. He could be quite convincing when he put his mind to it. 'And you're my best mate, so you should be there to protect me. I mean… I don't wanna end up tied to a lamp post with me shreddies round me ankles... And it's not like Nat's gonna be inviting you to *her* 'do', *is* it?'

Ed knew that the animosity between Nat and Jo was partly his fault. He could remember all too clearly the day he first used Jo as a scapegoat. It was shortly after the Lucy episode. And the idea of blaming his already despised best friend had come to him in what had seemed like a flash of genius at the time.

It started off innocently enough. He'd stayed too long at The Tapsters after work, and dinner was ruined. Nat had greeted him with 'that look'.... the terrifying mixture of anger and tears that only women seemed to be capable of. And floundering around desperately to head off her wrath, he'd hit on the idea of blaming Jo. It was all *her* fault, he said. She'd double-booked a job and he'd had to step in to save the day. He'd thought he could make it home in time. But then he'd got caught up in traffic and well... he was *so* sorry! It worked like a dream – Nat's anger towards Jo seized on the opportunity to express itself, like a terrier spotting a rat. And Ed went from zero to hero in the blink of an eye.

From that day, Ed knew that his best friend was a convenient patsy whenever he didn't want to feel too much 'under the thumb', and he'd found that he could really be quite inventive in thinking up ways to incriminate her...

'Jo insisted on buying another round.' (Legless).

'Jo rostered me in without asking.' (Going to the rugby match/cricket/pub and pretending to be working).

'Gotta just go round Jo's to pick up some stuff first' (Escaping to Jo's to cadge cigarettes, watch 'Top Gear' on video and drink coffee to avoid doing DIY jobs at home).

Not surprisingly, by now, the antipathy between the two women was legendary.

Jo rolled her eyes at the thought of Nat's 'do'. 'Well,' she said. 'That's a blessing. I'm not sure I could have coped with a pamper party and dancing round my handbag at Cinderella's.'

Ed's face clouded instantly. 'She never told me they were going clubbing.' His voice filled with insecurity at the thought, and Jo realised she'd slipped up. It seemed to be all she ever did where Natalie was concerned.

She cursed inwardly. She'd had no idea that the bloody woman hadn't told Ed about the club. And *she* only knew because Bill had confided to her that his wife was wondering how to get out of 'going to the disco' without offending anyone. She didn't think it boded well that Nat was keeping her plans secret from her fiancé. But female solidarity kicked in, none-the-less.

'I'm just talking hen-parties generally,' she said. 'Nat'll probably have Indian head massage followed by poetry reading and camomile tea before bedtime. So stop being such a dick.' She punched him gently on the arm to pull him out of his mood. 'The woman's completely nuts about you... anybody can see that.'

This was true – Natalie was still very much in love, and she'd thrown herself into the wedding preparations with all the enthusiasm for flower arrangements, dresses, and venues that Jo had seen so many times in the Brides-To-Be who came to organise their wedding cars at the office. Jo's heart always sank a bit when they came bubbling in with that tell-tale look about them... The look that kids get when they're over-excited and you just know there's going to be tears and sick before bedtime.

Thankfully, Jo was a smart operator when it came to women. She knew how to smile and look interested in all the right places - even when they showed her photographs. But she'd always been bemused at how delighted they were at the prospect of spending an entire day encased in an excruciatingly uncomfortable dress and high-heels. And the truth was that she'd just never really *got* any of that 'girlie' stuff at all. Handbags and shoes left her cold, she only really appreciated a nice dress if she liked the figure underneath it, and she'd come to dread the moments when her girlfriend of the day would come rushing in from the sales, clutching some trophy and saying 'Guess how much?' On the Richter-scale of panic, those awful no-win moments came only marginally below the times she'd failed to notice a new hair cut or make-over, or, on one particularly low spot in her dating career - a complete switch from blonde to brunette.

Ed was still feeling insecure.

'D'ya think?' he asked. He looked unconvinced. His bottom lip had crept into 'village idiot' mode. His shoulders drooped.

Jo wished she'd punched him a bit harder – just so he'd get a grip.

'*Totally* nuts about you,' she said reassuringly. 'Or... some might say... Just totally bloody nuts!'

Sometimes, insulting Ed was the only way to get through to him.

It worked. Comfortable with the idea that his fiancée must be crackers to marry him, he was happy again in an instant.

-0-0-0-

By the industry standard for such things, the stag night was probably a bit tame.

Only two of Ed's school friends turned up in the end. Algie and Chad – both total tossers with P.G. Woodhouse laughs and a leery way of eyeing Jo that left her in no doubt that they were entertaining 'girl on girl' fantasies about her. The cousins, Gary and Nick, were nice-but-dim, and 'the lads from work' comprised Bill, Andy and three others who hadn't been quick enough to make up prior arrangements - Ashad, Mo and James 'Jimmy-Lee' Watkins, the newest member of the team.

They were a motley crew. Ash and Mo, as usual, were drinking orange juice. Bill was on shandy and a ten o'clock curfew. Andy, anxious about getting into his Best Man suit, and secretly signed up to Weight Watchers, was trying to restrict himself to just a couple of halves of lager. And the rest of them were on a mission to get totally rat-arsed before the night was out.

By nine thirty, they were well on their way to success.

They'd started out at Wetherspoons in town, where they'd made good use of the 'Happy Hour'. But Ed's homing instinct had brought them all back, fairly quickly, to the 'Tapsters', where he was now buying for the whole pub. It was getting pretty rowdy in there. Smoke hung in the air like a London pea-souper. Algie and Chad were teaching the assembled throng a posh-lads rugby song with lots of innuendo about tackle and balls. And Jo was wondering if she *really* had to stick around for the whole evening just to save the groom from being kidnapped by his mates.

Then the stripper arrived.

She was maybe in her early-twenties, with dyed black hair, cut Uma Thurman Pulp-Fiction style. She was tall and busty, and wearing a long, rather ratty black faux-fur coat, leather gloves and *very* high heels. The collar of her coat was turned up, and 'Venus in Furs' blasted menacingly from her ghetto blaster when she put it down on the floor and switched it on. Everybody in the pub turned to stare, and a testosterone surge of whistling, jeering and snorting erupted from the more legless of the stag-nighters. The stripper flashed them a look of unmitigated contempt, and began, very slowly, to unbutton her coat to the menacing throb of the music.

This was all too much for Bill, who rolled his eyes and curled himself round his drink, blotting out the scene that was about to unfold in front of him. Andy blushed scarlet and stared down at his trainers. Ashad and Mo slipped quietly into the night.

Jo found herself uncomfortably transfixed by the pale flesh of the stripper as she slowly peeled back her coat to reveal a red satin bustier trimmed with black lace, a matching G-string, and black lace-top stockings.

'So where's the naughty groom then?' she growled, tossing the coat onto the floor beside her and adopting a *very* impressive dominatrix stance. The hooting and hollering died away as she stared down the group. As if from nowhere, she had produced a pair of red and black handcuffs that matched her outfit. She held them aloft with a stern flourish.

A sea of mesmerized and slightly awestruck fingers pointed towards Ed, who jiggled against his mates Algie and Chad in overheated gratitude for their stag night surprise.

Jo watched with a grisly kind of curiosity, taking in Ed's flushed look, a bit like the way he'd looked at *her* sometimes, that first summer of their friendship. The way he patted his knee for her to sit on it…. and how he roared with laughter when the stripper took up his offer and straddled him and pulled him towards her cleavage by his ears.

Suddenly, she hoped that Nat was enjoying a good last-ditch snog with some random lad at Cinderella's. But she knew she wasn't the type.

Unlike Ed, who'd now put his hand rather too high on the stripper's thigh.

The girl seemed unfazed. Jo guessed she must be used to it.

'They *told* me you were a very naughty boy,' she said, whacking his hand away. Jo heard the slap distinctly over the drone of the music and the snorting of the crowd.

Ed yelped. And his mates roared with laughter.

Bill finished his shandy. 'I'm off home,' he said in disgust. 'Reckon Mrs J'll have escaped by now.'

This broke Jo's trance. She dragged her eyes away from the grizzly scene and followed, with a relieved Andy hot on her heels.

She lit a cigarette as soon as they were outside in the warm night-time air. It was like dragging the taste of the pub outside with them, but she needed the nicotine.

'You should give that up lass,' said Bill.

'I know.' She *did* too. But she hadn't been able to kick the habit again since the Lucy debacle.

The sound of 'Love is The Drug' interlaced with ribald male laughter oozed under the pub door.

Bill sighed. 'That lad's an idiot!' he said, knowing how Ed would be playing up to his audience. 'Making a show of himself like that when he's got a lovely lass like Natalie to go home to!'

Jo pictured Bill on *his* stag night. Dominoes or darts and a fish and chip supper probably… mushy peas too, if they'd really pushed the boat out. She'd never known anyone more content with his lot.

'Why don't you just get yourself home now?' he was asking.

'I'm not sure,' she said, hesitantly. 'I *did* promise.'

'Well, he'll not know whether you're here or not… state he's in.'

Jo had to admit that she felt very tempted by the idea of an early night. Maybe she was getting old. 'Mrs J's not hanging around to get the dirt on Nat then?' she asked.

Bill shook his head. 'D'ya honestly think there'll *be* any dirt on Nat?... Unlike that idiot in there?'

Jo sighed. 'I really *am* supposed to be keeping him out of trouble.'

But she knew from bitter experience that Ed had reached the stage where he wouldn't thank her if she tried.

And so did Bill. 'Not a chance love. You might as well give up now and save yourself a lot of grief… I'll give you both a lift if y'd like.'

'Nah… thanks mate, but it's out of your way. We'll get a taxi.'

'Sure?'

'Yeah.'

'Okay… I'll be off then.'

They watched gloomily as he ambled across the car park.

Inside the pub, the music had shifted to 'Addicted to Love.'

Jo smoked another cigarette.

The music stopped.

Then the door flung open and the stripper bounded out. She was wearing the coat again.

'Filthy bastards!' The door slammed shut behind her. Her eyes lit upon Jo's cigarettes.

'Thank God... a smoker.... Thought they were all in there... I couldn't cadge a fag could I?'

Amused, Jo handed the pack to her. Then she clicked her lighter and held it out. It was a slightly old fashioned gesture – a habit from her early days with Veronica, who'd liked her women a bit on the butch side – though Jo wasn't particularly, and never had been.

The woman dipped towards the flame and sucked gratefully on the cigarette. Half of it vanished into ash as she inhaled. Then she blew a long, slow plume of smoke up towards the night sky. 'What's up love?' This was addressed to Andy. 'Wouldn't yer girlfriend let you watch?'

'I errrm... er...' He was struck dumb.

'I'm not his girlfriend,' said Jo, helping him out.

The stripper gave Jo an arch look. '*Thought* you might be batting for the other team!' she said. 'Saw you looking at me in there.' Jo felt herself blushing and started to protest. The woman plunged on regardless. 'Not that I mind. There's no harm in havin' a look. And at least you didn't try to touch. So what's up with him then? Cat got his tongue?'

'Something like that.'

'Right!' she continued to look at Andy, appraisingly, narrowing her eyes against the smoke. 'So, why'd you not wanna watch? You gay too?'

'No!' he sounded a bit indignant and Jo hoped she wasn't hearing any unconscious homophobia there. 'Not that I'd mind if I was,' he added hastily, redeeming himself.

'Well, that's good. It'd 'a bin a waste - handsome brute like you!'

Andy looked round to see who she was talking to.

Jo smiled to herself at this. He'd never quite got used to the idea that he was growing into a good looking young man.

'He's my brother,' she said, proudly.

'You don't look alike.'

'No – a lot of people have said that.' Her father included – on at least one of the occasions when he'd resorted to trading paranoid accusations with her mum…. It was ridiculous, of course. Her mother would never have had the energy to have an affair.

'Right….' The stripper finished the cigarette in one long hard draw. She tossed the butt on the floor and held out her hand. 'Krystal!' she said.

'Jo…. And this is…'

'Andrew,' said Andy, suddenly asserting himself.

Before that night, it had never occurred to Jo that her brother might actually prefer his name unshortened. She watched as the two of them lingered rather longer than necessary over their handshake.

Later, they shared a taxi and Krystal managed to manoeuvre herself next to Andy in the back. Listening to their giggling as she sat in the front passenger seat beside a grim faced Asian guy in full beard and kufi, Jo dreaded to think what might be going on back there. But it turned out that they were just swopping lines from Quentin Tarantino films and both of them seemed to know Reservoir Dogs by heart. Other shared interests followed – 'Dungeons and Dragons' in first place, with reading and collecting Manga comics coming a close second. As a couple they were made for each other, and not only because they were both a bit geeky and weird.

By the time the taxi dropped Krystal off at her flat over the Pizza Hut in town, they'd arranged a date for the next night, and by the end of the week, they were an item.

Andy didn't take her to the wedding though. It didn't seem appropriate, under the circumstances.

Chapter Nine

The day of the wedding dawned bright and clear, with a cloudless blue sky and promise of warmth to come.

For Andy, riddled with Best Man nerves, it wasn't immediately obvious that the groom was missing. He was too busy wishing that Natalie hadn't vetoed Jo, who had been Ed's first choice, on the grounds that he would look like a total 'Billy-No-Mates' if he couldn't find a biological male to stand by him at the altar.

The awful truth sank in quite gradually, after he'd run to the bathroom several times, sprayed liberally with 'fresh air' spray, gone downstairs, boiled the kettle, and finally taken a mug of tea up to Ed's room, thinking it was high time the lazy sod started to get himself up and ready for his 'Big Day'.

Finding the bed Ed-less sent him scurrying to the bathroom again. But it was only after he'd hammered on the door of the en-suite, looked in the lounge, checked the wardrobes, garden and shed, and peeped behind all the curtains just in case Ed was playing a joke on him, that he fully allowed himself to know that he really, truly, *had* committed the worst sin known to best-mankind, and lost the groom.

Hyperventilating with terror, he did what he always did when he didn't know what else to do. He reached for the phone, and dialled his sister.

-0-0-0-

Jo almost dropped the receiver as she juggled it to her ear. Her date from the night before (Christine), still slumbered next to her - flat out on her back and snoring her head off, as she had been all night. Jo had already decided that there wasn't much prospect of a long term relationship there. She felt seriously sleep deprived – and not because she'd been having a good time.

'Hi Andy,' she grunted sleepily, as she heard her brother gasp her name at the other end of the line. 'What's up?'

'It's awful Jo…. Ed's gone.'

'Hah… Pull the other one..' Beside her, Christine looked like she might be about to wake up, but then she just snorted and smacked her lips and went back to snoring. She sounded like a rottweiler in a very bad mood.

Jo wondered if she had sleep apnea. She'd read about it once in an article in a magazine at the dentist's. It might explain why she'd kept yawning over dinner last night whenever the topic had strayed slightly away from the awful time she was having with her ex-girlfriend.

She eased herself gingerly into a sitting position, careful not to wake her – though actually that would, at least, have brought some relief from the noise.

'No, honest Jo… I'm not kidding!'

The snores were making their way steadily up the decibel range. They seemed to have a cyclical pattern to them. The sound was loud enough to temporarily distract Andy from his panic. 'What the hell's *that*?' he asked.

'Oh God love… don't ask!' Jo ran her hands through her hair, wondering why she invariably got herself into these messes with women. 'So what's this about Ed?'

'He's gone Jo… Disappeared… I've no idea where he is… It's awful!' He sounded like he was going to cry.

Jo knew the feeling. But it was good to have an excuse to shelve the problem of Christine for now. 'Try not to worry,' she said, climbing carefully out of bed and hunting for the clothes she'd chucked on the floor last night in a vain attempt to ramp up some passion. 'I'll be with you in five minutes.'

-0-0-0-

Ed turned out to be in one of the garages at work, sitting in his beloved Ford Anglia. He was crying.

'What the hell are you doing in here?' asked Jo, opening the creaking passenger door and sliding in cautiously beside him. 'Andy's practically on the point of calling out the sniffer dogs.'

He looked at her through bleary red-rimmed eyes. 'I can't do it,' he sobbed.

'*Course* you can!' She patted him clumsily on the knee, trying to be firm and sympathetic all at the same time.

'I'll let her down.'

'Well, you will if you don't turn up mate.' She was trying very hard to keep the alarm out of her voice.

'Not just today... As a husband, I mean,' he sniffed back snot with the kind of noisy, viscous rattle Jo remembered from her brothers when they couldn't be bothered to use their hankies.

'Well, I'm sure you *will.*' There didn't seem to be much point arguing with that one. 'You *are* a bit of a plonker sometimes. But she'll forgive you. She always does.'

'She won't... I'll disappoint her... I *already* disappoint her.... And one day, I'll disappoint her one time too many and she'll leave me.'

'Don't be daft Ed. She loves you to bits.'

'*Does* she? Does she really?' He sounded angry, like a man who could prove otherwise and Jo wondered briefly if he'd found out that Nat had fibbed to him about going to Cinderella's on her hen night.

'Of *course* she does!' she protested. 'Come on mate, you're getting yourself all wound up for nothing here.'

But he wasn't in a mood to be consoled. '*You've* seen it,' he stuttered. 'That *look* she has. When I've done something stupid, or not been able to read her mind or something.... And you know how I am... I get drunk and make a fool of myself, and I fart in bed and watch Jeremy Clarkson on telly and read mucky magazines, and she hates all of that stuff. I see her looking at me sometimes with that disgusted look she gets... You know it... It's the same way she looks at *you*... like you're something she's trailed in on her shoe. And I feel myself just getting deeper and deeper in the shit... and I can't do it anymore Jo, I'm not cut out for it.'

He'd been drinking. Jo could smell it on him, sweet and cloying, like a morning-after kebab with a tell-tale overlay of nail varnish.

Cautiously, she weighed up the options. She wondered about phoning his parents. She was scared he might run if she left him though. He was getting hysterical. And she didn't want to move too fast and spook him.

She was still wondering what the hell to do when he skipped completely off topic and took her by surprise again.

'D'you remember that first summer?' he asked suddenly, turning to face her. 'We had a right laugh didn't we? You and me?'

'Yes,' she said, soothingly. 'We did.'

He buried his head in his hands again.

'Why did you have to be gay?' he sobbed.

This was a worrying new development. Jo patted harder in a 'don't even go there or I might just have to beat you up' kind of a way.

'You've always understood me,' he snuffled, through wet fingers.

'Yeah, well... we're mates, aren't we?' He was scaring her now.

'More than that Jo... It's always been more than that for me.'

'Don't be daft!' She might make a good job of pretending to dislike his bride-to-be, but she disliked the idea of seeing her humiliated at the altar even more.

'Run away with me Jo. We can start up again somewhere new. Just you and me. We could go to Scotland or Wales or somewhere. Or how about Cornwall? You like it there, don't you...? I could make you happy, I know I could.... We wouldn't have to... you know... if you didn't want to.'

He was clutching at straws, grown nostalgic for days that had seemed idyllic just because they were young. She could see that. And glancing surreptitiously at her watch, she knew she had to get him out of it... fast.

'For God's sake Ed, you're being stupid now. Come on. You've got a gorgeous woman who's desperate to have you 'for better or for worse' and there'll not be a bloke at that wedding... well, apart from Bill maybe... who won't think you're the luckiest dog alive today. God knows – even *I'm* going to be jealous and I can't stand the bloody woman... So come on mate... get a grip... This is just the drink talking.'

'I've only had a couple.'

'A couple of *bottles* maybe! You love Natalie, you *know* you do... So come on. Let's not keep the lady waiting, eh? We need to get you sobered up.'

Thank God for Andy. He'd been searching the offices and the other lock-ups, but now, as if out of nowhere, he was standing beside the car, looking in. For Natalie's sake, Jo hoped he hadn't overheard what Ed had just said to her.

She figured he *had* though, because something made him step in to take control of the situation.

'Come on now mate,' he said firmly, opening the driver's door and grabbing Ed by the arm. 'Let's get you home and ready for your Big Day, eh? Don't want you getting a bollocking off the bride for keeping her waiting now, do we?'

Jo felt proud of him as he took charge. For the second time in a fortnight, she was reminded that her baby brother had grown into a fine and competent young man.

-0-0-0-

'He's done a runner, hasn't he?' After four protracted laps around the church, Nat was fighting back tears and Ruth, her best friend and only bridesmaid, was trying to comfort her.

They were in the 'Classic Cars' Bridal Bentley. Ashad was driving and Nat's uncle, who was rumoured to be gay, but very much in the closet, had elected to sit beside him. His initial, rather too close interest in the handsome young driver had now completely given way to a ramrod stiff tension that showed even from behind. Ashad was sweating. Nat watched him running his fingers round the back of his starched collar. He'd worked for Ed for five years after all, and he knew what he was capable of.

'He's probably just held up in traffic,' said the Uncle trying to sound cheery.

They all knew that this was unlikely. The roads today had been unusually quiet, maybe because it was the school holidays and lots of people were away.

Nobody bothered answering him.

Ruth took Natalie's hand. 'If he has, he's an even bigger fool than I thought,' she said. It was the nearest she could bring herself to reassurance, bearing in mind the reservations she'd had about him all along.

'I'll have to move away. I won't be able to face people. Not after this.'

In her head, she pictured it... Her uncle making the announcement, and all those guests having to be sent home... Humiliation branding itself into her as the news crackled through the small town like wildfire.

As they came within sight of the church again, they could see the cluster of kids from Nat's school who had managed to find out where the wedding was. The group had started with just two or three who had detoured on their way to their customary pitch at the shopping mall, keen to take a low-key peek at their teacher in her wedding dress. But even before the widespread use of mobile phones, they seemed to have some telepathic way of swelling in numbers whenever excitement was brewing. They'd been chattering like hysterical magpies on the last two rounds, but now they were practically screaming with excitement, having seen the tall, blond and 'gorgeous' groom, finally belting towards the church with his slightly tubbier best man panting at his heels.

Ed's cousin Gary, on sentry duty by the lych gate, was sucking on a cigarette as if his life depended on it, afraid, now the groom was in place, that the bride had decided to call it a day and gone home. Then he saw the car too and chucked his cigarette away and stuck two excited thumbs in the air, grinning with relief. And Ashad swooped into the parking space in front of the gate as if the whole thing had been rehearsed like this all along.

It occurred to Nat, grimly, that this must be where the funeral cars parked too. But she pushed the thought from her mind as she saw her uncle stick his head out of the window.

'Are they here?'

'Yes!'

'Thank God!'

He leapt out and opened the door for Natalie. She didn't know him very well. He was from her father's side of the family and he wasn't someone who'd ever had anything much to do with her. But he was of the older generation, he was male, and her mother had suffered a panic attack when Natalie had dared to suggest that maybe her brother Ralph might be the best person to 'give her away'. Natalie's mother always hated it when Ralph showed Natalie any attention whatsoever. So the uncle had been drafted in and he was doing his best to rise to the occasion, offering his hand like a gentleman as Natalie stepped carefully out of the car in her wedding dress.

-0-0-0-

Showered and dressed, Jo had screeched her car into a parking space five minutes earlier, relieved to see the 'Classic Cars' Rolls parked by the kerb-side, and just in time to catch a glimpse of Ed and Andy sprinting through the graveyard, up the moss-covered path, past the ancient tombstones of the church's long dead parishioners. She'd nodded to Gary, and got halfway to the church before she decided to wait for the bridal car. She thought Nat deserved an explanation, even if it was a lie.

She was feeling pretty churned up by the morning's events, though there had been a tiny bright spot when she'd run up the stairs at home and found a note from

Christine on the bed. It was written in eye-liner, though there were plenty of pens lying around.... 'JOANNE COOPER - YOU ARE THE MOST IGNORANT WOMAN I HAVE EVER MET – HOW <u>COULD</u> YOU JUST GO OUT AND LEAVE ME LIKE THAT?!!!! PLEASE DO **NOT** EVER CONTACT ME AGAIN – CHRIS.'

Free of that particular worry, at least, she tried now to focus on the warmth of the high-noon sun on her face, tried to unknot her shoulders, and told herself that everything was going to be okay. Then she caught her first glimpse of the bride and felt her treacherous stomach flip as it always did when she saw Natalie.

Even from a distance, she could see that she had that look - the one that Ed had described - like he'd just gone down several more notches in his fiancée's estimation. And, as Jo always did with Ed, she felt the compulsion to try to make things better for him.

Nervously, she smoothed her hands over the navy linen trouser suit she'd bought specially for the day. She'd had to throw it on much too quickly in the end, leaving her with a slightly dishevelled look that she hadn't had time to correct in the mirror.

She made Natalie jump as she stepped forward from the graves. It wasn't a good start.

'I'm so sorry,' she said. 'We had problems with the car.'

'I might have known it would be *your* fault,' said Nat bitterly as she swept past.

Behind her, the bridesmaid gave Jo a quick once-over. She was porcelain-pretty with long auburn hair. There was a mischievous sparkle in her astute green eyes.

'I'm guessing you must be Jo,' she said. 'I've been looking forward to meeting *you*.'

Staring after her as she broke into a trot to catch up with Natalie at the door of the church, Jo couldn't shake the idea that she'd just been propositioned.

Chapter Ten

'So…' Ruth whispered to the new Mrs Mason, when they were finally seated at the top table in the 'Beresford Lodge Hotel', waiting for the melon balls to arrive. 'How come you never told me that Jo was so sexy?'

From the 'Classic Cars' group, Jo glanced up, bang on cue and realised that Ruth was talking about her. She felt herself blushing.

Ruth fluttered her fingers and smiled. Beside her, Natalie glowered.

'Well, that's probably because I hadn't noticed!'

Natalie now had a husband seated securely beside her, and proud parents-in-law beaming happiness round the room, delighted that their son had shown some signs of moving into adulthood at last. But she still felt unsettled and vulnerable and dangerously close to tears. And the very last thing she needed was her best friend suddenly deciding to launch herself into some kind of treacherous liaison with Jo.

'Mm… well, she's *very* hot… Is she spoken for?'

'I've no idea. She usually has some woman or other on her arm.'

Ruth deliberately ignored the tight tone. 'No "plus one" today though?'

'No, I don't think she's actually the "plus one" type.'

'So she's a "love 'em and leave 'em" kind of a gal?'

'Something like that.'

It was meant to be a warning. But right now, it was exactly what Ruth wanted.

She figured that some no-holds-barred, no-strings-attached sex with Jo might be exactly what she needed to distract her from the pain of seeing Natalie so finally and irrevocably hitched to Ed.

-0-0-0-

She continued to watch Jo through the meal. She was laughing with the lads from Classic Cars and making sure their girlfriends and wives didn't feel left out of the proceedings. She had a quiet, easy way of putting people at their ease that just didn't fit with the selfish, manipulative monster Nat had painted so consistently to her over the months.

She was a proud big sister too. Ruth could see that as Andy mumbled his way through his Best Man speech, his notes fluttering anxiously in his hands.

'First of all, I want to say sorry Ed…' He turned to face his friend and employer. 'You kind of got lumbered with me, didn't you mate?'

He paused, red faced, to give Ed chance to make a token protest, then ambled on. 'I know you'd have preferred our Jo. But she just wouldn't have that sex change… It's allus been the same with Jo… Totally selfish…'

Raucous laughter erupted from the Classic Cars table, while some of the older Mason clan looked bewildered.

'And then I reckon you'd have preferred Bill, but he's even shyer than I am, and wild horses wouldn't have got him up here making a total plonker of himself like this. And Chad and Algie and Gary and Nigel… I bet the missus warned you they'd all be off their heads by now. And look… she was right!'

More raucous and slightly relieved laughter from the lads who'd got away….

At tables near the back of the room, where people couldn't hear, one or two of the guests started to talk. Jo turned and glared at them to shut up.

'So, here I am...' He pressed on doggedly, knowing that somehow, no matter how much of a disaster it was, it would be far worse if he didn't actually get to the end. 'And when I was asked to do this, I thought I'd better come up with some funny stories about Ed getting drunk and falling over and all that... But then I thought "No!" because that's just the side of Ed that everybody thinks they know. And the Ed *I* know is different to that. The Ed *I* know's the bloke that took me straight out of college and gave me a job, so I've got a future now, when half me mates are still signing on. And he's the one who got up in the middle of the night and drove to Watford Gap to help me when one of our cars conked out there...' He started to speed up now as the end came into sight... 'And he's the one who's tekken me to his heart and done me the great honour of asking me to be his "Best Man" today... And, you know what Ed?' He turned shakily to face him again. 'What you keep hidden from people, is that you're a one hundred percent diamond geezer... And I might have been a bit low down on your best man list. But what I want to say is, as far as I'm concerned, you're the best mate any bloke could have. So cheers Ed, you're an absolute bloody star, and you deserve all the happiness in the world.'

Whether or not most people had heard or understood it, the speech had had its desired effect. Natalie reached for Ed's hand, and Jo was relieved to see the love back in her eyes. She smiled proudly at Andy for succeeding where she had always seemed to fail.

He grinned back, nodding and taking a deep breath. Then he continued. 'And now, I think it's traditional for the Best Man to cop off with… sorry… propose the toast to… the bridesmaid…. So, Ladies and Gentlemen… if you could just raise your glasses… because, here we have… 'Liiiive From Norwich…' (this was delivered in best "Sale of the Century" style, and raised a titter from the few older members of the audience who were close enough to hear it)... 'Ruth, our beautiful bridesmaid.'

'Ruth!' They all stumbled to their feet and a few chairs fell over.

Ruth thought it was sweet that Jo was wiping tears from her eyes as she stood to make the toast.

-0-0-0-

At 4pm, there was a late-afternoon lull before the evening 'do', and Jo was in serious need of a lie-down. The champagne and sleep deprivation had just collided head-on. And the coffee, taken black at the end of the meal, had piled into the back of them, leaving her with the jazzy, multi-coloured, double-helix light-show she recognised only too well as the onset of a migraine.

Andy was fretting about his speech as he trotted beside her on the seemingly endless red-carpeted corridor to their rooms. His voice was starting to sound a bit weird.

'Are you sure you don't think the "cop off" joke was too near the mark?' he asked. 'Krystal said she thought it'd get a laugh.'

'It was great.' Jo tried to inject some enthusiasm into her voice. She didn't want to poop the party by acknowledging that she was ill. 'Krystal was right. People expect things to be a bit cheeky at a wedding.' She knew that Andy's anxiety was a bottomless pit once it became aroused, and much as she loved him, she needed to get some Migraleve down her *now*. She thanked her lucky stars that, even though she'd been in a rush that morning, she'd remembered to put her tablets in her case.

'You don't think she was offended then?'

'Who...? Sorry love..?'

'Ruth?'

'*Not at all!*'

The carpet had muffled the bridesmaid's footsteps and neither of them had heard her sprinting up on them from behind. The fact that she was carrying her shoes helped too, obviously.

She grinned as they both jumped. 'In fact, I thought it was sweet,' she said. 'If I were straight, I might even have been tempted to take you up on your offer. But as it is, I was wondering if your sister might be free tonight instead.'

Ruth may have been talking to Andy, but she was looking at Jo. Even through the flashing aura of the migraine, Jo couldn't help but notice that. She wondered gloomily if she'd ever been chatted up at a less convenient time.

They were drawing level with her door though and she really needed to take action quickly if she was going to stand any chance of functioning again by the evening.

'I'm really sorry,' she said. 'I'm not feeling very well.'

She fled inside.

Ruth stared at the door as it closed in her face.

'I don't normally have that effect on women,' she said, nonplussed.

Andy shrugged apologetically. 'She's having a bad day,' he said. 'I'm sure it isn't anything personal.'

Chapter Eleven

'Feeling better?' Ruth forced herself to smile as she made a rather less confident than before bee-line for Jo. She'd had to peer amongst the wedding guests for ages before she located her. All the tables had been moved to the edges of the room so that people could dance. And Jo, who had changed into a long, soft, powder blue shirt, had her back to the door, sitting at a table with Andy and a middle-aged couple she recognised vaguely from earlier. The rest of the Classic Cars team had gone now, though some were expected back later. Ruth remembered overhearing Ed saying that they had jobs that evening. The remnants looked up in unison when she spoke, as if they practiced in their spare time.

Jo leapt to her feet. She'd convinced herself that she'd completely burned her bridges with this particular woman, so she was shocked to find her by her side again now.

'Yes... thank you,' she said. 'I'm really sorry about earlier.'

Ruth had also changed her outfit. The bridesmaid frock had been replaced by a short, figure hugging dress in purple. She wore it well. The richness of the colour was a perfect foil to the Pre-Raphaelite hair that rippled down over her shoulders. And the dress – well, Jo couldn't help but notice that it didn't leave much to the imagination.

She wondered if she'd been granted a second chance. If so, she figured she'd really better watch her manners this time. 'Ruth…. This is Bill…' She dragged her eyes away from Ruth's cleavage and nodded across the table at her trusty work mate.

Ruth flashed him a brilliant smile.

'Hi Bill,' she mouthed, over the racket from the bar.
'And Mrs J....'
'Fiona...' Mrs Jones interjected.
'Hi Fiona!' The smile bounced across to Bill's wife.

Mrs Jones stood and reached for Ruth's hand, patting it between both her own, as if she were making cookies. 'You looked lovely today,' she said. 'And I thought you were a great support to Natalie.'

Ruth allowed herself to be patted. She even looked like she was enjoying it.

'Thank you, Fiona. It's good to meet you at last. I've heard a lot about you. I was sorry I couldn't get to the hen night.'

She's a right charmer, is this one, thought Jo.

'And, of course, my brother Andy's already propositioned you...' Jo flipped Andy a fond smile to tell him she was only joking. He looked almost pleased with himself under his customary squirm. Clearly Krystal was going to be good for him.

'Seems she prefers my sister though!' he grinned, outing Ruth to Bill and Fiona and anyone else within hearing range of their table.

Thankfully she didn't seem to mind. 'That's right,' she said, awarding him one of her best flirtatious looks.

Mrs J looked even more interested than before. She was on a mission to find a 'nice young lass' for Jo, and she figured she might be onto a winner here. She patted harder.

'Would you like to join us?'

'That would be lovely.' Ruth sent up a silent prayer of thanks that she hadn't just been knocked back again. She pretended not to have noticed the table full of old

University buddies beckoning her from the other side of the room.

Jo pulled out a chair and tucked it expertly behind Ruth's knees as she sat down. This was another of the habits she'd retained from her formative days with Veronica. At sixteen, adopting all the traditional butch gestures her older lover had insisted upon had imbued Jo with a certain kind of boyish charm. Now, in different circles – different times, it seemed quaint and a bit old fashioned. Ruth thought it made her look like a waiter, but she was wondering if it had implications for the bedroom too. She'd done a lot of reading about lesbian and gay history when she was in her 'coming out' phase. She surprised herself by feeling turned on at the thought of a night of naughty one-way pleasuring from someone as quietly attentive as Jo.

'Can I get you a drink?' This was Jo again - looking after her. The signs were all good.

'Thank you.' Ruth's smile locked onto Jo's eyes, and stayed there. Even in the dim light, she could see the blue of the shirt reflected in them, like the sea playing with the sky on a hot summer's day. She could also hear the faint sound of her friends yelling 'Ruuuthhh, we're over here,' from their table on the other side of the dance floor. But they were relatively easy to phase out now she had her back to them. 'I'll have whatever you're having.'

'It's just fizzy water.'

'Great! That's fine by me.'

-0-0-0-

From the bar, Jo watched as the newlyweds kicked off the dancing with 'Three Times a Lady.'

After a polite interval Bill and Mrs J joined them. Then Mr and Mrs Mason. People in love, after all those years. Though that image was spoiled somewhat when Natalie's mother and brother decided to take to the floor...

Jo knew that Ed had been scared about that first dance and had asked Bill to give him lessons. She'd discovered the two of them stumbling round the office after hours one night and nearly scared the wits out of them. 'It isn't how it looks!' Bill had protested leaping out of Ed's arms like a scalded cat. Jo still found herself chuckling at the idea that he'd thought he needed to say that.

But he'd been a good teacher, because Ed danced perfectly that night.

And they looked so good together, Ed, tall and strong and handsome, and Natalie, dark and soft and flowing in his arms.

Watching them, envious and just a little bit wistful, Jo wondered if she'd ever find a woman who'd want to melt into her like that.

And Ruth felt fury and grief in just about equal measure.

'What the hell does she see in him?' she asked, when Jo returned.

'Who?' Jo was taken aback by this sudden outburst.

'Natalie... in Ed?'

'Well, he's a nice looking bloke, and he's kind, and funny, and great company,' she said, puzzled. 'What's not to like?'

'You mean, apart from the fact that he almost jilted her at the altar this morning?'

'Well, that was hardly his fault.... You know what those old cars are like.'

'Huh!' Ruth's face indicated that she didn't buy the car excuse. 'Or maybe the fact that he's permanently pissed then?'

Jo looked across at Ed. He was relieved at being out of the spotlight now the dance was over, and guffawing loudly with Chad, while Natalie stood, looking disconnected again, by his side. He was certainly a very long way from being sober.

As always, though, Jo felt pulled to defend him. 'He's a good mate of mine,' she said indignantly. 'You heard what Andy said about him earlier. And it's true. Neither of us would be where we are today without him.'

Ruth scoffed. 'And I'm guessing *he* wouldn't be where he is today without you and the lads doing all the hard work for him…. Anyway…' she took her glass. 'Let's agree to differ, shall we? Nat's always had bloody awful taste in men…. About as good as my taste in women, probably.' She seemed unaware that she'd potentially just insulted Jo. 'So what was it with *you* this afternoon? Had you *all* been at the cooking sherry before you set off?'

Jo's Perrier fizzed gently around ice and lemon as she stirred at it with her straw. Despite herself, she couldn't help but smile at the image of Andy, Ed and herself necking cheap Amontillado with their cornflakes.

She shook her head. 'It was just the start of a migraine. We'd had a stressful morning…. I mean, what with the car troubles and all that.' She figured she'd throw that in again - on the grounds that if you repeat a lie often enough, people might just start to believe it.

Ruth didn't even dignify it with a response. 'But all better now?' she asked.

'Pretty much.'

'Good. Because my offer still stands, if you're interested…. Look, I suppose I'd better go talk to the Uni crowd before they decide to descend on us here.'

She took her drink with her. This was usually a sure sign that people weren't planning on coming back in a hurry. Jo felt as if she'd been tagged for later though. And she found her eyes helplessly following the leisurely sway of Ruth's backside across the room.

'Nice bum!' said Andy, showing more Krystal influence.

'Can't say I'd noticed,' said Jo.

The band were belting out a medley of sixties music now. They were four aging demons in dinner jackets, playing lead guitar, organ, bass and drums and taking turns to harmonise on vocals. And they certainly knew how to rock and roll. After a couple of numbers Mrs J was delivered back to the table by her sweating husband, on his way to the 'Gents'.

'It's "The Twist",' she said. 'Gets him every time.' She noticed the direction of Jo's gaze as she sat down. 'Nice girl!' she added, hopefully.

'Yeah!'… But *was* she? After her outburst about Ed, Jo wasn't so sure.

'Very pretty… Nice legs!'

'Yes, I guess so.'

Andy raised his eyebrows at Fiona and shrugged. 'I'm just off to phone Krystal,' he said. 'She's out on a job later.' He'd been restless ever since he'd seen Ed and Natalie's loved-up first dance. Jo dreaded to think of the phone bill he'd be presented with in the morning. She also wondered how he coped with his girlfriend working as a stripper. She knew she'd worry herself sick in his position.

She watched as Ruth spoke to her friends, standing slightly back from them, not sitting down. Something in the self-consciousness of her stance reminded her of the scene in 'Pride and Prejudice' where the ladies walk around the room so that the gentlemen can observe them. She figured that Ruth was well aware that she was watching her. She also wondered if she'd said something to her friends about her intentions for the night. Certainly there was a lot of raucous laughter. And glances were being cast in her direction.

'You could do a lot worse,' Mrs J persisted. It wasn't unusual for her to have this kind of conversation with Jo. She had a naïvely optimistic view of Jo's chances of happiness in love.

'Except she lives in Norwich.'

'That shouldn't matter, if you like each other.'

'And she's Natalie's best friend. It'd go down like a lead balloon.'

'Well, I've never understood Natalie's attitude towards you. She's such a sweet girl in every other way.' She nudged her husband, who had returned to the table, checking his flies and tucking his shirt in, as he always did when he'd been to the loo. Jo sometimes wondered why he never remembered to do any of that while he was in there. 'It's a mystery to us, isn't it love?'

'Sorry sweetheart, I didn't catch that.' Bill's hearing wasn't great, especially when there was a lot of background noise. Though on this occasion, he was playing for time.

'I said… I've never understood why Natalie can't get on with Jo.'

'Nay lass.' Actually Bill thought he had a pretty good idea. He'd heard Ed on the phone, on many occasions, using Jo as an excuse. He'd tried to challenge him about it a couple of times, though he'd just been called an 'old misery' for his pains. He'd even tried hinting about it to Jo once. But that had fallen on stony ground too. So now he figured it was safer to keep his thoughts to himself. After all, where other people's business was concerned, 'Least said soonest mended' was generally the best policy. 'It's beyond me,' he said.

Jo took a guilty gulp of Perrier. She remembered the Tandoori Knights debacle only too well. 'I think she misunderstood something I said once,' she confessed. 'And she's never really trusted me since…. Last thing I want to do now is upset her on her wedding day by bunking up with her best mate.'

'Well, I wasn't suggesting "bunking up"… More, having a bit of a dance and swopping phone numbers. You young people have no sense of romance… And you never know. It might improve things between you and Nat if you were "seeing" her best friend. It would give her chance to get to know you better.'

Jo doubted that very much.

'I think I'd better steer clear,' she said. 'I'm pretty useless with women all round. I always seem to mess it up.'

'Don't be so defeatist, love. You just haven't found the right one yet. When you do, you'll know.'

Jo smiled. And she hoped her old friend was right. But her parents, Veronica, Lucy, and even Ed, that morning, had left her tired and battered and cynical about love. And looking at Ruth through the multi-coloured blur of dancers on the dance floor, she doubted that anything on offer from her that night would lead to any kind of phone hugging, '*You* hang up…' 'No… *you* hang up,' kind of long distance romance.

-0-0-0-

And so the evening progressed. The swirl of dancers thickened as the band launched into a Frankie Valli medley and a crowd of Natalie's colleagues from school took to the floor. It felt weird for Jo, seeing her old teachers in this new setting, tipsy, and with partners in tow. 'Wiggy', the old Latin teacher danced like a cross between Mick Jagger and John Cleese in 'The Ministry of Silly Walks', and Miss Wilks, the Deputy Headmistress, who may have been attempting to dance with him, appeared to be doing a duck impression. Jo guessed that they must still be single, as they had always been. But how on earth had weedy Mr Bobs the music teacher managed to snare such a gorgeous trophy wife? And was Suzi Hardcastle the ex-Head Girl *really* with Miss Brotherton the gym mistress? Jo shuddered, remembering freezing cold hockey matches and Miss Bro's intense discussions with Suzi on the sidelines, and figured she could make a good guess at just *how* long that particular liaison had been going on.

She was wishing she had some of her old class mates with her to share the experience, or at least a camera to record it, when across the room, she noticed Natalie approaching Ruth by the University Friends' table. The pair of them flickered in and out of view like an early cinema reel in the gaps of Mr Wigston's increasingly rubbery dance-moves. Then they appeared and disappeared behind Miss Wilks' large wobbling backside. From a distance, their conversation could have been seen as 'animated'. But in those first weeks before she blew it with Natalie, Jo had observed her far too closely to be taken in by any such appearance. No. There was no doubt about it. Ruth and Natalie were arguing. Big time!

Then suddenly Ruth was stomping across the room and catching her by the arm.

'So, do you *want* to shag me, or not?' she demanded.

Fortunately Bill and Fiona didn't hear this. They were big fans of Frankie Valli too, and had just decided to chance Bill's bladder on the dance floor again.

Jo glanced up at Ruth, then back across the room at Natalie. She looked like she might be on the verge of tears and Jo didn't like to see it.

'I don't want to cause a rift between you and Nat,' she said, cautiously.

'Not even after the way she talked to you this morning?'

Well, since she put it like that….

'When you were just trying to help.'

Yes, it was true. Nat had always thought the worst of her…

'And when I could show you a *really* good time.'

Oh God, don't do this to me!

Jo took a deep breath. 'Okay!' she said quickly, standing up and taking Ruth's hand. Suddenly she didn't want to see this from Nat's point of view anymore. Suddenly she wanted to be out for what she could get, just for once. 'Your room?' she asked. 'Or mine?'

-0-0-0-

Jo wasn't sure when it dawned on her that Ruth was in love with Natalie. It must have been sometime after they'd kissed, despite the CCTV cameras, in the lift going up to the fourth floor. And after Ruth had pulled her into her room next to the honeymoon suite, and closed the door with just the softest of clicks. Sometime, even, after they'd French-kissed like teenagers, for a long time, on the bed and Ruth had started to run her fingers in the soft, downy hair at the back of Jo's neck.

Looking back, Jo knew it must have been then... when Ruth stopped kissing her, just for a moment, and said, 'I can't believe she still thinks she has the right to dictate who I can sleep with!' and tried to start kissing her again almost without missing a beat.

Once it had dawned on her, she couldn't believe that she hadn't seen it right from the start.

'Whooah there!' She caught hold of Ruth's arms and pulled herself back. 'I'm starting to think there are three of us in this bedroom.'

Ruth tried to chase after her with her lips. 'Don't be silly.'

'I'm not!'

'I could say the same thing about *you*, with your beloved Ed.'

'No!' said Jo firmly. 'You couldn't.'

Ruth looked like a kid caught with her fingers in the cookie jar. Scared, but still wondering if she could play the 'cute' card and wheedle her way out of it.

'Please forget it,' she pleaded, sticking her bottom lip out ever so slightly.

Jo would have liked to. She was turned on and she'd been enjoying herself. But she had no intention of continuing with this until she knew exactly what she was dealing with.

'Have you two been an item at some point?' she asked.

Ruth gave in. 'I wouldn't go *that* far,' she said. 'I loved her... like we do, and she loved me "like a sister" as she puts it. Good to tell she's never had any sisters, 'cos I hate all of mine... We ended up in bed once, when we'd both drunk too much ouzo.... God I had a foul hangover the next day.... Mouth like the bottom of a budgie cage... But I "had" her, and she bloody well liked it. And then the next day she told me it had all been a massive mistake, and she was "sorry"... Maybe it was the morning-after ouzo-breath that put her off, eh?'

Jo saw the grief in her, pushing at the back of her eyes, reddening them.

'I guess you must have felt like that about someone, at some point,' she said, seeking common ground as she allowed Jo to fold her in her arms, to comfort her.

Jo wondered about this. But she didn't think she had. It had always felt like a relief when women told her she wasn't right for them, because no-one had ever, really, felt right for her either.

So she didn't answer. And they lay like that for a long time. Ruth staring into space. And Jo stroking her and kissing her hair.

Finally, just before they fell asleep, they made love. And in the end, it was so much gentler than either of them had ever imagined it would be.

-0-0-0-

At The Retreat, Jo pulled the blanket closer round her shoulders. It was 4am and freezing cold. Ice patterns were forming on the inside of the window, like they used to at home when she was a kid and her parents couldn't afford to put money in the electricity meter.

Her fingers felt frozen. She could feel the skin beginning to crack at the tips.

Shivering, she wrote '**RUTH?**' on a new page of the note pad, circling the name before tearing the sheet out and blu-tacking it to the wall with all the rest.

At the edges of her vision, a worm of light began to shimmer. She blinked to erase it, but it was soon joined by another, dancing like a firefly with its mate. Cursing, she shuffled to her bag to get her migraine tablets.

But they weren't there. She'd left them behind, in her other bag, at home.

Resigned - her whole vision edged now by dancing light - she braced herself for the onslaught to come, crawled back into the uncomfortable bed and pulled her pillow over her head in preparation for the pain.

Chapter Twelve

Sunday 28th December 2014

Ed was already up and in the kitchen when Natalie emerged the next morning.

He had the radio on, so he didn't hear her as she stood in the doorway, tuning out the early morning DJ chatter, watching him glugging milk straight from the carton then topping it up with water and putting it back in the fridge. Dottie had been absorbed in sitting and gazing up at him with her usual mix of adoration and hope, tail-tip flicking softly against the tiled floor. But now she spotted Nat and padded over to prod at her with a slightly dry doggy nose.

Nat leant down automatically to rub her hand along the dog's curly head.

'I always wondered where Jake learnt to do that,' she said, as he closed the fridge door.

Ed jumped, and gave her a guilty, sideways look. Two slices of white bread were folded on a plate on the worktop. Sticky globs of red oozing from their sides gave them away as jam sandwiches. A pack of co-codamol was open beside them. The sandwiches began to unfurl themselves, slowly. Ed pressed them down again and licked his fingers.

Nat eyed him, dispassionately.

He was wearing the 'Kiss My Arse' boxer shorts with a mistletoe design that someone had bought him for his 'Secret Santa' present at work. She wondered, sadly, quite how long it was since she'd have thought he looked cute in those.

'I didn't want to wake you,' His voice was tentative and he seemed to be finding it hard to make eye contact. 'But I thought I'd better go into work, seeing as Jo's run off and left us all in the lurch.'

'It's Sunday, Ed.'

'So....? We've got a lot of bookings on!'

Natalie felt sure that the 'Classic Cars' lads would be fine without Jo or Ed nannying them for a few days.

'I thought Jo had asked Fiona to cover for her?'

'Yeah, she has. But they might need somebody with more authority there.'

Natalie shrugged. Fiona might be a gentle soul in general, but she'd never noticed her struggling to assert her authority when she needed to.

She could only assume that this was just a ploy to get out of the house and she wasn't going to argue with *that*.

She changed the subject. 'Don't forget we're going round to your gran's for tea tonight.'

'Oh, shit!' He crinkled his nose and sighed. 'I *had* done..! What time?'

'Six o'clock.'

'Ok.' He knew he couldn't get out of it. It was a Christmas tradition. 'I let the dog out,' he added, in search of Brownie Points.

He didn't get any.

'She needs some water too,' said Nat.

'Okay – sorry!' He picked up the dog's water bowl and half-filled it from the cold tap. The truth was that he was rarely the first person up in the household and the needs of the dog were a bit of a mystery to him. 'It looks icy out there. Be careful when you go collect Alyssa... Can I get you a coffee?'

Nat watched Dottie making a bee-line for the bowl as he slopped it down onto the floor. She wondered about asking him to wipe up the puddle of water around the base and decided against it.

'No thanks.'

'Tea?'

'No, thank you.'

'Jam sandwiches?' he grinned, trying to look cute. It had always worked in the old days.

Nat ignored the question. 'Did you do it on purpose?' she asked.

'What?' He still couldn't make eye contact with her. But she saw that he was looking at the bruising on her wrists where he'd held her.

'You know what,' she said, disgustedly, turning tail and going upstairs to lock herself in the bathroom until she knew he was gone.

-0-0-0-

Sometimes she wondered if they should ever have had the kids.

They hadn't planned on getting pregnant so soon. It happened when Natalie was between Pills, and Ed was careless with a condom. He'd never liked wearing them anyway, and he tore this one putting it on. He daren't admit to Nat that he'd known it was broken, and in the heat of the moment, had gambled on it being alright. But he knew that she'd always suspected it. And it played on his mind, and added itself to the growing list of things he sensed she held against him.

They were just eight months into the marriage. They hadn't even finished decorating the house. Nat was on the verge of a minor promotion at work. At first, they both secretly hoped it was a false alarm. When it wasn't, Ed would have liked her to have an abortion, but he couldn't bring himself to ask for that. And anyway, he knew she wouldn't. Not when they were married, and had both said that they would like kids someday.

He wasn't sure he'd ever thought *that* one through properly either.

-0-0-0-

'So, how's "Thick Ed" coping with it all?' This was Ruth, on a visit, during the pregnancy. She was staying for the weekend, and Ed was out 'on a job'. Nat was brewing coffee for her in the half-finished kitchen. Her own herbal infusion was filling the air with the warm scent of strawberry and hibiscus. It smelt good, but it was the bitter tang of the coffee that called to her. She could have murdered a cup. But she'd told herself she wouldn't caffeinate the babies. So she made herself be strong.

'I wish you wouldn't call him that,' she sighed. She felt stressed and ill and really in need of some TLC from her best friend. Despite his strained smile and apparent enthusing at the prospect of parenthood, she'd sensed that Ed was not thrilled about the pregnancy. She'd noticed how his voice went up when he talked about it, and she wondered if he felt repulsed by the idea of the life growing there inside her. He'd barely touched her since the pregnancy test. And he'd been even more evasive since he'd actually seen the tiny bean-like images on the first scan. 'He's delighted,' she said. 'He's working very hard now, so he can take some time off later.'

'Yeah… right,' Ruth wondered which it was this afternoon – rugby or the pub. She knew from Jo that he didn't work half as many shifts as he said he did. 'So he's looking forward to having a new brother or sister to play with, is he?'

Natalie didn't have the energy to challenge her again. 'Actually,' she said. 'That should be in the plural.'

'Twins?'

'Yes. We found out when we went for the scan.' She hadn't had the heart to phone Ruth with that particular bit of news. And her friend's response now made her glad that she hadn't bothered.

'Good God Nat! You two don't cock up by halves, do you? Have you told your mum she's about to be a granny twice?'

'I have!' Natalie remembered her mother's hysterical reaction on the phone. When she was younger, she might have been hurt by it. But it was a very long time since she'd taken her mother seriously. 'The news has sent her back into therapy apparently. And she's already told me that if the children ever call her by any variation of the 'G' word, she'll disinherit them…. Ralph's quietly pleased though. I think he likes the idea of being an Uncle. And Ed's mum and dad are thrilled, of course.'

Ruth laughed. 'I can imagine. They're getting a couple of little rug rats to inherit the carpet empire. They must be over the moon.'

'Yes, so the kids will have at least one set of doting grandparents to spoil them.' Nat smiled. The Masons were the nearest thing she'd ever had to 'proper' parents. Ed's mum, in particular, thought the world of her, and it was mutual.

She poured Ruth's coffee and handed it to her. 'Let's go sit down with this, shall we?'

-0-0-0-

The sitting room was warm, and sunny, and finished. Nat had decorated most of it while Ed was working on late shifts. It had a pale oatmeal coloured carpet, and a large painting of a poppy field over the fireplace. Nat slightly regretted the oatmeal now the kids were on their way, though with Ed's tendency to come tramping in with muddy boots, she *had* already had the foresight to have the carpet Scotchguarded.

'I suppose you'll be seeing Jo at some point this weekend?' Her face clouded at the thought of her friend's unwelcome relationship with her bête noir. She steadied the cup of herbal tea between both hands as she backed onto the sofa.

Ruth sat down opposite her in the large leather armchair next to the coffee table and helped herself to a Viennese Whirl. They were her favourites and Nat had bought them especially for her from a nice little family bakery in town.

As always, looking at Ruth, Natalie was struck by how pretty her best friend was. Pretty, and surprisingly petite, despite her love of biscuits. Nat had always felt huge beside her. She guessed she'd be feeling even bigger soon.

'No.' Ruth shrugged like it wasn't important. 'She's working. And anyway, we've decided to call it a day. It was fun. And she's ***amazing*** in bed!' She wiggled her eyebrows for effect, and Nat wondered if this unwanted piece of information was added specifically to hurt her. 'But it wasn't going anywhere.'

Natalie closed her eyes with relief. She hugged her 'tea' close to her chest, breathing in the fragrant steam that she always thought was the nicest bit. 'Is she seeing someone else?' she asked.

'Yeah... we both are. But that was always the deal. It was never serious. We live much too far apart to be tying each other down.'

Natalie looked across at her friend. She'd never really understood the idea of relationships not being serious. But then, she was a serious kind of a person. And Ruth wasn't, in general. Right now, she envied her that. 'I know this is probably unfair of me,' she said. 'But I'm glad it's over with Jo. I never really trusted her... So, tell me about this new woman. You've been keeping *her* pretty close to your chest.'

'Pretty close to other bits of me too!' Ruth grinned cheekily and tucked her feet up into the chair. It was all show though. She didn't *really* want to talk about Justine, who had seemed like a contender a couple of weeks ago, but was rapidly downgrading herself into the 'nice but boring' camp frequented by most of the women she'd toyed with over the years.

She licked her finger and dabbed at the final crumbs of biscuit on her plate, observing her friend through narrowed eyes. The sun, slanting into the south-facing room, spotlighted the sallowness of her skin and the dullness of her hair. She looked weary and unwell. Pregnancy, or marriage to Ed, or both, seemed to be sapping the life out of her.

Ruth didn't see any point in revisiting the old ground of how much happier she could have been with *her*.

She sipped at her coffee. It was strong and black and burnt the back of her throat.

'You're wrong about Jo,' she said. 'She's a good person. And you're not normally stupid, so I really don't know why you can't see that.'

-0-0-0-

Natalie was right about Ed though. The pregnancy scared and repulsed him in just about equal measure. And, of course, eventually, when he couldn't bear it any longer, he confessed his feelings to Jo.

'They're like little maggots,' he said with a shudder. 'You shoulda seen 'em on that scan.'

He was in the inspection pit where he was working on a bright red 1959 Austin Healey. He wiped his hands on his already grease-streaked blue overalls and reached for the mug of tea she'd brought in for him. The overalls had been clean that morning when he climbed into them. Jo wondered what kind of industrial grade washing powder Nat used to get the stains out. She was sure they'd never actually been washed at all before he was married.

'Well, *you* were like that once,' she said cautiously. She wasn't sure that she wanted to get drawn into a conversation about this. She breathed in the air of the place, heavy with oil and petrol. It was cold.

'Yeah, but I don't like thinking about it… you know… Them *in* there… Growing… It gives me the heebie-jeebies.'

'Well, *don't* think about it then.' This was Jo's favourite coping strategy. It had helped her survive her childhood and she found that it generally worked okay for most situations, even now. 'D'you want a biscuit with that? I've got some Fruit Clubs in the office.'

'God, yeah, I'm starving! Nat's got us on muesli for breakfast now. Bloody rabbit food!'

He wasn't going to let the pregnancy thing drop either. He launched into it again when Jo returned with the biscuit.

'If only it were that easy!' he said, going back to the 'don't think about it' advice. 'But she's on about it all the time. And she's gone all clingy… All that "You *do* still love me don't you…? Will you just give me a cuddle…? Don't you *fancy* me anymore…? You're not going off me are you?"…. *Jesus!!!*' He unwrapped his biscuit and demolished it in two easy bites.

Jo wondered if her father had felt the same way when her mother was pregnant. Certainly he'd stayed well away when she was expecting Andy. And Nat's minor insecurities wouldn't have even registered on the Richter scale of the Cooper household back then.

'She'll be feeling vulnerable,' she said, reasonably. 'You're just gonna have to man up and support her. She probably needs reassuring that she's still attractive to you. It's not easy being pregnant, you know.'

Clearly she *wasn't* attractive to him though. Not right now. And Ed had never been a great actor.

He looked glum. He'd hopped up onto the edge of the pit and was swinging his feet, slurping at his tea. He looked too young to have kids, sitting there all frightened and covered in grease. He'd even got it in his hair, and there was a long streak that went diagonally across his cheek and eyebrow.

'But what about *me*?' he asked, plaintively. 'Who's gonna support *me* while Nat's being all weird and hormonal?'

Jo sighed. She could see both sides of this. And she knew that Nat could be a pain.

'Guess that's gonna have to be me,' she said. 'Look… if the old lady's starving you at home, how about I get you a bacon sarnie for your lunch?'

She knew that she shouldn't be siding with him against his wife. But she thought muesli for breakfast was a bit mean for a guy who had to work in a garage all day. And it was always just a bit too tempting to be kind to someone who could be cheered up so easily – just by the mention of a bacon buttie.

-0-0-0-

Cindy was a tart, but in a good way.

'Oh yeeeesss! Oh My God.....Oh sweet Jesus... there... that's right Baby.... Oh yes... right there! Don't stop!!!'

Jo certainly had no intention of stopping. She was enjoying herself way too much. But somehow, from somewhere, permeating the continental quilt and Cindy's hands clamped rather tightly over her ears, she could hear a distant ringing. It sounded ominously like the phone on her bedside table. She paused and cocked her head to listen.

'Oh Jesus, Jo, don't bloody stop now... Just ignore it for fuck's sake!!!'

Jo's head popped up from under the quilt. Her hand groped for the phone, which was flashing, as well as ringing, in the darkness.

'Bloody hell Jo!'

'It's past midnight. It might be an emergency.' She juggled the phone to her ear, almost dropping it as Cindy aimed a petulant slap at the side of her head. 'Shit Cind... that bloody hurt! ... *Hello?'*

On the other end of the line, Natalie sounded hysterical. 'Jo... thank God you're there... Have you any idea where my bloody husband is?'

'Ed?'

'No, Jo... King Charles the Bloody Second... How many bloody husbands do I have?'

'This is it,' muttered Cindy, setting up a wave of bounce on Jo's mattress as she flounced over the edge and picked

up the strapless little number she'd worn, but not for very long, earlier in the evening. *'We are finished!'*

Jo was normally pretty good at multitasking, but she was struggling to hear over her girlfriend's tirade. She raised her hand to try to ask Cindy to just hold on while she dealt with Natalie. Cindy looked as if she might actually like to kill her, but she paused in her tracks, long enough to aim another slap at Jo's head.

Jo was ready for it this time. She ducked.

'Well, there's no need to swear at *me*,' she protested down the phone. 'He should have been back hours ago.'

'Well he's not!' Natalie's voice shrilled out in panic. 'And I need to get to the hospital.'

'You're kidding me!'

'Do I *sound* like I'm kidding you?'

'Oh shit! Hang on… Hey Cindy…' Cindy had struggled into her high heels and was stomping towards the door. Jo put her hand over the telephone receiver. 'Cind… please come back.'

'Not till hell freezes over!'

'No… seriously… Cind… please… we've got a situation…'

Thankfully, Cindy just happened to be a nurse and it seemed she could switch into work-mode at the drop of a hat.

'It's alright darling,' she cooed down the phone to the terrified and distraught Natalie. 'Just breathe nice and steady. You remember, how they taught you at ante-natal classes? Thaaat's right… Goood…. Now how are those contractions going? …Okay… okay… There's nothing at all to worry about. Where are you sweetheart? ….Oh that's just around the corner from us isn't it? ….Well you just get your overnight bag now, and my **arsehole** of an ex-girlfriend will drive me there in just two shakes of a dog's tail.'

'She's gone into labour,' she announced as she put the phone down. 'We're taking her to hospital.'

'But... the Jag!' spluttered Jo. 'It's got cream leather upholstery!'

'So? ... We've got a woman in labour here.'

'But it's not mine.'

'It's not **what?**'

'It's not mine. It's one of our hire cars. And it's booked out tomorrow night. We can't have somebody giving bloody birth in the back of it. Can't we just phone for an ambulance?'

'Jesus... you don't even own the Jag?' Cindy shook her head and clicked her tongue contemptuously. '*You*,' she said. 'You really *are* just totally chucked you know!'

-0-0-0-

It's not easy finding a parking space big enough for a Jaguar XJS in a hospital car park, especially when you're not really all that used to driving one. But having dropped the two women at the door Jo was quite relieved to have the excuse to stay away as long as possible anyway. In fact, if Ed had shown any sign of making an appearance, she would have just sloped off home to try to clean the car before drowning her newly single (again) sorrows in a few double brandies and bed.

Ed, however, was still not answering his mobile, so she figured it was her duty to feed an inordinate number of pound coins into the Pay and Display station and make her way up to the maternity ward to stand in for her best friend until he deigned to show his face.

Cindy was long gone when she got there... presumably back to the nurses' home where she lived. So she had to ask the fifty-something Sister on the nursing station for directions.

'I'm looking for Natalie Mason,' she said, shuddering at the spine chilling screams coming from one of the side wards. She reckoned it was going to be a miracle if her already disheartened sex drive survived the horrors of this particular night.

'Ah, yes... I've just come on duty.' The Sister took in Jo's smart black trousers and open necked shirt, the first clothes to come to hand, having been hurled onto the back of a chair in the bedroom as she backed in there with Cindy earlier. 'You must be...' she leafed through her notes.... 'Ed... I guess that's short for Edwina, perhaps.'

'God, no.... I mean....' Jo struggled to explain her relationship to Natalie. 'She's just a... friend.'

The Sister patted her hand reassuringly. 'It's alright dear. I understand. I've had Equal Opportunities Training you know. I was sent specially... There was a bit of a misunderstanding a few months back, so they taught me all about 'heterosexism' and how I should never assume that people are in nuclear families... Anyway, I'm sure you don't need to know that. The important thing is that Mother and Babies are doing just fine... They're in Bed Seven.... Just down there on the right.'

-0-0-0-

Natalie looked exhausted, washed out and, as always, stunningly, frustratingly, gorgeous.

She looked up expectantly as Jo came round the corner. 'Oh,' she said. 'It's you.'

No thanks there then.

'I'm sure Ed will be here soon.'

'Well, I hope he's okay.'

'I'm sure he will be. He's probably just broken down somewhere in the wilds of Shropshire.'

It was one of the regular hazards of the classic car business. Breakdowns miles away from the nearest cell phone signal or phone box. Jo had lost track of the number of miles the lads had walked over the years looking for civilization and a tow-truck.

'Do you want to look at them?'

Nat appeared to be referring to the babies, and Jo thought it might be rude not to. She peeped cautiously into the cribs at the side of the bed.

'What do you think?'

Actually, they were nowhere near as sweet as Andy had been when he was born. He'd already been plump and round faced, with wisps of thin blonde hair. These two were more like Jo's great grandpa Obediah; bald and wrinkled and with skin that looked several sizes too big for them. Some latent instinct of self-preservation stopped her from saying it though.

'I think they're beautiful,' she said. And in that moment, as if the words were magic, they became so. And her heart went out to them, enraptured by their vulnerability and their innocence.

To her surprise, when she looked up, she saw that Natalie was smiling at her. She smiled back, tentatively, like someone trapped in a yard with a Doberman that's suddenly, inexplicably begun to wag its tail.

Then she heard Natalie talking, and to her amazement, she was actually being *nice* to her.

'Thank you so much for everything you did tonight,' she was saying.

But the Equal Opportunities Sister ruined the moment. 'Aren't they lovely Ed?' she called, as she trotted down the corridor towards someone who was screaming blue murder on yet another of the side wards. 'You must be really proud of them all.'

And Natalie rolled her eyes in disgust. 'Oh thank you *very* much!' she muttered. 'Coming in here, looking like Radclyffe Hall on a butch day. Now everybody thinks I'm a frigging lesbian, don't they?'

-0-0-0-

Natalie suffered from post natal depression, and Ed never really 'got' it.

He wasn't particularly interested in the babies, but he worked hard, brought in good money, and was tired at the end of the day. With Natalie opting to stay at home, he figured that, at the very least, the house should be tidy and his tea on the table when he got in.

He also thought she should be the one to get up in the night when they cried. After all, he told himself, she could always have a nap during the day if she wanted to.

When the house began to look a mess and he'd heated up his umpteenth ready meal, he found himself looking for excuses to stay away more often. And secretly, he began to feel more and more critical of the wife he'd always felt slightly in awe of before.

Then, one day, Jo called round to drop off some papers and found Nat sobbing in the still-unfinished kitchen. Her hair was greasy. She had purplish dark rings under her eyes and her cheeks were hollow. The unwashed plates from breakfast were still in the sink and the bin had the distinctive pong of dirty nappies.

From upstairs came the loud, insistent yowl of two babies who took it in turns to wake each either up. They were both in full force now and they sounded like an alley full of fighting cats.

'Oh,' said Natalie, looking up wearily as she came in. 'It's you!'

Jo recognised the greeting from the hospital. It was said in the same tone – flat – disappointed – and with the unmistakable subtext of 'Why aren't you Ed?'

'Bloody hell!' she said. 'They've got a fine set of lungs, haven't they?'

'I can't bear it. They're driving me mad.'

This felt shocking. Jo had never heard Natalie sound *this* low before.

She glanced at her watch.

It was 7pm and Ed was on an overnighter.

She reached in her pocket for her house keys.

'I'll see to this,' she said. 'My spare bed's all made up. There's food in the fridge. You go get a good night's sleep at my place.'

-0-0-0-

When Natalie returned home the next morning, there was no sign of Jo. And her first, awful thought was that she had abandoned the kids.

She hesitated at the babies' bedroom door, mentally berating herself for leaving her precious offspring with an irresponsible idiot like Jo. Then she registered the sound of 'Smoke on the Water' playing quietly within. Dreading what she would find, she turned the handle and went inside.

It took a moment for her eyes to adjust to the gloom, and her nose searched first, groping for the sharp ammonia laden smell of wet nappies, but finding only the soft, soothing scent of Johnson's Baby Power. When she looked from cot to cot, she saw that Jacob and Alyssa were sleeping soundly. And, on the floor between them, with a pillow and blanket from the spare bedroom, Jo, still very much on sentry duty, and lying in something akin to the recovery position, was fast asleep too.

Wonderingly, Natalie stared at her. She looked so peaceful. It seemed cruel to wake her. But it was 7am and she probably needed to get ready for work.

She went downstairs to make a cup of coffee for them both.

When she came back, Jo was stirring. She stretched and looked up into Natalie's eyes. Then she saw the coffee, and reached for it. 'You are an angel!' she said quietly, so as not to wake the kids.

'And *you* are a miracle worker!'

They looked at each other with something like a return to their original fondness.

'Not me!' Jo protested. 'I just hit lucky with the Deep Purple – You should have seen Jacob cooing along to 'Child in Time'. They both like Genesis and Rick Wakeman too. Alyssa quite likes Spandau Ballet and Lionel Richie, but Jacob hates 'em. And neither of them like that weird spooky 'Whale Music for Tots' CD you had in the player.... I mean... God... what warped mind thought of *that?*' She shuddered.

Nat smiled. 'It was a present from Ruth,' she said. 'I think she read somewhere that babies like it.'

'Yeah... baby whales maybe... God, it was creepy... Anyway, did you manage to get a good night's sleep?'

'I did! Thank you so much. I feel almost human again.'

They were still sitting together on the floor, closer than they had been since that first night in the Tennis Club. For a brief crazy moment, Natalie felt her eyes blur and felt an almost magnetic pull towards Jo. In that moment, she wondered if she might actually kiss her. She certainly wanted to. She told herself it was an aberration brought on by sleep deprivation and extreme gratitude. *My hormones are probably still all weird too,* she thought. She took a deep breath and sipped at her coffee. 'You need to be getting ready for work,' she said.

Jo glanced at her watch, gasped and leapt to her feet, waking the babies.

'Oh shit! I'm sorry!' she said as they began to wail.

'It's alright, truly!' Natalie struggled to her own feet beside her. 'Thank you again Jo. You were a real lifesaver last night… And please… you won't tell Ed, will you? He already thinks I'm totally pathetic.'

Jo looked as if she was going to try to deny this, but Nat stopped her. 'Please,' she said. 'He *does*… I know he does.'

And so it became their secret.

But once or twice a week, when Ed was working away, Nat slept at Jo's house and Jo stayed over with the kids.

-0-0-0-

'Jo – you're a woman… right?' Ed was fixing the Bentley, which had developed a problem with its head gasket.

'Well, I *was* last time I looked.' Jo figured she'd better proceed with caution. This question, in that tone of voice from Ed usually preceded discussions about Natalie. Impossible questions like, 'What do you think Natalie would like for Christmas?' or 'Natalie's in a mood with me, what do you think I might have done wrong?'

Jo didn't like being set up as an expert about any of that stuff. After all, her track record with women wasn't great either. And Natalie was every bit as much of a mystery to her as she was to her husband.

'Well, how long does it take for 'em to get back to… you know… normal? …. after they've had babies, and that?' His embarrassed glance downwards left her in no doubt that he was talking about their sex life.

'God, Ed, how would *I* know? It varies from person to person, I guess.'

'Yeah… but some kind of ball park figure would be good.'

Jo remembered that she'd come in to bring him a mug of tea. It was burning her fingers now. She passed it to him as a diversion.

'When you say *normal*…' she ventured, 'How… kind of… *often*… are you thinking of?' She wondered if he'd ever actually got over his aversion to 'the maggots' during the pregnancy. If he hadn't, it was probably hard to even know what 'normal' meant anymore. She decided against asking.

'Well, any kind of ever would be good.' He sounded anxious.

'Oh… right!' she winced. 'Well, look, she's got a lot on with the twins. She must be tired. And she's been depressed…'

He looked sulky.

'I don't know what she's got to be depressed about, sitting around on her backside all day.'

Give me strength! Jo resisted the urge to slap him, and went into problem solver mode. If nothing else, she wanted to draw this mortifying conversation to a close.

'She's probably just knackered,' she said. 'And, distracted, you know, listening out for them all the time. Why don't you two have a nice romantic weekend away? I'm sure your mum and dad would love to babysit for you. And you could have a bit of 'adult' time together. Nice hotel… candlelit dinner… Give her a break from the kids and the cooking and washing up. Get some flowers and champagne in the room. Romance her a bit. Women *like* a bit of romancing from time to time.'

This had always been one of Veronica's mantras, and she'd absorbed it unthinkingly when she was sixteen. But as soon as she'd said it, she wondered if it was, actually, true. It never seemed to have worked particularly well for her. In fact, it had always seemed to put a lot of pressure on things, and had invariably ended badly.

It appeared to make some kind of sense for Ed though. He looked like she'd just given him the answer to the whereabouts of the Holy Grail.

'And you reckon that'll work?' he was asking. 'Cos, you know, I'm going nuts here. My balls are practically dragging on the floor!'

Jo shuddered. 'God, Ed… too much information!' She *hoped* it would work, if only to prevent a recurrence of this kind of conversation. 'Like a dream,' she said reassuringly. 'Trust me, she'll be putty in your hands.'

-0-0-0-

She'd got a bit of romancing of her own planned, as it happened. Nothing too 'over the top'. Just a minibreak in London with Cindy, who she'd finally managed to sweet-talk back into her life. She was looking forward to it. Well, all except the afternoon of shopping on Regent's Street that Cindy seemed to think would be the highlight of the trip.

They'd got an upgrade to First Class on the train, a hotel just off Leicester Square and tickets for 'Cats'. Cindy had swopped shifts and bought new underwear specially.

Then Ed phoned. He didn't normally phone unless he needed something. 'Jo…?'

She recognised the tone. He'd messed up. She knew it. Her heart sank.

'I've booked that weekend away like you suggested.'

'Great!' She hoped, if she managed to stay upbeat, that whatever the problem was, it might just go away.

'Yeah… Lovely hotel in the Lakes… Fantastic views…. Michelin Star restaurant… Four poster bed…' He paused, and she knew he was picturing that bed, and what he hoped to be doing in it, several times, probably, in the course of the weekend.

'Sounds great!' Maybe he'd just messed up his shifts. Maybe it would be as simple as getting one of the lads to cover for him….

'But I forgot that Mum and Dad are at a Ruby Wedding in Hemel Hempstead.'

'Oh God Ed… you *plonker…!* You didn't think to check with them before you booked it?'

'Well, they *never* go anywhere, do they?'

This wasn't strictly true.

'Can't the hotel just shift the booking to a different weekend?'

'I've already told Nat we're going.'

'I'm sure she'd understand.'

'Well, I don't know…. She didn't seem that keen on the idea at first to be honest. She said she didn't want to leave the kids for a whole weekend. I had to lay it on a bit thick to persuade her to go. You know… How neglected I've been feeling…. How I'm scared that we're drifting apart…. All *that* crap.'

Jo thought of how it wasn't so very long since Nat had been frightened of Ed backing away from *her*, and she felt puzzled. She'd assumed that she would have welcomed some romantic attention from her husband.

'So you guilt-tripped her into going?'

He laughed uneasily. 'Only a bit… But she's looking forward to it now. So, I thought, 'strike while the iron's hot' and all that, and I booked it without checking. And now I haven't got a babysitter and y*ou're* pretty good with kids, aren't you?'

God, this was a right can of worms! Jo tried very hard to think on her feet…

'Nat would never agree to it. She hates my guts. You know she does.' Now she felt guilty. She'd been keeping Nat's secret about the overnighters for the past three months, but this was the first time she'd actually lied to Ed about it. It felt horribly disloyal.

Thankfully, Ed was clueless.

And he had his argument all planned out.

'Well, I think she seems to be warming to you since you and Cindy took her to the hospital. I actually heard her saying something nice about you to Bill the other day.'

'Really?' Despite the impending catastrophe, she was gratified to hear that.

'Yeah – she was saying that she didn't know how the business would survive without you. Weird, eh..? But anyway, I know you practically brought Andy up, cos he's always going on about how you were more of a mum to him than his mum was. So how about we at least *see* if she'll go for it?'

'I dunno.'

She could picture that wily look of his as he wheedled away at Nat... That 'I'm so cute, how could you possibly even *think* of saying no to me?' look.

'This *was* your idea after all,' he said.

And how the hell did he do that? Making it her responsibility all the time?

'Which weekend are we talking about?' She knew that he would have gone for the first possible opportunity.

'This weekend coming.'

'Right.' She'd already absorbed the feeling of responsibility. After all, it *had* been her stupid suggestion. She should have just kept out of it. Particularly now it was clear that Nat wasn't exactly desperate to get Ed's pants off. 'But only if Nat's one hundred percent happy with it,' she added, hoping that Natalie might jump at the chance to veto the idea and save the day with Cindy.

'Cheers mate!' Clearly Ed didn't think this was likely. 'You're a star.'

And, of course, Natalie agreed to it. She still loved Ed, and she wanted to make him happy. And she figured, if she drank enough of the champagne he'd hinted might be waiting for them in their room when they arrived, maybe she'd disconnect from the part of her that resented him. Maybe she'd be able to relax and forgive the times he'd let her down, and come to want him again, urgently, desperately, physically, like she used to.

So, Jo had to prepare herself to break the news to Cindy. She was dreading it. And she knew it would end with her being single again. But she was also picturing Jacob and Alyssa and their tiny cabbage-patch faces and distinctive baby smell. And she was thinking how nice it would be to look after them for a whole weekend. Nicer, definitely, than shopping on Regent Street. Nicer, maybe, even, than seeing 'Cats', or unwrapping Cindy from that sexy new underwear she'd bought.

And when she realised that she'd rather babysit than spend time with her (soon to be ex) girlfriend, she knew that she was in very deep trouble indeed.

-0-0-0-

Ed looked disgustingly smug when he turned up for work on Monday morning. He put his thumbs up as he came into the office. 'You're a frigging genius, mate!' he said to Jo with a sly grin.

Jo forced a smile.

'You had a nice time then?' she asked, trying to keep it clean. She'd thought that Nat seemed quiet when they'd got back on Sunday night. But maybe she was still trying to keep up the illusion of aloofness with Jo.

'She couldn't get enough of me!' he said, like the self-satisfied dick he was.

'Well, that's good!' It didn't feel it. The urge to slap him was creeping up on her again. 'D'you fancy a cup of coffee?' she asked, in an effort to change the subject.

'Yeah…' he yawned, and stretched so hard he gave her a flash of navel as his T-shirt and jeans parted company. He really *was* good looking, the bastard! 'Reckon I'll need *something* to keep me awake today!'

He ambled out towards the body shop.

And a distant blast of dirty laughter told her that he was sharing his success with all the lads in there too.

-0-0-0-

Nat didn't have anyone to talk to about how she'd had to get drunk to have sex with her husband. She knew that Ruth would be secretly pleased. It was hardly the kind of thing she could discuss with her mother-in-law. And Jo, of course, was Ed's best friend. So she kept it to herself and hoped it would get better.

It didn't.

And she just kept getting closer to Jo.

Those early years were full of her. Jo on her back on the sofa with the giggling kids held aloft, or posing with (clean) Pampers nappies on her head, or singing 'Ice Ice Baby' as she heard the jangling 'Greensleeves' of the ice cream van and disappeared, only to burst back moments later with tubs of cold, white, whipped up goo and raspberry sauce dripping over her fingers.

Then there were the buggy races with the kids, digging in the sandpit, splashing in the paddling pool, snail hunts in the garden and trips to the woods to liberate the captives.

And the long, warm summer evenings before the kids started nursery and Natalie returned to work (part time at first, though the thought of having to juggle everything still filled her with dread), when Jo would just 'pop in' on her way home from work; careering round the garden, achieving the impossible and tiring Jake out before bedtime; telling magical stories about heroic princesses to Alyssa; and disappearing, as if by magic, just before Ed started to feel hungry and prised himself away from the pub to come home.

Nat had once heard a theory that the natives of Hispaniola literally couldn't see Christopher Columbus approaching because his giant sailing ships were so far out of their existing experience of the world. It was rubbish, of course. We *see* things. We just don't always understand their significance.

It was like that with Nat's feelings for Jo. She knew that she'd been drawn to her right from the start. But, back then, while she still defined herself as 'straight', she'd filed Ed's undeniably attractive side-kick in a 'potential friend' category. She realised now that her heterosexuality had never been as total as she'd told herself it was. Long before she'd ever met Jo, she knew that she'd been turned on by the films she'd seen with Ruth – 'Desert Hearts', 'Lianna,' even the depressing older stuff like 'The Killing of Sister George' and 'The Loudest Whisper'. And she knew that her treacherous body had whispered the truth to her on that first night at the tennis club when Jo had leant so close to play 'cupid' for Ed.

It wasn't that she was homophobic. She'd been *so* 'politically correct' back in those old university days. She knew that there were rumours about her relationship with Ruth. She made a point of not appearing to care.

But she *did* care, because deep down, she didn't want to be gay, especially not with Ruth, who she didn't love like that at all.

The night they had sex had proved that to her. The clumsy drunken madness of lying there and pretending she didn't notice Ruth's hand running down over her stomach. Feeling sick and excited all at the same time. Wanting to know how it would feel. Knowing it was crazy. But knowing she had to let this run its course now, and hopefully prove that it really, truly, wasn't for her.

In the event, she'd enjoyed the things Ruth did to her. She just didn't want to do them back. And, lost for any other way of handling it, she'd conveniently fallen asleep, under cover of being drunk, before she could be asked to reciprocate.

She'd always felt like a bitch for doing that. Though she was relieved to find that she really *wasn't* 'in love' with her best friend. What she failed to realise was that Ruth was just that little bit too close, too petite, too girlie, and, back then, when Nat was still hooked on chasing after the emotionally unavailable, far too besotted with her, to ever be anything other than 'not her type'.

But then again, there'd been the films she'd watched sometimes with Ed. He had a bit of a 'thing' for that kind of viewing. And she went along with it in the early days when she was still crazy about him, tempting him home early on a Friday night with the lure of a couple of bottles of wine, a takeaway and a 'mucky video' that he'd choose personally from 'Blockbuster' on the way. Such things were outside her comfort zone, and slightly against her principles. But it's hard to separate all the things that go into turning you on. So she wrote those particular nights off under the guise of being a 'good wife'.

But now, finally, there was Jo, on her sun lounger, the highlights of her hair glinting amber in the golden late afternoon sun, her eyes soft as she smiled over at her from under the shade of her hand. Jo, who was very much Nat's 'type' - tall, blonde, good-looking, strong, and frequently, comfortably, silent.

And suddenly, she couldn't deny her furtive reading of Jo's books when the kids were babies and she stayed there overnight. She couldn't deny that after the initial exhaustion had begun to wear off, there were nights when she had touched herself, secretly, in Jo's spare bed.

She didn't have the excuse of alcohol, or hormones, or sleep deprivation anymore.

And she realised that she couldn't deny to herself any longer that she was wondering how it would feel to touch Jo like that... to kiss her... and to hope that Jo would kiss her back.

-0-0-0-

Jo had never had the benefit of denial as far as Nat was concerned. And she knew that she was now fulfilling her own worst fears and falling, hard, fast, and deeply in love with this woman who should have always been off-limits for her. She told herself that she should stay away. But Nat always seemed so pleased to see her. And so she just kept digging herself in deeper.

Eventually, she figured she needed to find a way of making sure that Ed could be at home with his family more. That way, she hoped, he might become the kind of husband and father Nat had always wanted him to be, and *she* could stop mooning around after her best friend's straight wife and get a life of her own.

When she came up with the brain-wave of recruiting a team of nationwide 'Classic Cars' freelancers, she wondered why the idea had never occurred to her before.

'I've been thinking,' she said to Ed one afternoon shortly after the twins' fourth birthday.

'Uh-huh!' he looked anxiously at her as he pulled on his chauffeur's jacket. They were in the office portacabin at the garage. He'd had last minute parts to order for a 1962 Citroen DS, and now he was about to head off with Ash, Mo and Jimmy-Lee to a huge Sikh wedding over in Leeds. He was running late, but 'Parts' was a job he wouldn't entrust to Jo. She never *had* been able to tell a gudgeon from a gasket – or a piston from a poppet, for that matter. It was one of the very few areas where she'd always been a total 'girl'.

Ed studied her in the mirror as he flipped up his collar and lassoed himself with his already knotted tie. 'Well, fire away,' he said. It wasn't like Jo to propose stuff when he was on the run, so he figured it must be important. 'I've got five minutes – max!'

Through the window, on the forecourt, he could see that Mo had finished decorating the cars and was leaning against the Bentley for a smoke.

Jo took a deep breath. She'd picked her time carefully. She didn't want Ed to have the chance to say 'no' without at least thinking about the idea.

'I think we should set up a freelance register of cars and drivers,' she said. 'We could recruit at rallies. We've got to 'man' our stalls there anyway and we always get talking to people. We could personally hand pick decent people with great cars – see if they'd be interested in doing a bit of chauffeuring in their spare time. I've got a few in mind already who'd probably bite our hands off at the opportunity. If we *do* get people interested, we could police check them and do the bookings centrally. I think it could be a real goer. And if it works, it could take a load of pressure off you and the lads. The chauffeuring's just going crazy at the moment, and we're having to turn away a lot of bookings. It would mean that we could offer a much bigger service. You wouldn't have to work away so much while the kids are little. And if we're taking a commission off each job it could be a really nice little earner for the business.'

Ed straightened his tie, and pulled his collar down. He turned and looked at Jo.

Part of him liked the idea and part of him didn't. The part of him that really enjoyed working away wanted to say no. Home wasn't a comfortable place for him. Nat always seemed intent on finding him jobs to do when he was around, and his chauffeuring got him out of shopping and DIY and baby sitting and all that tedious stuff. It also provided perfect cover for extracurricular activities – like rugby and cricket, and the pub. But the part of him that was actually a fairly shrewd businessman knew that this idea could earn him a lot of money. And that meant he couldn't just reject it out of hand.

'Has Nat set you up to do this?' he asked, suspiciously. He'd noticed that 'the girls' had been spending quite a lot of time together recently and he hoped they weren't starting to gang up on him.

Jo shrugged. 'No... But would it be such a bad thing if she had?'

He skipped answering that one. 'There'll be all sorts of legal complications,' he said. 'Like who'd be responsible if a driver didn't turn up, or had an accident... all that stuff.'

'Yes, I've been doing a bit of research on all that.'

Outside, Mo beeped the horn on the Bentley.

Ed sighed and capitulated. 'Okay,' he said. 'Put some proposals in writing. I'll run it past my dad. If he likes the look of it, I'll give it a try.'

-0-0-0-

It was amazing how many classic car enthusiasts were thrilled at the opportunity to chauffeur their beloved 'babies' at weddings, anniversaries and prom nights.

Classic Cars had to add extra pages to their website to cope with them all.

It meant that the Yorkshire lads no longer had to travel the length and breadth of the country on jobs.

Jo thought she'd solved her problem.

But Ed just thought up new excuses for not being at home.

Chapter Thirteen

In the bathroom, Nat heard the door slam and the car engine revving. She listened to the crunch of tyres on the driveway as Ed reversed onto the gravel in front of the house, then out of the gate.

The bathwater cooled around her and the foam crackled quietly around her ears. She turned on the hot tap, careful to keep her feet away from the scalding water as it steamed into the bath, kicking up thousands of tiny fragrant bubbles. Then she turned it off again quickly, just as the temperature headed for unbearable.

Slowly Ed's absence and the heat began to soothe her.

And she thought of Jo.

Jo's hands and lips and tongue all over her – the delicious softness of her – and the love in her eyes.

Desire kicked in, despite the soreness. She raised her hips above the surface of the water, poured almond oil into her hand, and tried to imagine that it was Jo touching her now where she slid to touch herself.

-o-0-o-

The Sunday Service at the Parish Church of St James always ended promptly at 12 noon. It was arranged that way so that people could get home and finish preparing their Sunday lunch. Nat stood by the gate, scanning for Alyssa, as the congregation filed out in their thick winter-best coats and scarves, stopping to pull on their woolly gloves after they'd shaken hands with the vicar, and walking gingerly on the mossy, uneven paving stones, still slippery in places where the sun hadn't reached to burn away the morning frost. Nat was a familiar face there now. Several of the church goers greeted her as they went past.

St James's was the church where she and Ed had been married, and whenever she came to collect Alyssa, she couldn't help but find herself haunted by that day. How bright it had been, with the sun shining from that perfect blue sky above the squat and rather ugly stone tower with its unadventurous bell ringers. She remembered the excitement tinged with gut-wrenching stage fright as she'd sipped a glass of Buck's Fizz with Ruth for 'Dutch Courage' before setting off. The 'Classic Cars' Bentley driving round and round the small housing estate that circled the church, witnessed by the embarrassing clump of students determined to catch a glimpse of 'Miss' in her wedding frock. She remembered her drafted in and obviously gay uncle - dead now and never officially 'out'. His futile and slightly pathetic flirting with Ashad, and his sweet but clumsy attempts to find reasonable explanations for Ed's absence as the grim possibility of defection began to dawn.

She wished now that she'd made more of an effort to get to know that uncle. He was the only one of her father's family who'd ever made the slightest bit of effort towards her. And she imagined he couldn't have had an easy time of things, growing into manhood in Britain in the late 1950's.

She wished too that she hadn't snapped at Jo when she'd leapt out from behind the mossy grave of Joshua Arkwright and his widow Dora, and tried to tell that well-intentioned lie about Ed and the car. Jo had forgiven her, of course, long since. But she was full of regrets, and full of guilt. Without Jo's easy going, comforting presence, she felt as people feel when someone has died, trawling back through all the stupid, careless, selfish things they've ever said or done, agonising over all the many ways they've neglected to be kind.

At the church, Alyssa had appeared in the doorway with her friend Roxanne. She was chattering away to the vicar who looked desperate to escape, home to his family, roast beef, and Yorkshire puddings.

Nat started up the path to rescue him.

Sometimes she wondered about her daughter's friendship with Roxanne.

But she knew that experience had put her way ahead of Alyssa on *that* one.

-0-0-0-

Andrea phoned just after lunch. 'I wondered if you might fancy a walk on the moors with the dogs,' she said. 'Blow some Christmas cobwebs away.'

Natalie looked across the sitting room to where Alyssa and Roxanne were sprawled on the rug in front of the fire, playing a board game based on the London Underground. Their heads were almost touching, intent and giggling as Alyssa read the instructions on one of the forfeit cards aloud. The TV was playing a Christmas movie to itself. Jake was out for the day in Blackpool with his girlfriend's family and wouldn't be home till late. And Ed, who was always last minute for everything, was unlikely to be home much before five.

'Would you two like to come out for a walk with Dottie and Auntie Andrea?' she called.

They wrinkled their noses. She'd known that they would.

'Do you mind if *I* do? I won't be long.'

They looked up at her as if she were crazy.

'We're not *kids*,' said Alyssa, with the slight tone of contempt that had recently, despite her general good manners, begun to creep into her voice when she was with Roxanne and talking to her mum.

Nat assumed it was a teenage thing. Finding parents stupid and embarrassing made it easier for them to prepare for leaving home. And it probably made it easier for parents to wave them goodbye too.

'Phone me if you need me,' she said, indicating that she was tucking her mobile into the pocket of her dog-walking jacket.

Alyssa's scornful expression told her exactly what she thought of *that* idea.

-0-0-0-

The air felt sharp in her lungs as they wove up through the rocks and dead bracken towards the moor-tops. It was still a bright day with a pale cobalt sky and high white cloud. The sun was almost warm as it touched her cheeks through the chill of the air.

The dogs ran in circles just ahead of them, Andrea's rescue lurcher, Rags, hot on the heels of Dottie, who loved being chased more than any other thing in the whole wide world. She yapped giddily into the moorland wind as she swerved and swooped and tantalised him with her agility.

'I don't know where she gets her energy from,' Nat laughed. 'Just look at her teasing poor old Rags.'

'Oh, it'll do him good. He's always like a puppy again when he gets home from a walk with Dot…. Well until he collapses in a heap and snores for a week, anyway.'

'I can identify with that,' said Nat, smiling.

'*You...?* You're still a kid. Just wait till you reach *my* age... *Then* you'll know about it!'

They paused, as they reached the plateau at the top of the moor, gazing out over the villages and towns dotted with church spires and the occasional mill chimney, and stretching out to the borders of South Yorkshire.

'God's own country!' said Andrea, with that smug look that Yorkshire folk adopt whenever they talk about their home county.

'Mm.' Nat was non-committal, though she had to admit, the view was nice.

'Ah... I forget sometimes, that you're a southerner.' She looked pityingly at Nat as she changed the subject. 'We got home to a raid last night. Stephen had decided to put a party announcement on Facebook and the place was heaving with kids in various stages of consciousness. We found Rags quivering in the shower cubicle. The police took away two bags of cocaine, a whole stash of MCat and enough 'legal highs' to keep the clubbers of Leeds happy for a month.... We were at the police station most of the night.'

'Gosh, Andrea, how awful for you! Was everybody ok?'

'Well, they kept A & E busy for a few hours... but yes, apparently so.'

'Are they charging Steve?'

'Hopefully not,' she sounded grim. 'Though I imagine we'll probably hit the front page of the local rag. I can imagine the headlines now, "Local Businessman in Midnight Drugs Raid". It should keep the neighbours scandalised for a week or two. The house looks like a bomb's hit it. We've left Steve cleaning up. Martin and Gemma are helping him... which is very good of them since they were both out when it happened. Gem's directing operations, and you know how bossy *she* can be, bless her, so hopefully some kind of order will have been restored by the time we get back. They've packed us off 'to chill out'. So Robert's having a nice soothing round of golf, and me.... I'm here with you.'

They walked for a while in silence, Andrea, picturing the state of her house, and Nat finding that, as always, no matter how hard she tried to distract herself with other things, her thoughts had returned to Jo.

Unbeknownst to her, Andrea's thoughts had now begun to hover in the same ball-park.

'And speaking of scandalising the neighbours,' she said suddenly. 'I think you should know that Ed believes you're having an affair with Joanne Cooper.'

They'd reached the edge of the plateau. Huge outcrops of millstone grit reared up and out over the dizzying drop to the rocks below. Andrea stared across the cold, veined rock towards the horizon, allowing Nat the privacy to process this particular bombshell without being observed.

'Oh God!' she heard her gasp, as if she'd just been punched.

And they both knew then, that their suspicions of the night before had been correct.

Chapter Fourteen

Sister Ulrika was used to retreatants missing breakfast. Arriving exhausted and weighed down by the cares of the world, they often slept late, wandered off into the grounds, or locked themselves away like hibernating bears until the gong for elevenses tempted them with the promise of coffee and freshly baked cake.

But Jo had not responded to the cake's siren call. And when she missed lunch too, Ulrika's mild concern slid up a notch and she tapped, first gently, then more firmly on Jo's door.

'Joanne?' she called, with her lips close to the heavy oak.

Her voice echoed weirdly through the pounding in Jo's head.

'Yeurgh,' she replied. This was meant to be a 'Yes,' but her tongue felt too big for her mouth, and the effort of forming the word seemed to have drained the last dregs of energy from her. She felt a wave of coldness as she pushed her face out of the covers.

'Are you decent? May I come in?'

Jo tried to make sense of this question. *Was* she decent? She wasn't sure. She shivered and dredged up another 'Yeurgh.' It sounded even weirder than the first.

But she heard the heavy metal latch of the door clunking, and the creak of un-oiled hinges.

And a voice saying, 'My goodness, it's *freezing* in here!'

Ulrika crossed the room in two steps and bent to fiddle with a valve on the radiator.

'The last guest had practically turned it off,' she said, embarrassed. She remembered the grim-faced padre who had been the room's previous occupant. He'd eaten his bread dry and sneered at cake. She should have known that he'd prefer his temperatures sub-zero.

Gratefully, Jo tried to lift her head, feeling herself swimming in waves of chilly nausea. She felt Ulrika's warm hands guiding her gently back to the pillow. She forced herself to form words. It seemed like her last best hope of recovery.

'I'm sorry,' she said. 'It's just a migraine. I forgot my tablets.'

Ulrika seemed to be swimming too, in and out of focus, as she gazed down at her like the Holy Mother in a renaissance pietà. 'Oh my poor sweetheart,' she said. 'I'll get you some of mine.'

-0-0-0-

It was four o'clock before Jo fully regained the power of speech. She propped herself, limp and full of gratitude against her pillows and sipped at the mug of steaming chicken soup that Sister Ulrika had brought for her. It was thin and smelt of Italian seasoning, nothing like the tins her mother had opened for Jo and her brothers for their tea when they got home from school. She remembered the distinctive smell, Heinz Cream of Chicken, the packet of sliced white Mothers Pride bread open on the table, a tub of margarine and a knife beside it. It had always been Andy's favourite meal. She felt tears rising into her eyes and blinked them back. Migraines always made her emotional.

'I'm afraid it's our relief cook today, and she isn't very good at soup,' said Ulrika apologetically.

'It's nice,' Jo lied, adding, 'And it's hot,' which was a whole lot closer to the truth.

Ulrika glanced across at the paper blu-tacked to the wall around the crucifix. 'It looks like you'd been busy before you got ill,' she said.

'Yes, I've been trying to piece it all together.'

'And *have* you?'

Jo sighed. 'I'm not even sure that's possible. But there's something I need to tell you about, I think.'

'Are you up to it now?'

'As up to it as I'll ever be.'

-0-0-0-

One instant, she thought.

Wrong place. Wrong time.

And nothing's ever the same again.

It started out okay. It was Andy's birthday and they were all at 'Giovanni's', for pizza, his favourite.

They had a round table, with a red and white striped cloth. Krystal and Andy had been married for just over three years by then and they were still as besotted as ever. She was resting her hand on his on the table, running her thumb over his wedding ring as if she still couldn't quite believe her luck. Liam was there and his wife Angie. Cliff was out of prison again, looking thin and scruffy and eating quickly, as if he didn't do it very often. Bill and Fiona, not great fans of 'foreign muck', were persuading themselves, as they always did, that it was just like cheese on toast really. And then there was Jo, and Natalie, and Ed.

The kids, six years old already, were on an overnighter at Ed's parents.

Looking from Krystal to Ed, Jo sometimes wondered how everyone managed these occasions, bearing in mind the embarrassing circumstances of their first meeting, but

Krystal, and Andy too, had always seemed to be able to compartmentalise her work. Bill knew how to keep a secret. Natalie was oblivious. And Ed – well, Ed had never shown the slightest sign of recognising Krystal from that night.

So, there they all were. Jo remembered it as if it were yesterday. It was February and cold outside, and the restaurant was snug and warm, with the pizza ovens working at full tilt just behind the counter. The whole place was noisy and garlicky and familiar. Andrea Bocelli was belting out pop-opera on the sound system. Ed was on good form, buying Chianti and keeping everybody's glasses topped up. Nat looked a bit disconnected. It was a particular expression she'd started to have when Ed got drunk. A sort of dullness in her eyes, as if she was dreading what might happen next. Jo could see that she was struggling to make small-talk with Angie. Nat loved Fiona and got on well with Krys, though she didn't always entirely know when she was joking. But she had nothing whatsoever in common with Liam's no bullshit, heavily tattooed, army wife, and somehow, she'd ended up next to her, hemmed in by Ed on her other side.

The food, as always, was good. Jo remembered they'd had dough balls for starters, then pizza and salad and garlic bread. There was homemade ice cream – Amarena, nocciola and cioccolato - for dessert. Then Tia Maria for 'the girls' (including Andy, much to Ed's amusement), and brandy for the 'lads', with coffee and cream and chocolate mint sticks. Sometimes she wondered if it would have turned out differently if they hadn't all been, at least, a little bit tipsy.

Andy and Krystal made their announcement over coffee. Holding hands even tighter, and giggling a little, smiling proudly into each other's eyes.

'We're going to have a baby,' said Andy.

Nat couldn't have failed to notice how different he was to Ed in his euphoria at the prospect of fatherhood.

There was a lot of hugging and backslapping then. And Ed snatched up the bill at the end of the night, waving Andy's protests aside and telling him he'd need to save every penny now he was going to have a little 'ankle-biter' to feed.

It was almost eleven o'clock by the time they gathered their coats.

They'd ordered taxis. And the smokers were keen to light up before they arrived.

'I'd better just slip to the loo… *again!*' said Krystal.

'We'll wait for you outside!' Ed called after her.

'Okay!' She disappeared into the 'Ladies'.

Jo remembered that Puccini had been playing softly in the background. It was the recording of Tosca they tended to put on when they wanted people to leave…. *'L'ora è fuggita – e muoio disperato'…. That moment has fled and I die in desperation.*

The tragic aria had seemed almost comical in contrast to the bubbliness of their group that night.

She remembered Ed swaying a little, laughing too loudly as they gathered by the door. And she saw the strained look deepen on Nat's face. She knew it was closely related to the look Ed had spoken of when he tried to run away on the morning of his wedding day. She tried to pretend to herself that she hadn't noticed.

She remembered the feeling of her arms sliding into the sleeves of her coat, shrugging it up in preparation for the cold outside, wrapping her scarf around her neck. Beside her, Andy was wrapped in his own happiness. There was such quiet joy in his face - such gentleness and pride.

'I'm just so lucky!' he said, very quietly and privately to Jo, and she hugged him again, breathing in his soft blonde hair, wondering how her baby brother ever became old enough to have children of his own.

'You'll be a lovely dad,' she said, with tears in her eyes. 'I'm *so* proud of you.'

-0-0-0-

The restaurant was at the top of a cobbled side street lined with tall, semi-deserted Victorian offices. One or two of them were still in use, though their windows were grubby and no-one had bothered to pull the dandelions from the paving around their doorways. Most of them were boarded up. It was quiet. A few half-hearted snowflakes fluttered down and melted on their shoulders as they waited in the pool of light by the door.

Only Cliff registered the hunched figure in baggy jeans and hoodie who looked as if he'd been waiting for someone and lurched towards them now. He recognised him as he got closer, and jumped to one side as he lunged, sending the lad stumbling, like someone drunk, into Andy who, seemed, bizarrely, to hug him for a moment, before stepping back, shocked, and clasping his hand to his side.

The lad cursed as he took flight down the street with Ed, hot on his tail.

Andy turned his palm upwards and stared at it bewildered. It was wet, and in the half light, it looked as if it had been smeared with tar.

He was still standing like that when Krystal appeared in the door of the restaurant.

Their eyes met.

She screamed as his legs buckled from under him.

-0-0-0-

'My younger brother was killed in a knife attack,' said Jo.

'I'm so sorry,' said Ulrika. She covered Jo's hand with her own.

Jo stared down at it on the quilt – arthritic, the joints bent at painful angles – the thinning skin, the age spots, the knotted blue of the veins. It brought back a long distant memory of her grandmother, who had died when she was five.

She turned her face into the pillow and sobbed.

-0-0-0-

She knew the story by heart. In the days after Andy died, it had run continuously like a horror film in an endless loop inside her head. Sometimes, even now, it would just start up, at strange times, seemingly at random. It was always dark in that film. And the sound was always on full, so that it startled her at unexpected moments in the daytime, and shrieked her awake at night.

She took a deep breath and plunged back into it.

The cobbled street.

The grim Victorian buildings.

The lurch of the hooded figure towards them.

Then Cliff, pressed against the menu in the glass case on the wall, his hands lifted to cover his face, whimpering.

And Ed… crazy, stupid, half-cut Ed, who thought this was just some mugger… giving chase automatically, as if he were back on the rugby pitch at his old school, trying to stop someone scoring a try.

Jo remembered the clatter of footsteps bouncing up from the slippery cobbles, ricocheting off the walls, as her best friend careered down the street after a man who could have turned at any moment and killed him.

She remembered Nat screaming at him to come back.

And Liam, the only one trained to recognise immediately what was going on with Andy, hurling himself down into the gutter beside him, muttering 'Stay with me mate... come on now... fucking stay with me Andy you bastard!' ripping off his jacket to press into his brother's side, cradling him with his left arm, and rocking him like a baby.

There was no mobile signal. She'd jabbed 999 into her phone and it was dead. The signal was blocked by the tall buildings around them. So she'd had to run back into the restaurant, yelling hysterically at them to phone an ambulance. And when she got back outside, she remembered Liam's stricken look, and the unnatural stillness of the group.

'Nothing was ever the same after that day!' Jo finally allowed herself to look into Ulrika's eyes.

A cold wave of desolation washed over the nun as she sat in silence beside her.

She understood only too well how some moments can change everything.

Chapter Fifteen

The police investigation meant that the funeral was delayed for weeks.

The blade, it seemed, had been meant for Cliff, who had been entrusted to carry drugs for one of the local dealers and 'lost' them. In fact, he'd been jumped by a rival gang and had them beaten out of him. No one cared how it happened. You don't get away with things like that. He knew who'd stabbed Andy, but he wouldn't tell. And Ed, who'd finally brought the lad down in a rugby tackle at the bottom of the street, on the precinct in front of Waterstones, had felt him kick and punch and wriggle out of his grasp. Clumps of Saturday night clubbers stood by and stared as the killer escaped. They thought that Ed was attacking him. They parted like the Red Sea as he scuttled through them and away up a side alley. And not one single person was able to give any kind of description of him to the police.

-0-0-0-

Somewhere, sometime later, Jo read that grief is a physical as well as emotional experience... and it was. It ate into her bones, leaving her bruised and raw and sickened. Her teeth, her throat, her eyes, her head, all ached. She had no tolerance for anyone. She said what she thought. She told people they were talking rubbish even when they weren't. She judged them all as idiots. She was a liability at work. And even *she* knew that she shouldn't have been working at all. But she couldn't bear the silence if she stayed at home.

-0-0-0-

Then, finally, there was the funeral.

People sometimes say these things pass in a blur. But it was all in sharp focus for Jo.

She remembered the daffodils banked along the steep slope from the car park, shivering in the wind. And the tulips standing tall, pale and red-lipped, waiting, in the flower beds amongst the primroses. There were two magnolia trees full of blossom, white and pink, looking like they should have been at a wedding.

Inside the chapel, there was a small blue stained glass rose window and yellow ochre walls. The hard wooden pews had flattened cushions and a funeral service book on the shelf in front of every mourner.

She remembered the noise that Krys made when the men carried the coffin into the chapel. It was a muffled howl as if the knife that had killed Andy had just entered her too. And there was an answering chorus of sighs that swept through the room like the wind through the heather on the moors.

Andy had never known how much people loved him. Even Jo had never realised *quite* how much until that moment. Part of her wanted to reach out to comfort Krys. But her heart was frozen. So she was grateful when Angie drew the girl into her arms, crying into her hair as Krys wept silently into her shoulder. And she was glad she could stay very still and very cold, her arms wrapped around herself - alone.

She was sick of always having to take responsibility for her family. Though, of course, she'd ended up being the one to organise the funeral. Krys couldn't cope with it, and no-one else was capable. They'd wanted her to 'do' the eulogy too, but she refused because she knew she couldn't. She knew that she would be speechless in the face of the total disgusting pointlessness of it all. And in the end Liam did it.

He stood behind the lectern with the notes he'd made shaking visibly in his hands. His round face was flushed. His collar was too tight, digging into his beefy, ex-army neck. He talked about how Andy had been 'A diamond geezer… his little bro…. his pal.' He forgot to mention anybody but himself, and he collapsed in tears while Cliff the fucking idiot who'd caused it all sobbed into his mother's neck like a baby in his black puffer jacket, shiny, grubby looking pants, and trainers.

Then the sound system played 'Angels'. She remembered Andy and Krys dancing to it at their wedding. Everyone smiling as Andy's new wife guided him gently round the dance floor with his two left feet. Jo knew that Krys must be remembering that too. She had known it would be too much for her. But she'd been so insistent about wanting it. And she saw her half collapsing then gently eased to her feet by Angie as the family shuffled out of the chapel to stand next to an arrangement of purple and white lilies in the foyer.

Jo took her place at the end of the line and allowed herself to be hugged and kissed by people who had no idea what to say. The flowers smelt sickly and put yellow stamen stains on people who brushed too close to put folded tens or twenties or handfuls of copper into the collection for the benevolent fund of the Ambulance Service. It was as if it helped, making that small gesture of thanks to the men who had gently lifted her baby brother's body out of a gutter clogged with blood soaked cigarette butts, knowing that they could never have been in time to save him.

She remembered how old her parents looked. They seemed dazed in the crowd of well-wishers. Her mother was like a terrified child, with her thin, lined face and greasy grey hair tied back in a ponytail. And her dad looked broken now, and very small. In a sudden shock, it dawned on Jo that this shattered man had always loved them after all, and had just been incapable of showing it. She felt an overwhelming sense of pity for him then. And more than anything, she wished that Andy could have seen it.

Outside, there was a photographer from the local newspaper. He snapped them as they came out into the cold grey daylight.

She said something unkind to him as they left the chapel. And then she wished she hadn't.

-0-0-0-

They gathered afterwards in a nice hotel, with soft music in the lobby and filter coffee and freshly made tea in stainless steel pots when they arrived. There were the obligatory sandwiches; ham, egg and cress, and something that smelt like salmon. And there was quiche, and chicken legs, and scones. Natalie guessed that Jo must have paid for the funeral, and she was struck, as always, by how poor the Cooper family looked. They seemed out of place in those smart surroundings. The muffin-topped women had short skirts and high heels and clouds of celebrity perfume. And the balding and beer-bellied men wore cheap suits and black ties and piled their plates high with food they couldn't eat, congregating at the bar instead with Andy's mates from work and drinking pints and whisky chasers as fast as Ed could pay for them.

Nat could see no trace of Jo in the tall, ashen faced stranger drifting among the guests. It was as if she had been avoiding her for weeks, not answering her phone or her door. She'd been glazed and distant when Nat had called in at the Classic Cars office to try to see her there. And she hadn't even spoken to Jake or Alyssa, though Alyssa had made a card to tell her how sad they were and Jake had signed it, and they still cried themselves to sleep sometimes at night, for the loss of Jo now, as well as for the death of 'Uncle Andy'.

Now, with the children at their grandparents, Nat tried to do what little she could to ease the pressure on her friend - comforting Bill and his wife who were still shocked and pale and oozing grief, and talking to the more distant aunties and cousins and friends. She was good for all *that* at least. She'd learnt it from her mother, an ability to make conversation at a superficial level.

'Yes, I'm Ed's wife,' 'The service was lovely,' 'Liam did very well,' 'Have you travelled far?' 'Will you be going back tonight?'

Cakes arrived with fresh pots of coffee and tea and made the women's eyes light up. She pretended to be tempted by them as she glanced over anxiously from time to time at Jo who was still listing amongst the mourners in a daze. She looked like some doppelganger provided by the funeral parlour. It frightened Nat to see her like that.

At the bar, Ed and his crowd of hangers-on were getting hammered. He'd bottled up his feelings about that awful night. She knew he was traumatized by it all, though no-one would ever know by looking at him. There were gales of laughter. For the umpteenth time, 'The Boss' was recounting how Andy had got a wedding car stuck in a ford and heroically waded through the water with the bride on his back... And how, racing against time on his way to a different wedding, he'd had to stop to deal with a puncture, earning himself the nickname - insensitive in light of his constant struggles with his weight - 'Spare Tyre.'

Ed's laugh hacked across the room towards her, like a road drill, head and shoulders above the rest. She'd forgotten long since why she'd ever found it attractive.

Then she spotted Cliff outside, hovering by the French windows, next to a heavily topiaried ball of holly in a wooden tub. He was clutching a pint and a roll-up and staring out over the gardens as if scanning for some impending attack. Nat guessed he must always be on high alert like that. She wondered why he'd let his guard down the night Andy was killed.

She felt sorry for him though, out there in the cold, alone.

'Hi Cliff,' she said, joining him. 'How're you doing?'

'How d'ya think?' he glanced at her with hollow eyes.

'I'm sorry,' she said. 'It's hard to know what to say.'

'Yeah!' He went back to staring bleakly into the distance. His bony fingers were stained with nicotine, the nails cracked and rough. He was shaking with cold.

She remembered how he'd quaked against the glass-fronted menu display at the restaurant, the night Andy died. And then her thoughts jumped back to the first time she'd ever met him. It was Andy and Krystal's wedding. He'd almost certainly been 'on' something that day. There had been an unfocused look in his eyes and track marks on his arms. He'd disappeared early. She knew that people noticed. But nobody said a word about it.

'Our Andy thought the world of you,' he said.

It was good to hear that, particularly now his sister seemed to have abandoned her.

'Well, I loved him to bits too. He's…. I mean, he *was*, one of the nicest people I've known.' She heard her voice shake as she wondered if it had even *begun* to sink in that she'd never see him again.

'Aye!' said Cliff, bitterly, gulping at his lager and wiping his mouth with the back of his hand. 'Andy was very nice.' He made it sound like a *bad* thing to be. 'He'd still be here today if he hadn't invited me to his birthday. He was the only one 'at ever did. Our Jo and Liam never have.'

Nat wondered how it must feel to carry that level of guilt… and such a sense of being not-wanted. She couldn't even begin to imagine.

'Nobody could have known, Cliff. You mustn't be hard on yourself….. Look, why don't you come back inside? It's cold out here.' She could feel the dampness of the air, seeping through the thin layers of her black jacket, through the plain white blouse, chilling her skin.

She wrapped her arms around herself for warmth.

'They don't want me in there,' he said simply. 'They think it should 'a bin me. I don't blame 'em. *I* wish it'd bin me too.'

She understood why he thought that. She would have thought it too, in his position.

'It was an accident,' she said. 'You mustn't blame yourself.'

'Why not?' he asked. 'Every bugger else does.'

'I'm sure they don't.'

'*Jo* does. She's said as much. It was always Andy for Jo, right from day one. Four years old, and changin' his nappies. Rocking him to sleep, reading him comics in bed. She's like that... Typical bloody Taurean. They're all the same. She loved him from t'first minute she set eyes on 'im. I used to be jealous. Nobody ever read me no bedtime stories nor kissed me goodnight. Liam always hated the fuckin' sight o' me, and me mam was good for nowt most o't time. And Dad...' He worked a stray wisp of tobacco to the tip of his tongue and spat it on the ground for emphasis... 'Well, I'm sure Jo's told you about Dad.'

She hadn't. Nat made a mental note to ask her, if she could ever get her to speak to her again.

'And then I discovered Mam's 'Moggies' and I didn't need any o' that rubbish anymore.' He smiled his thin, bitter, self-pitying smile. 'How's Ed tekkin' it? ...Proper "have a go hero" on the night, wasn't he?'

Nat jumped, shocked and temporarily confused by the sudden change of topic. She remembered from Andy's wedding that he was like this. Jumping about from one subject to another like a disorientated frog. 'He doesn't say much,' she said.

'No... he's like me, is that one. Self-contained. Likes his comforts predictable.'

Nat saw the shift in him. The slight easing of tension as he landed on someone almost as flawed as himself to think about. He must have liked the feeling, because he jumped again, and she was next. 'It's a shame Jo dun't have nobody to look out for 'er,' he said. 'I thought that Cindy were a nice lass... But she was never gonna get a look in with *you* around, *was* she?'

'I don't know what you mean.' Nat felt like she'd been slapped, suddenly and by someone who'd seemed benign. She felt herself flushing despite the cold.

A wily look hovered around his eyes as he checked for the effect of his words on her.

'Yes you do,' he said. 'People think I don't notice stuff. But I've seen the way she looks at you. And I've seen how you *like* it too... And I've often wondered... do you ever actually *give* her any? Or is she really stupid enough to just stick around out of love?'

He didn't look at her as he said it. But his pale grey eyes had grown cold as he scanned the horizon. Nat knew that he was probably still at risk from the people who had killed Andy. And it occurred to her now that maybe *she* was at risk in a different way from him.

'You don't have to be vile just because you're feeling guilty,' she said.

He laughed, and his eyes warmed slightly. 'You know what,' he said. 'You're right.'

They stood for a while, silently, looking out. They were both scanning the horizon now for invisible threats.

'Does Ed know?' he asked, eventually, conversationally, as if they were swopping thoughts about the weather.

Nat didn't answer.

'About you and Jo, I mean? I guess some blokes wouldn't mind.'

Nat hadn't needed him to clarify this. She knew exactly what he was talking about. She continued to ignore the question. It seemed like the best strategy. 'They'd all forgive you in an instant if you helped the police catch the person who killed Andy,' she said instead.

'I know,' he sounded subdued. 'But I can't.'

'I know you must be scared that they'll come after you.'

He laughed, a short sharp cough like the crack of a starting pistol. 'They'll come after me anyway,' he said. 'When the heat dies down. They won't do it publicly like last time. No… one day I'll just disappear and that'll be the end o' me. I'm not bothered about that. Dying don't frighten me, but I'm scared a'what they'll do first. If I had the money I'd get well away from here. Go to Scarborough - get some work on the rides for the summer. Get clean. Get out of you and Jo's hair.'

He looked sideways at her and she wondered if she was being blackmailed.

She told herself that Jo might be happier with him out of the way.

'How much?' she asked.

'To keep me quiet?'

'To go to Scarborough.'

'A hundred should do it – cash.'

She hadn't expected him to be so cheap.

She took four twenties and two tens from her bag, sensing that she was making a big mistake.

'So,' he said. 'She *is* shaggin' you then!'

He gave her a narrow-eyed look as he reached for the notes. Then he changed his mind. 'Keep it,' he said. 'I'd only spend it on smack anyway.'

He tossed the final crushed half centimetre of his roll-up into the shrubs beside him, handed his empty glass to her, and slouched off down the drive without a backward glance.

-0-0-0-

Nat felt sick as she went back inside and found that even the pale wraith pretending to be Jo was gone. She looked frantically around the room for her, feeling panicked, like a kid who's got over confident and wandered off from her mother and suddenly realised she's lost.

Anxiously, she checked the 'Ladies' and investigated the front entrance of the hotel to see if she was talking with the smokers there. Jo's parents were gone too – and Bill and his wife – and Krys. Realising she must have been outside with Cliff for longer than she'd thought, she headed for her husband, who could usually be relied upon, at least, to know where Jo was.

He had his arm round Liam as if they had always been best buddies. She noticed he had the sweaty look she'd come to hate. His tie was pulled down, and the top button of his plain white funeral shirt was open.

' 's my beautiful girl…' he slurred, swaying a little and patting her on the bottom. 'sn't she chuffin' gorgeous Lee?'

'Chuffin' belter mate!' Liam punched Ed rather harder than he meant to, and nearly knocked him off his barstool.

Despite her anxiety, Natalie found that she wanted to smile at that. She managed to suppress the urge. 'Where's Jo?' she asked.

'Dunno!' Ed's eyes made an unfocused sweep of the room.

'She's teken Mam and Dad 'n Krys 'ome,' said Liam. 'They've 'ad enough.'

If Jo had gone, Natalie didn't see any point in sticking around either.

'I think maybe *you've* had enough too,' she said quietly to her husband.

Ed gave Natalie a sideways glance. She was giving him *that* look. He knew he ought to care, but he didn't. He'd seen it far too many times for that. 'Aye up,' he announced to his assembled 'mates'. 'I'm gettin' the chuffed off look from the Ball and Chain.' He concentrated hard, swaying as he took out his wallet and pulled two fifties out of it. 'Same again all round,' he said to the barman, slamming his money on the bar, just to make a point. 'What'll *you* 'ave love?'

She could have hit him.

'I'm going to see how Jo is,' she snapped. 'Get yourself a taxi when you're ready to come home.'

She turned her back on her husband, hearing his defensive splutter of laughter following her out of the room.

And in that moment she knew exactly what she was going to do.

-0-0-0-

On the way to Jo's, it occurred to Nat that she might not be in. The idea felt unbearable, because she knew that if she didn't do this now, she may never have the courage again.

She was relieved to find Jo's car parked on the driveway. The door was unlocked.

'I didn't knock,' she said, finding Jo in the kitchen, pouring a large tumbler of Courvoisier. She'd changed already out of her funeral clothes and into a thick grey sweatshirt and jog pants. 'I wasn't sure you'd let me in.'

'Maybe there's a clue in there somewhere,' said Jo coldly. 'I saw you talking to Cliff, by the way.'

'He was upset.' Nat felt emboldened by the sight of Alyssa and Jake's card taped to the fridge door. It meant, at least that Jo still had some feeling for the kids.

'Oh dear!' The sarcasm didn't fit Jo. It sounded tight on her. 'I saw you giving him money,' she added 'You *do* know he'll buy drugs with it, don't you?'

'It was to go to Scarborough, and…'

'He'll go straight to his dealer, Nat.'
'He didn't take it'
'Yeah... right!' she scoffed. 'How much was it?'
'A hundred.'
'Good. He'll be able to get enough to kill himself then.'
'He didn't take it Jo.' She felt herself becoming desperate, and angry with Jo for being like this. 'And anyway, you know you don't mean that.'
'*Don't I?*'
Maybe she did.
She shook her head angrily as she lifted the glass to her lips.
Natalie's heart was pounding. 'Don't!' she begged. 'Please... It's bad enough with Ed!'
'Yeah...? Well, there seems to be a common factor here somewhere.'
Natalie tried to ignore the accusation in Jo's voice. Again, she told herself that she didn't mean it.
'Cliff thinks that you're in love with me,' she said.
Shock registered on Jo's face. Her eyes flickered briefly then glazed again. 'Don't flatter yourself.'
'I don't,' said Nat. 'But I know that I'm in love with *you.*'
Jo blinked. She put the glass down.
Nat held her breath as she saw the tears welling in Jo's eyes, her hands creeping up over her mouth. She slumped against the worktop, shaking her head as all the anger seemed to drain away from her.
She looked helplessly at Natalie. She didn't respond to her declaration, though there was no doubt that she'd heard it.

'He was my little brother,' she said, her voice so small Nat had to lean forward to catch the words. 'I was supposed to look after him.'

She looked haunted.

Nat had no idea how to take that away.

'You always did, sweetheart…. God knows, you *always* did.'

She stepped forward and reached for Jo. It was a relief to be able to take her into her arms at last. 'Please,' she whispered. 'I can't bear it when you shut me out. Just use me however you like… Whatever helps you get through this.'

And she was relieved to feel Jo clinging to her as she sobbed.

-0-0-0-

'I was a total mess,' Jo ran her spare hand through her hair and found that her scalp was starting to feel less tender now as the pain subsided. 'Andy was so precious to me and I just didn't know how to go on without him. Nat comforted me. She gave me a reason to live. But we never should have crossed that line. I don't think we ever *would* have, if Andy hadn't died.'

Ulrika's hands were clasped together now on her lap. Her gnarled fingers tightened their grip on each other.

She understood more than she could ever say. And Jo felt it as she looked at her.

-0-0-0-

It was a hot Saturday afternoon early in June when they finally betrayed Ed.

The twins were at a birthday party.

Jo had been working in the morning and Nat was waiting for her when she got home.

It was as if they had arranged it, though neither of them had said anything out loud.

'I need a shower,' said Jo. And Nat just nodded and followed her up the stairs.

The water battered over them like monsoon rain, flattening their hair to their skulls, running down their faces in rivulets, dripping from their noses, their chins, into their mouths as they kissed.

Jo remembered how her hands had felt, sliding over Natalie's shoulders, her arms, her waist, her hips. She was used to being in charge. Used to doing this, with other women, in other showers, and in this one. She knew how to please women. But she'd never wanted to please anyone as much as she wanted to please Nat.

She remembered how her hands had felt tangling in Nat's long dark hair. The feel of her skin. The smell of citrus shower gel. Fresh. Cupping her face. Drawing her into a kiss that pulled them deeper, wet tongue on wet tongue. Pulling away, to her ear lobes, her neck, her breasts. And all the time, the water coming down like hard summer rain.

'Is this okay?' she'd asked, breathing against Nat's cheek, one hand pressing softly against her back, holding her, as she ran the other down over her stomach to the triangle of hair below.

'Very,' Nat smiled, in an attempt at sounding confident, blasé, even.

And then Jo went further, and her fingers pressed in, and Nat bit down harder than she'd intended on her shoulder, bruising her, and pulling her in closer as she braced herself against the cold, wet tiles of the shower in a long, slow, gasp of surrender.

-0-0-0-

'It was just our secret,' said Jo. 'No one else was ever meant to know.'

'Did you feel guilty?' She already knew the answer to that.

'Yes, of course. But it was our space. Separate from everything else. We told ourselves that it was okay as long as no-one got hurt. But of course, it hurt *us*. It hurt us every time we had to fix those stupid inane smiles onto our faces and go back to our real lives as if nothing was wrong.'

'You never thought of being together?'

'We dreamed of it constantly. But how could we? Nat had the kids and it would have destroyed Ed.'

'People find ways of dealing with that.'

Jo looked up at Ulrika. 'Well, *we* didn't!' she said fiercely. Then her face crumpled in uncertainty. 'We thought we were doing the right thing.'

In the distant chapel, the bell rang for Vespers.

'I must go,' said Ulrika.

Jo nodded. 'Yes… thank you… so much.'

The elderly nun struggled painfully to her feet. She smiled down at Jo. 'I'll pray for you,' she said. Then rushing on before Jo could ask her not to, 'Maybe it would be good to sleep now. At least your room's not so cold anymore.'

'No, it's positively snuggly.'

She hesitated at the door. What she wanted to ask felt risky. She took a deep breath.

'What do you think Andy would have said about all this?' she asked.

Jo closed her eyes. She exhaled slowly.

Ulrika could see that she was searching for her lost brother in her mind.

'Andy loved Ed,' she said, after a long pause.

'I think that's partly why I'm asking.'

'I don't know.' She shook her head. 'He would never judge me, *that's* for sure. Andy never judged anyone… I think he'd have just found his own way of keeping right on loving all of us, no matter what we decided to do.'

The thought was strangely comforting.

Jo pulled the covers up to her chin. She felt drowsy and peaceful in the aftermath of her tears. She was asleep almost before Ulrika had closed the door.

Chapter Sixteen

'Auntie Krys phoned.' Alyssa barely looked up as Nat came into the room. This was usually a sign that she was being shifty, though with Roxanne there she could just have been showing off. Dottie bounded towards her, snuffling and squiggling and sending the pieces of the board game flying in all directions. Roxanne giggled and tried to scoop the dog away from the board.

For once, Nat was glad of the distraction. 'Oh?' she asked, trying to sound normal, though she had to raise her voice slightly to be heard over the rumpus. 'How are they? Did Jorge have a nice Christmas?' Jorge was Andy and Krystal's son, eight now, and spookily like his dad. Nat felt bad for not phoning them herself. She'd meant to, but the shock of the card, and Jo leaving, and Ed's behaviour, had all driven her good intentions from her mind, and she'd forgotten.

'They're fine. She said she's sorry she hasn't been in touch. And she wondered if we'd baby sit Jorge. She's got some new bloke in tow and they want to go to the pictures.' Dottie was licking Alyssa's ear now. Big, slobbery dog-breath licks that made her scrunch her face and lift her elbow between herself and the dog. Dottie dodged round it, thinking it was a wonderful game and nibbling playfully at her neck.

Nat pretended it wasn't happening. As far as Dottie was concerned, she'd always figured it was best to act like one of those mothers who can tune out their own child's annoying behaviour. She *was* after all, the only member of the family who'd never wanted a dog. 'Oh, well, that's nice.'

Fleetingly, she wondered if Jo was aware of this 'new bloke'.

She hoped he was better than the last one, who'd turned out to be married with three kids and another girlfriend in Doncaster.

'When do they want to go?' It was hard to keep the underlying feeling of panic out of her voice. She wasn't sure how she'd got through the rest of the walk with Andrea. She vaguely remembered making superficial conversation about their plans for New Year, and Andrea's hug as they said 'Goodbye'. There had been some comfort in that brief moment of physical contact. It seemed to be saying. 'I don't reject you for this.' But away from Andrea's reassuring presence, Nat was only too aware that her world was collapsing around her.

'Tonight.' Over the dog, Alyssa gave Roxanne a half-secret little sideways glance that showed clearly that she knew she should already have said 'no'.

'But you're supposed to be coming with me and your dad to see Great Grandma Mason.' Nat heard how weak her protest was. She didn't have the strength to argue.

'Well, it's not fair. *Jake's* not going.'

Nat looked at her daughter. The petted lip was almost out. And the last thing she needed right now was a teenage tantrum. She shrugged, defeated. 'You'll have to check with your father,' she said wearily, heading upstairs and away from her daughter's casual adolescent disdain.

-0-0-0-

At the small desk in the corner of the spare room, she sat and stared at her mobile phone. She'd been checking for more texts from Jo all day, feeling the now familiar dread as she saw that there was still no news from her. She tried to tell herself that it was just because there was no signal. Jo would contact her soon and everything would be okay again. More than anything right now, she longed for Jo's sweet lopsided grin, the warm lilt of her voice, and the comfort of feeling her arms around her. It didn't have to be sex. After all the stresses of the past few days it was the very last thing she wanted anyway. To be honest, what she really wanted was to cry, but she wanted to cry in Jo's arms, and there, alone in that tiny room, she couldn't.

She told herself that there were lots of things she *should* be doing. She was a mum with teenage kids and a husband who could have been the inspiration for 'Men Behaving Badly'. There was washing to do, and ironing – always lots of that. There were thank you letters and emails to write. She doubted that it would have crossed Alyssa's mind to empty the dishwasher, though it must have ended its wash and dry cycle while she was out, and it would certainly have beeped loudly enough for her daughter to hear.

Hesitantly, she picked up the phone. She was torn between her desperate longing for Jo and her knowledge that the woman she loved was doing what she needed to do right now... seeking peace and quiet and a place to think about what she really, truly wanted.

Taking a deep breath to steady herself, she did what she thought would be the next best thing, scrolled through the names in her address book, and rang Ruth.

-0-0-0-

'Hi Nat,' Ruth was slightly breathless. A couple of minutes earlier and she probably wouldn't have answered at all. She'd just been 'enjoying' some hot lesbian erotica on DVD. She held the phone with her left hand.

'Sorry love, were you in the middle of something?'

'No.' There was a kind of grim satisfaction in lying to Nat about that. 'I just had to run to get the phone that's all…. Hey, you're sounding a bit low. Is everything okay?'

Grief shuddered in Nat's chest, crept into her throat like a strangler's grip, burning, then leaping, hot and stinging into her eyes. She struggled to compose herself enough to speak. Tears oozed down the side of her nose.

'Nat?' Ruth might be furious with her friend right now, but she still loved her, and she was concerned as it dawned on her that everything was most definitely *not* okay.

'I'm sorry!' Nat chewed on her lip and scuffed impatiently at the tears with her hand. She realised that she didn't have a tissue. She sniffed.

'What's up? Is Ed upsetting you again? I'll come and bash him if he is.' She was trying to get a smile. She'd never 'bashed' anybody in her life… well, apart from her sisters when they were all kids and getting on each other's nerves.

She heard her friend taking a long, deep breath. It still had that distinctive, snot-heavy, congested sound to it.

Eventually Nat collected herself. 'I've got something I have to tell you,' she said. 'I know you'll hate me for it. And if you don't want to be friends with me anymore after this, I don't blame you.'

'Jesus,' said Ruth, startled. 'There's *nothing* you could do that would stop me being your friend.' She shoved the bitterness to one side. 'What the hell's going on?'

There was a long pause. Ruth could hear a clock ticking in the background. On her TV, with the sound muted, 'Lesbian Brief Encounters - Volume Two,' was entering a dark new chapter. A woman had appeared on screen. She was wearing a lacy red thong and brandishing something that looked ominously like a butt-plug. Ruth grabbed the remote and killed the image.

'I've been having an affair.' The words seemed to tumble out of Nat.

It was true then. Ruth had been furious from the moment she'd begun to suspect it. It was a deep, seething, wounded fury that ate into her and kept her awake at night. She figured she deserved an Oscar for hiding it from Nat. Ever since that grim November weekend when she'd been staying with them and overheard.

She put the phone on speaker and held it away from her. She felt like she needed to distance herself from this particular confession.

Nat's voice took on a hollow, echoing quality. 'With Jo...'

Ruth's hands crept to her mouth. She'd known, but she'd wanted to be wrong. Even when she'd realised that they loved each other, she'd wanted it to be hopeless... tragic even... but above all, platonic.

'You bitch!' She couldn't help it. It just exploded out of her.

'I'm sorry.'

'All that shit you gave me about how ***fucking*** straight you are!'

'I know. I'm sorry.' Nat's voice was choked

And if you're not straight, Ruth thought, *it **was** me that you rejected back then.*

She didn't say it out loud. It was too painful.

'Why are you telling me this?' She heard the coldness in her voice and hated it.

'Because Ed knows.'

Slowly, Ruth's heart pumped up its volume in her ears. She listened to it, aghast.

'Please, Ruth... say something... anything.'

But Ruth was feeling suddenly, horribly sick. 'I'm sorry,' she said, retching. 'I've gotta go.'

Nat stared at the phone, lying dead in her hands.

-0-0-0-

In Norwich, Ruth clutched the side of the toilet seat as she threw up violently, shaking and sweating and trying to keep her hair out of it. She'd never thrown up in terror before. But then, she'd never been this scared. Not even when her father used to come home drunk and get into fights with her mum. *That* had been grim, but it had been predictable, and it hadn't been her fault. *This*.... Oh God, this was a whole different ballgame.

Standing shakily, she flushed the loo and washed her face and hands in the basin, tying her hair back, and catching an unwelcome glimpse of her grey, guilty face in the mirror.

She reached for the toothbrush to try to scrub away the vile taste that lingered in her mouth.

And she railed against herself for her stupidity.

-0-0-0-

It had seemed like a good idea at the time, that stupid thought that maybe she and Jo could get back together. But the truth was that it had developed in the absence of any kind of reality check.

It had come in the slow dawning of the knowledge that Ms Right probably was never going to exist for her. That being in love with her best friend meant that she didn't have the energy to overcome reservations about women who seemed boring to her, or crazy, or addicted, or just plain lacking in any kind of chemistry.

Hitting forty that year, it had occurred to her that out of all the lovers who, as Kylie might say, 'had gone before', Jo was the only one who had ever actually 'got' her. She was also nice looking, relatively sane, unusually good in bed, and apparently single.

In retrospect, the 'single' thing should have set off warning bells.

But then Ruth was single too and *she* wasn't having an affair with her best friend's wife.

So, it had seemed like a good idea at the time to combine a weekend at Nat's with an attempt to revitalise the relationship with Jo.

She'd decided to go for a casual approach, phoning her apparently on the spur of the moment while Nat was taking Dottie for her morning walk.

And she should have known that Jo was distracted, right from the start. But she was too busy delivering the 'impromptu' speech she'd been practising for well over a week.

'Hi Jo, how're you doing?'

'Great.... Yeah... and you?'

It had taken a deep breath to start on the next bit. She'd found it surprisingly difficult and a bit embarrassing. 'I'm good... Look, I'm staying at Nat and Ed's and I was just wondering, while I'm local... if you might fancy to...' She tailed off, shocked, hearing Nat's voice, very faintly, in the distance.

'Oh sweetheart, I thought I'd never get away. I've been going crazy without you.'

Jo had called back deliberately loudly. 'Hi love… I've just got a friend on the phone. Don't come up. I'll be down in a minute!'

'It sounds like you've got a visitor,' she'd said suspiciously.

'Yeah… New girlfriend… Nothing serious.'

Ruth recognised the false laugh. Jo always *was* a lousy liar. And Ruth could have recognised Nat's voice in a football stadium full of people singing 'You'll never walk alone.'

For some reason she felt scared to challenge the lie though. 'Oh well.' She'd forced a smile into her voice. 'No worries. I was wondering if you might fancy to get together for a coffee while I'm here, but it sounds like you're going to be busy.'

'Yeah…' Jo laughed again, uneasily. 'Next time maybe. It'd be good to see you. Text me in advance, eh. I'll make sure I'm free.'

Shaken, Ruth had managed to say, 'I'll hold you to that. Don't do anything I wouldn't do.' She'd even managed to sound teasing, a bit flirtatious.

But now she knew, she wondered why she'd never suspected it before. *'You devious **shits!**'* she'd snapped into nowhere as she hung up the call.

-0-0-0-

Reluctantly, now, she picked up the phone receiver, sat down weakly on the sofa, and hit 'One' on speed dial.

Nat answered immediately, her heart flooding with relief that her friend had phoned back.

Ruth started to take a deep breath, then swallowed it. She still felt sick. 'I'm so sorry Nat,' she said. 'I think this is my fault.'

-0-0-0-

Ed was driving home after an unproductive day at work. As Nat had predicted, Fiona had got everything nicely under control in the office, so he'd ended up skulking in the garage, working on a Citroen DS that could quite easily have waited until after the New Year. He'd had a long lunch hour in the 'Tapsters' and he wished he could go back there for the evening now. Hard as he tried, he'd been unable to shake off the memory of Nat's face that morning. He'd seen the contempt there. And he knew he'd sunk to a whole new low in her estimation. He didn't feel all that great about *himself* either. He'd hurt her and he felt ashamed. He'd never been the kind of man who'd do that. In fact he'd always hated men like that – men who got pleasure out of hurting women.

Bitterly, he found his thoughts turning to Ruth. How he couldn't stand the woman. How she'd always had it in for him.

He'd fancied her at first, secretly turned on by her delicate frame and flaming red hair. He'd tried hard with her, in his own way, making an effort to show an interest in her, telling (clean) jokes, doing the cute little boy act that usually worked quite well with women. And he'd had a few ultra-top-secret fantasies when he'd found out that she was sleeping with Jo. But it hadn't taken him long to realise that she hated him, irrevocably, and with no discernible good reason. Once he'd realised that he was 'onto a loser' with her, he'd fallen into his other strategies - avoiding her whenever he could, and trying to keep things as superficial as possible when he couldn't. It was a strategy that worked okay for him, up to a point. But sometimes he really wished that the two of them would just have some major girlie bust-up so he wouldn't have to endure the emotional sniper-fire of Ruth's all-too-regular weekend visits.

At first, on that fateful weekend in November, he'd half dared to hope that his wish had come true.

It had started off normally enough. Ruth arrived late, as usual, on the Friday evening, having driven up after school. There had been the standard flat, 'Oh, hi Ed,' delivered in the tone he'd never heard her use with anyone but him. And he'd felt Nat's anxiety rising, as it always did in her knowledge that her best friend existed in such a state of antipathy towards her husband.

Dottie had provided a diversion, leaping on her like a doggie dervish. And then the kids had been treated to their customary cuddles and small gifts. They all loved Ruth and always seemed to bask along with Nat, in the warmth of her approval. Ed wondered if Nat knew that he *had* noticed and *did* care that he was always the one out in the cold. Like most women, his wife liked to 'talk' about things. But she'd never talked about this.

The first night of the visit had progressed pretty much along its usual lines. The kids had gone to bed, ostensibly to sleep, but actually to check Facebook and text their friends into the small hours, and Ed had taken the dog round the block, as he occasionally did when Ruth was there, to give 'you girls a chance to catch up'. Then he made his excuses, 'Early morning tomorrow – rush job,' and disappeared upstairs with a whisky 'night cap'. As he drifted away, he'd heard the faint melodic sound of Nat and Ruth laughing together, still downstairs, probably sharing some 'teacher' or student-days joke he wouldn't have got anyway.

-0-0-0-

By the next evening, everything was different.

Ruth always liked to sleep in on Saturdays, so, thankfully, he didn't have to see her until he got back home from work. He knew that the plan had been for Nat to take the dog out and make brunch for Ruth when she emerged. Then the two of them were going Christmas shopping together. It was the kind of thing women seemed to enjoy doing - a trip into York on the train and a whirlwind tour of the shops, followed by afternoon tea at 'Betty's'. Nat had tried to get Ed interested in doing that kind of thing in the early stages of their relationship. He'd even pretended to enjoy it the first couple of times. But it hadn't been long before he began to show that he hated it really, and she'd got the message soon enough.

He'd expected for them to be all bubbly and excited when he got home. Normally after a pre-Christmas jaunt like that they'd be hiding presents and bending the kids' ears about something 'funny' that had happened during the day.

But he felt the atmosphere the minute he walked into the house.

'What's up with *her*?' he asked Nat, quietly, grimacing towards the lounge where Ruth was tucked, barefoot in a chair, looking sulky and watching a repeat of 'Are You being Framed?' with the kids.

'I don't know.' Nat looked edgy. She hated it when people were upset or angry. It distressed her. And being distressed, she opened up rather more than she would normally do with Ed. 'She's been like it ever since I got back with Dottie this morning.'

'Probably wrong time of the month,' said Ed, unwisely.

Nat wondered if he might be right – though she was generally more vulnerable to PMS than Ruth ever had been; and the feminist in her was always annoyed when he said stuff like that anyway.

He grinned cheekily as she shot him a disapproving look. Sometimes he thought it was fun to play at being a 'male chauvinist pig'. And he'd never really managed to suss out that there never was a good time to do that with his wife.

-0-0-0-

It was later, after dinner and coffee, when the kids had gone to their rooms, and Nat had headed off with Dottie for the last walk of the day, that Ruth delivered her bombshell.

She was drunk, which was unusual for her. Ed had noticed that she'd been drinking quickly earlier in the evening, and he'd kept her glass topped up in the hope that it might lighten her mood a bit. It didn't seem to have worked. And the moment the door clicked behind Nat, she turned on him.

'Come on then,' she said. 'Let's get the dishwasher loaded.'

'Yeah, okay. I'll do it in a minute.' Ed stretched back in his seat and yawned. He'd learned way back in his teens that if you delayed long enough with jobs like that, someone who cared more about things being tidy would usually do them for you.

Ruth shot him a look. 'You really *are* an idle sod, aren't you?' she said.

This was unexpected enough to make Ed sit up straight. Normally, Ruth kept her criticisms beneath the radar, delivering them under her breath or in the sarcastic raising of an eyebrow. He suspected that she dripped them like poison into Nat's ear when he wasn't around. She'd probably tried it with Jo too when they were sleeping together, but he'd always trusted that they'd fall on stony ground there. Jo knew, better than anyone, what he was like, and she loved him anyway. Or, at least, that was what he'd always thought.

Anyway there he was, alone with Ruth, and finally, she was telling him what she thought of him. In a funny sort of way, he was glad. It gave him the opportunity to defend himself.

'I work my nuts off for this family,' he said.

'Oh sure,' she scoffed. 'It must be *really* hard on your 'nuts' lifting all those pints down the pub... And, sneaking off to watch the rugby... *that* must really wear them out.'

'I work bloody hard!' he protested. 'The business doesn't just run itself, and it buys my family a bloody good lifestyle... I don't notice you turning down free holidays here anytime you feel like it.'

Ruth gave a swift internal brush-off to the 'free holiday' comment, which had stung somewhat, and went for the first line of his defence instead. It felt like she was on safer ground there. 'The business?' she sneered. 'Well, as far as I can see, Jo runs the business.'

'Well, that's her job.'

'Her job...? I used to go out with her. Remember? I saw how you've got her on call 24/7. You say 'jump' and she asks 'how high?' If it weren't for her, you'd still just be some little back street grease monkey.'

Ed knew this was true. He'd never really attempted to claim otherwise.

'Yeah, Jo's great,' he said. 'She does a brilliant job, and she *does* work long hours, but she's paid bloody well for it!' He wished he could manage to keep the hurt out of his voice.

Ruth crinkled her lip. She could be merciless when she got going. She'd inherited that from her father. 'She could have done a whole lot better if she hadn't been joined at the hip to *you*.... What is it everybody calls her..? 'Ed's gopher'... Some interesting stuff in her job description too, isn't there? "Get me tickets for the cricket Jo... Tell Nat we've been let down by the driver in Warrington... Tell her I've had to go stand in for him, will you Jo?"...'

Ed grimaced guiltily. Ruth must have overheard the Warrington excuse when she was at Jo's. It was a long time ago, though there'd been plenty of similar excuses since. He wondered if she'd blabbed all this to Nat. He knew women talked about stuff like that. He remembered his mum and her friends sitting in their sunny lounge at home, with coffee in china cups, and Kunzle Cakes and scones on the tiered cake stand. They'd all laughed affectionately about their husbands' little foibles. He'd always thought it was a *nice* part of family life. Not bitter, like Ruth was making it out to be.

'Look,' he said. 'We've both had a few too many. Let's just drop this now, shall we?'

The memory from his childhood had made him nostalgic for those happier days before school made an idiot of him. A blond haired, blue eyed kid, adored by his 'aunties' - snuggling against his mum's legs, silky in 'nylons'. He remembered the warm cosy smell of her as she passed him the plate with those special treats, letting him have first choice. He'd always liked the one with the tiny, crystalized orange segment on the top. He remembered the crunch of the chocolate shell in his mouth, and the tang of orange and sugar.

He wondered, in a hazy, drunken kind of way, if they still made those cakes. He hadn't seen them for such a long time. Not even at his mum's. He reckoned, if they still made them, his mother would have hunted them down for the kids when they were staying over, or for the rare occasions when he took them round there himself. She wouldn't have done it in front of Nat, who'd always discouraged sugary treats. She believed, probably correctly, that they made Jake hyperactive.

Ruth was still talking. She had no intention of 'dropping' it.

She put her finger to her chin in an affected gesture, as if the next bit were an afterthought… 'And then there's, "Get an anniversary card for me Jo…. A nice big one so she'll think I've made an effort… And order some roses from Interflora will you…? Which colour does she like best? I can never remember… What do you think she'd like for Christmas? I'm useless with all that girlie stuff… Will you just get that for me?".... God knows how Nat puts up with you Ed. You've never had the faintest, foggiest idea how to make her happy.'

Ed struggled back into focus. He was tired and he wanted to go to bed. He wondered if he might be able to persuade Nat to give him a blow job once they got there. And he was sick of this woman needling at him. He eyed her sullenly. 'You're just pissed off that Nat's not gay,' he said, bang on target for once. 'Aren't you? That's been the problem all along.'

It was like baiting a sore-headed bear. She'd been seething ever since she'd overheard Nat that morning. And she was getting more and more angry now at the sheer bloody injustice of it all. Nat, the only woman she'd ever truly loved, sleeping with Jo, of all people! So much for Nat's awful, heart breaking rejection of her all those years ago!

'Not gay?' she sneered. '*Really..?* Are you *sure* about that? She sounded pretty gay to me this morning when I heard her round at Jo's.'

Now she'd got his attention. His eyes locked on her, shocked into focus. 'That's crazy!' he said. 'She wasn't even *at* Jo's this morning.'

'That's what *you* think!'

He ran through the morning's timetable in his head. The room swam a little. He felt slightly queasy.

Ruth knew he was on the ropes. She went in for the kill. 'In fact, I wondered if *that* might be part of Jo's job description too.' She adopted a Yorkshire accent and lowered her voice to mimic him, 'Could you just warm the wife up a bit Jo…? Get her going for me, will you…? Then I can just slip it in when she gets home.'

She knew as soon as she said it that she'd gone too far.

Ed stared at her transfixed, and she ground to a halt, shocked at the words that had just spilled so angrily from her mouth. Appalled, she stared at the wine that had made her do it.

Ed shook his head as the full impact hit him. 'You've seriously got a screw loose,' he said, trying to dismiss her revelation as an act of insanity.

But she had blushed and she appeared to be trembling. 'I'm sorry,' she said, shaking her head. 'That was a terrible thing to say. Please forgive me. And please forget I said it.'

Maybe if she hadn't apologised... Maybe he could have dismissed it. Apologising made it seem more real somehow. He looked at her carefully to see just how serious she was being.

'Are you telling me that Nat and Jo are...?' He couldn't say it. It stuck in his throat.

Ruth pretended to laugh. 'No... don't be daft, Ed. You know they can't stand each other.'

'That was *ages* ago.'

'I was just winding you up. You know what I'm like. I'm sorry. I'm obviously drunk.'

The door flung open and Dottie came ploughing in.

'God, it's cold out there!' Nat's voice called through to them from the hallway. They could hear her, innocently rustling out of her coat, hanging up the dog's lead.

'Please believe me. I was just trying to hurt you,' said Ruth, pleading.

The dog veered off its initial trajectory towards her, repelled by her anxiety, snuffling instead at Ed's hand, wagging the last two inches of her feathery tail in the sudden crestfallen hope of cheering him up. Ed tickled her ears to comfort her, but he never took his eyes off Ruth.

'Oh, I can believe *that*!' he said.

Ominously, he stood and went into the kitchen to load the dishwasher, casting his wife a suspicious look as he went.

-0-0-0-

It was eight days before Jo had a morning off. Sunday 7th December. The second Sunday of Advent.

Ed waited until Nat had set off on her walk with the dog. Then he got into the car, drove through the streets by a different route and parked round the corner from Jo's house. There were trees at the bottom of the road, and Nat wasn't looking anyway. She was too focused on where she was going.

For a moment he thought Dottie might give him away, tugging on her lead in his direction and wagging her tail in a blur of recognition. But Nat didn't even notice, just spoke softly to the straining dog and manoeuvred her up Jo's drive, almost tripping over the lead as she went.

The bark of the tree was cold and damp and rough against Ed's cheek as he pressed himself into it. Something felt tight in his chest. It crawled like a silent wounded creature into his throat. He could feel it clawing in there to be let out.

He stumbled back to the car and drove home with the creature screaming silently within him. It felt like it wouldn't be satisfied until it had tasted blood.

-0-0-0-

Now, three weeks later, he was driving home again. It was four thirty. The streets were dark and almost deserted. Even the Christmas lights seemed fainter now, as if they knew their days were numbered.

His heart was heavy. The bleak, bitter pain had taken up residency within him. It hurt to breathe.

In a way, his plan had worked. That stupid bloody Christmas card. He'd almost given up and taken it back as it sat there, day after agonising day in the untidy pile on Jo's desk. He'd never meant for everything to explode on Christmas Eve. But it had. And now, Jo had done the decent thing and run. He missed her. And he was already halfway to forgiving her. He couldn't, after all, guarantee that he might not have succumbed to the temptation of several of her girlfriends if they'd decided to throw themselves at him. Those were *girlfriends* though... not wives. He didn't know why it felt different, but it did. And Nat, as always, had confounded him with her defiance and her sadness, and that unfailing talent she had for putting him in the wrong. He felt bewildered that she could do that even now, when, God knows, he *should* have been able to hold on to the moral high ground, just for once.

The pub sign for the Fox and Hounds beckoned to him as it so often did on the final leg of his journey. The craving was always there, nagging at him like Nat used to when she could still give a damn. The warmth of the Tapsters was a faint memory now, the soft focus of the two lunchtime pints wearing thin. The thought of an evening with Grandma Mason clinched it for him. He pulled in for a 'stiffener' before going home.

-0-0-0-

And, of course, he allowed Alyssa to babysit for Krystal. She'd already texted him and he'd already agreed.

So it was just Ed and Nat driving home over the high moors that night.

The visit to his grandmother had been strained. At ninety, she had early signs of dementia, which she tried, fiercely, to hide, along with her loneliness. It was hard not to notice the faint smell of incontinence vying with the more welcoming tang of the cold buffet - the ham and pork pie with egg and home-made potato salad that the kids had loved when they were younger. The old lady had always felt slightly intimidating for Ed. She'd been widowed in her twenties, and she was shy and sharp and not cuddly like Granny Moffat, his mum's mother. She was, in fact, very much like Ed's father, who also, had always scared him. Ed understood why the kids didn't like visiting her. But even so he felt sad at her disappointment that they hadn't come - particularly Alyssa, who was her favourite, and who she'd still been expecting. He felt guilty about that. And he felt bad that her furtive jibes about 'liberal parenting' were all too obviously directed at Nat, who had always been a softer target than her adored grandson.

Now, driving back with the kids' presents, still wrapped, on the back seat, Natalie seemed wrapped too… in an ominous, brooding silence that Ed found almost unbearable.

The headlights cut into the blackness ahead and swept like wartime searchlights over the snow, banked high at the side of the road, and glistening with frost.

'Don't you think we'd be safer on the main road?' she asked, as he took the moorland route.

'This is quicker.'

She shrugged, hardly caring anymore.

He took a deep breath, 'I've been wondering if we should go to Relate,' he said.

Nat shook her head. There had been a time when she would have felt relieved to hear him make that kind of effort. That time was long gone.

'It's too late.'

'It's only ten o'clock.'

It was so typical of him - trying to make a joke of it.

Nat remembered the song 'Don't Speak' and how sad it had always made her feel. She knew that was what he was doing now, trying to stop her from finally delivering the death sentence on their marriage.

'I want a divorce,' she said, as tears welled in her eyes. She couldn't get the song out of her head.

His hands gripped the wheel as he stared ahead into the darkness.

'Is this because of Jo?'

'No.'

He knew she was telling him the truth. After all, he'd predicted this moment, right from the start. But then they'd lulled him into a false sense of security, the pair of them, making him think that things had become easier because Nat had somehow managed to come to terms with how he was.

He ignored her denial.

'You *have* been sleeping with her though, *haven't* you??'

'Yes... I have.'

'How could you do that to me?'

'Because she was there when I needed her, and *you* never were.'

He knew that in the darkness, her jaw would be set. He knew that she had acted against her own principles. That she must be feeling humiliated and ashamed.

The road had been cut out of sheer rock. It banked up sharply alongside a snow-covered quarry where generations of people had lived and worked and died in harsher times. In the daylight, this place had a wild, eerie, haunted beauty. Ed remembered he'd cycled up here with Jo, that first innocent summer. It would have seemed unthinkable then that someday, she would be the one to betray him.

'And because I love her,' Tears began to pour down Natalie's cheeks. She was surprised at their force. They were hot and full of grief. 'She's the only person who's ever actually made me feel good about myself. And, for a long time, she helped me to feel better about *you* too.'

Ed cast back in his mind. He couldn't place exactly when the pressure eased in his marriage, when Nat stopped 'pecking his head' about his time-keeping, his absences and his drinking. The change had started gradually, a few months after the kids came along, but it had accelerated with the horror of Andy's death. He'd thought, at the time, that maybe the tragedy had put things in perspective for her. That maybe his bravery in chasing after the killer had made her respect him more. Certainly she'd seemed more appreciative of him – kinder and more accepting – more like she had been in the very early days of their relationship. She'd still occasionally give him a 'bollocking' when he let the kids down. But for herself, she seemed much less in need of him, much more secure. He thought they'd turned a corner. He'd felt that he could relax more. He'd believed that he was experiencing unconditional love. How could he have known that she'd simply given up on him, and, actually, it was convenient for her when he wasn't around?

'How long?' he asked.

'Does it matter?'

'Yes, it matters, to me.'

'About eight and a half years.'

'You fucking…..'

'Go on,' she said wearily. 'Say it, if it makes you feel better.'

'You BITCH!'

It was milder than she expected.

She glanced across at him. He was crying, and she reached out to try to comfort him.

'Ed... I'm sorry. I never meant for it to be like this.'

He snatched his hand away, shamed by her pity. He could see his future... His parents' distress, the kids tolerating him on access visits, Jo gone from the office... The two of them *living* together while everyone laughed at him behind his back.

He wished he'd never found out. It was all alright before he found out.

'Don't you DARE fucking touch me!' he spat, feeling the tyres sliding slightly on the bend as the blackness of the quarry beckoned and offered him a get out clause.

Nat knew what he was going to do a split second before he did it. She felt the car accelerate, and closed her eyes. She heard the sharp splintering sound as they hit the low white crash barrier and flipped over it. For a long time, it felt like they were flying. Then there was an explosion of sound, tearing metal, and the feeling of being shaken like a rag doll.

Then silence.

-0-0-0-

At the retreat house, Jo burst into consciousness like a diver trapped too long under water, lunging up into the air.

Fear had leapt onto her as she slept, and she fought against it, unsure where it was coming from, kicking and screaming as she tried to struggle out from beneath its weight. Eventually, along with a terrified kind of hyper-alertness, came a memory of where she was. She felt her heart pounding as she pulled at the light cord and pressed herself against the bare, painted wall, whimpering and praying that she hadn't frightened the retreatants in the neighbouring rooms with her cries. She held her breath and listened.

Finally, relieved at the absence of any running footsteps, she reached for her phone on the bedside table, clicking it on and trying to focus on the screen. Ten thirty. She'd expected it to be later. Her head still felt sore with the aftermath of pain. And she was still frightened. She told herself it had just been a night terror. She'd experienced them regularly when she was small, along with bouts of sleepwalking. They'd returned again, intensely for a couple of years after Andy died. She wondered if she'd triggered this by raking all that up again. But she couldn't settle back to sleep.

-0-0-0-

Ed was swimming underwater too. Then he was back at his grandmother's. And then a faint clicking pulled him away from there and he was in the car. An acrid smell hung in the air, like dust burning. Something had punched him in the face. And when he coughed to try to dislodge whatever was silting up his throat, his ribs felt like they'd been stoved-in by a size ten jackboot.

Dazed, he raised his hand to the pulpy mess of his broken nose, trying to piece together where he was and how he'd got there. Ahead, through the shattered windscreen, a thin white ribbon of light stretched from his side of the car in a crazy angle up against what looked like the side of a cliff. And then he felt Nat's silent presence beside him, and remembered.

Everything was ominously quiet, except for the clicking of the engine and the ragged sound of his breath, tearing through the pain in his chest. He reached for his wife and felt the rough woollen fabric of her jacket, and something sticky around her hair. He recoiled, feeling a sharp twist of nausea. And gasping, he released his seat belt and struggled to hoist himself up against the tilt of the car to reach the cabin light and switch it on.

She was pale, bloody, and motionless, her head on one side, facing away from him, leaning with the crazy angle of the car, towards the passenger door. She looked, in the half-light, as if she were asleep – except for the white ghostly fog from the airbags – and the dark, spreading stain across the side of her face and down her grey winter jacket.

Desperate, suddenly, to get away from her, he rammed the door with his shoulder and hurled himself out into the snow. It was deeper than the tops of his shoes and slid icily into his socks, soaking his feet. He tried to take stock of the situation. The driver's side of the car had mounted a pile of rock, lifting and tilting the whole thing to the left. The passenger side looked half caved in. He didn't dare look any closer at Nat.

Frantically, he began to run, taking clumsy, giant steps through the snow, stumbling along the floor of the quarry, then heaving himself inch by painful inch up the sharp escarpment, clutching at icy rocks, feeling his finger nails ripping and burning on the ice, clinging to the tough, sharp moorland grass and scrambling for each painful, hopeless foothold as tiny shards of rock skittered away from him over and into the snow.

He didn't know how long it took. Ten minutes, maybe twenty, scrambling a few feet up, then sliding back, soaked to the skin in ice and blood, his hands torn to shreds, sobbing into the still cold blackness of the night.

-0-0-0-

Paul Braithwaite had just passed his driving test the week before Christmas, and he was the designated driver that night, coming home from Skipton with his girlfriend Bev in the passenger seat, and his best mate Matt with some Skipton bird in the back. He'd got his IPod plugged into the stereo with Wiz Khalifa blaring, all the better to drown out the noises from the rear.

The figure stumbling out into the road in front of him looked like it had just emerged from the Zombie Apocalypse. Its clothes were torn, and it was bloody and gruesomely pale. Paul slammed his foot on the brake and just managed to stop the car going into a skid. The figure... a man... he could see that now... felt its way round the bonnet of the car and to the side window, where it hammered with gory fists.

Shaking, Bev, wound down the window – just an inch. Ed stooped, sobbing, to peer into the car at her.

'Please help me,' he gasped over the racket of the music and the screaming of the unnamed girl in the back seat. 'I think I've killed my wife.'

Paul took in the grey and wild eyed look of him, the blood smears on the side window of his elderly Suzuki Swift, and the abject terror on his girlfriend's face. Without hesitation, he floored the accelerator and skidded away down the hill, leaving Ed running after them, pleading for them to come back.

He watched the desperate figure receding in his rear view mirror, then turned a corner and lost him. 'The minute you get a mobile signal,' he yelled at Bev. 'Call the freakin' police.'

-0-0-0-

At 5am, Ulrika found Jo in the Small Chapel. She was huddled in the middle of the front row of chairs, wrapped in her quilt, one solitary candle flickering on the altar in front of her.

Ulrika had grown accustomed to finding retreatants here. At first she'd thought that they must have sensed that the place was special – a 'thin' place, where the veil between heaven and earth was more permeable. But then she'd caught a particularly stressed company executive attempting a 3G Skype call and had discovered the secret of the mobile signal. She smiled sometimes at the many ways people were drawn to the holiest of places. And then she smiled at how far her beliefs had diverged from those of the church she had surrendered herself to, all those many years ago.

'How's the headache now?' she asked, sliding onto the seat next to Jo and making her jump.

'Almost gone.'

'Good!' Ulrika smiled. 'And Natalie? How is *she?*'

Jo looked down guiltily at her phone.

'I don't know,' she said, sheepishly. 'She texted last night, about 9.30, but, of course, I didn't get it then, so I didn't text back, and... I don't know... I can't put my finger on it... I just feel... *weird...* Like something's not okay.'

Ulrika nodded. She'd felt that all along. It was a relief to know that Jo, finally, was seeing beyond her shame, and sensing it too. 'What did she say in the text?' she asked.

'She said that she loves me. She misses me. She wants me to come home.'

'*Will* you?'

'I think I have to. I think it's time to face the music.'

Ulrika reached out and squeezed Jo's arm through the quilt. 'Go now,' she said quietly. 'It's time.'

Chapter Seventeen

At 6.30am, Jo stopped at a petrol station for a microwaved Breakfast Panini and Costa Express. The air was still dark and ice cold. Her breath billowed around her as she came out of the forecourt shop. Then her phone started vibrating in her pocket.

'Oh shit!' she cursed, juggling the cardboard Costa cup onto the floor and perching the Panini on top of it. She caught the call just in time to stop it going to voicemail.

'Hi?' she barked into the receiver. If this was a PPI, she was going to be seriously pissed off.

'Jo?' Anxiety crackled in Krystal's voice, making it louder than it would normally have been and scaring Jo half to death. All her irritation drained away. 'God, Krys. What's wrong?'

'Jo, you've gotta come home... now!'

'Why...? Look, I'm on my way, anyway. But what the hell's going on?'

'We're at the hospital.'

'What..? Who..? Who's we...? What's happening?'

On the other end of the line, Jo heard her sister-in-law draw a deep breath. 'I'm here with the kids. Nat's in surgery... There's been an accident.'

Jo felt sick as the anxiety she'd been feeling all night latched itself onto the words 'hospital', and 'surgery'. 'Is she gonna be alright?' she asked, not sure that she wanted to know.

'I don't know. She was in the car with Ed. They came off the road at Quarry Tops. She's smashed up pretty bad.'

Unbidden, Jo saw the road, the crash barriers, the sheer drop beyond. Her heart quaked as she pictured it.

'Where's Ed?' she asked, terrified.

There was a very long pause. And Jo felt the pre-emptive grief of losing them both.

Finally, Krystal spoke. 'He's at the police station,' she said. 'Look, Jo… just fucking shut up and get here as quick as you can, right? The kids need you.'

-0-0-0-

She found Krystal in A & E, by the 'Cold Drinks and Snacks' machine, bashing the glass with the heel of her hand.

'Bastard machine,' she snarled. *'It's stolen my money. And if I don't have chocolate, I'm gonna kill someone!'*

Jo didn't doubt it. She'd been on the receiving end of Krystal when she was hypoglycemic. She reached in her bag and produced a Twix.

'What's the latest?' she asked, as Krys ripped into the packaging.

The reply came through a mouthful of chocolate, biscuit and caramel. 'Nat's still in surgery,' she said. 'There's a bleed on her brain. She's got a broken pelvis. Her left foot's mangled. God knows the rest… They went straight over the edge… That 4x4 of Ed's is built like a tank, but it's not designed for *that* kind of a crash landing.'

Jo felt her legs weakening. She sat down on one of the grey plastic chairs beside the vending machine. Krystal sat beside her and offered her a bite of the Twix. 'Might help with the shock' she said.

Not if I'm sick, thought Jo. She shook her head. 'And Ed just walked out of it unscathed?' she asked.

'Not exactly "walked", more *crawled*, I think…. all the way up the edge of the quarry. He flagged a car down to get help. He's hurt, I'm sure. But he's nothing like as bad as Nat. You know how it is with drunks. They bloody bounce... Anyway, I imagine the police doctors will have patched him up by now.' She sounded grim and unforgiving. But then, Krys often sounded like that. And Jo knew how fond she actually had become of Ed.

'Where are the kids?' she asked.

'They're in the relatives' room... Look, Jo, are you okay taking over here? I've left Jorge with my new bloke, and they get on okay, but, I haven't known him long, and you can't get 'em police checked.'

Jo swallowed. 'If you'd prefer to stay, I can take over with Jorge,' she said.

Krystal gave her a disgusted look. 'Are you fucking crazy?' she demanded.

Jo had never realised till then that Krys knew their secret. It came as a shock. They'd always been so careful to hide it.

'How long have you known?' she asked.

'Jesus, Jo... since the kids were in nappies, at least. It's written all over the pair of you. Me and Andrew had a quid on whether you'd ever actually have the balls to tell him.... I guess I won that one.' She gave a funny, twisted little half smile as the loss hit her again and her eyes misted. 'We always figured that Ed knew too... Though maybe we were wrong on *that* score, eh?'

Jo stared at her. It seemed pointless and irrelevant somehow to tell Krys that they hadn't been lovers back then. In a strange kind of a way, anyway, she knew that they'd been lovers from the moment they met.

'Thank you,' she said.

Krys continued to look at her as if she'd gone crazy. 'Thank you for what?' she demanded.

Jo smiled and shook her head. She knew why Andy had loved this woman so.

'Thank you for not judging us,' she said, very quietly.

-0-0-0-

Jo stood back as Krystal hugged the kids goodbye. Alyssa had already hurled herself at her as she came into the room. She was red-eyed and guilty about her rudeness to her mum earlier in the day, and she'd held onto Jo as if she'd never let her go. Jake, was undemonstrative as ever, giving her one of his reticent sideways boy-hugs before turning and introducing his girlfriend, Tamzin, who she'd recognised immediately from Nat's description.

Now she felt Krystal's arms around her.

'I'll pick up Dottie on the way home,' she promised them all as she headed for the door. 'And you must phone me the minute there's any news.'

-0-0-0-

At 10.08am, Ed's father arrived to take the kids away.

Alyssa was asleep across two of the stained hospital chairs, her head in Jo's lap. Jake was sprawled with his legs stretched out in front of him, Tamzin snuggled into his side, her head against his shoulder. They were playing a game on his mobile phone, deep in their shared concentration on the small screen. Jo felt moved by their closeness, and relieved that the girl's parents had given her permission to stay. She thought that whatever happened next in this family's drama, Jake, at least, would not have to face it alone.

Mr Mason looked as if he'd dressed too quickly. One side of his shirt collar was tucked into his sweater. His thinning, grizzled hair looked uncombed. He had a navy blue anorak draped over his arm. He glanced coldly at Jo as he stepped into the room.

'I've come to take them home,' he said, nodding towards the children as if they were parcels in a depot.

Jo tensed and stopped stroking Alyssa's head. It was something that she'd always done for her, ever since she was a baby. Alyssa found it soothing when she was upset. But now, Arnold Mason's expression made it feel akin to some form of child abuse. Alyssa stirred, missing the soft, reassuring contact, and looked up sleepily to see her grandfather. She smiled as she struggled, yawning, into an upright position. 'Oh, hi Granddad,' she yawned. 'Is Dad here?'

Jake glanced up too. He loved his Granny Mason, but he'd never been more than polite with his grandfather. As a boy, he'd always come up much more sharply than his sister against the cold rules and conventions of the man. Jo noticed that he shrank away from Tamzin under his grandfather's stern gaze too, sitting up more stiffly so that they were no longer touching.

'He's at *our* house.' He'd always had a harsh voice. It was even harsher now.

Jo wondered if Ed had been cleared, or simply bailed. Either way, it seemed that he had returned to his childhood home. The place where all of this had begun.

'Is he okay?' she asked.

'He's with his mother,' he said, without looking at her. 'Alyssa, get your coat.'

She was torn. Jo saw her glance in the direction of Jake, then back at her grandfather. 'But Granddad...'

'Jacob, you too... I'll drop your...' he looked down his nose at the short skirt, thick tights and cherry red Doc Martens of Jake's girlfriend, '... *friend*...' His voice oozed contempt that must have been the final straw for his grandson, 'home on the way.'

Jake missed just one beat. His eyes narrowed and he looked down and away from his grandfather, his hair flopping over his face. 'Get stuffed!' he muttered, under his breath.

The old man's jaw tensed and Jo wondered if he would have lashed out if they'd been alone. She saw his hand on the door handle, tightening into a fist and wondered if he had, in fact, frequently hit Jake - Ed too, in his youth.

'Jake!' she remonstrated. 'Don't talk like that to your grandfather!'

Jake's chin tilted ominously. She knew that look… had known it ever since he was a toddler. 'I'm not going anywhere until I know Mum's okay,' he said.

She knew that would be his last word on the subject.

Tamzin squeezed his arm. Clearly he'd found himself a cheerleader there.

Alyssa glanced from her grandfather, to Jake, to Jo. She was tired. She wanted to please everyone. And she'd always been 'Daddy's Girl'.

Jake understood. There was that kind of telepathy between them. 'You go see Dad,' he said. 'I'll phone you the minute there's any news here.'

Alyssa reached for her coat. She looked tiny and bewildered. She hugged Jo and Jake and Tamzin, reluctant to leave them all.

But her grandfather was implacable. He put his hand on her back to guide her in front of him through the door. He cast a vicious look over his shoulder at Jake as he followed her. Then he turned on Jo. '*I'll* be looking after the business for the next few weeks,' he snapped. 'It goes without saying that you're fired. I'll send one of the lads round to collect your laptop and anything else that's ours. Don't even *think* about asking for a reference.'

Jo didn't actually blame him. She nodded, showing that she understood.

He was halfway out of the room when he turned to face her again.

'My son dragged you out of the gutter,' he snarled. 'I wish to God he'd never bothered.'

As the door slammed, Jo could have sworn that she heard Jake mutter the word *'Tosser!'*

But she didn't tell him off. She was too busy absorbing the fact that the old man had never once asked after the well-being of his daughter-in-law.

Chapter Eighteen

Jake was asleep. He was snuggled in Tamzin's arms. She twisted her fingers softly in his long hair, her own streaked blonde locks tumbling over him as she leant to kiss his head.

In the Family Room, people had come, and waited, and gone. There was a thin faced mother with a toddler who screamed constantly, rubbing at his face with tiny fists and smearing his cheeks and hair and the upholstery of the battered chairs with bubbling candles of snot. They overlapped with an Asian family with women in headscarves and men in traditional shalwar kameez. The women had wailed just outside the door when the doctor came to give his news, and Jo saw Jake's face freeze at the sound of their grief. And then there had been a solitary old man in a sports jacket and grey M&S slacks, sitting stiffly, wringing a white cotton handkerchief in his hands, sipping from a plastic cup, tears brimming and dribbling from time to time in his rheumy eyes. He drew them into conversation for a while, distracting them, before he too was called out, never to return.

And now the three of them were alone, and Jo was wondering how any of them would ever manage to drag themselves on through life if Natalie didn't survive.

Tamzin looked across at her and smiled.

'You mustn't worry,' she said, quietly, for fear of waking Jacob. 'At least, not about you and Mrs Mason…. I mean, it's worrying about Mrs M…. And it's worrying about your job…. But not the other stuff. We all know about that. And it's okay… we're all cool with it.'

Jo was starting to wonder why they'd ever bothered to try to keep it secret. First Krys, and now the kids…

Clearly their love had been proclaiming itself in flashing neon lights for years. She was grateful to Tamzin for telling her though. It struck her that this sensible young woman was only a year younger than *she'd* been when she first met Ed. She remembered how everything had seemed so black and white then, before life had introduced her to all its many shades of grey.

'Even Alyssa?' she asked. It was Alyssa who worried her the most…. Well, after Ed, of course.

Tamzin smiled reassuringly, 'Even Alyssa,' she said.

When the nurse appeared in the doorway she made them both jump.

They held their breath. Jake stirred in Tamzin's lap and looked up, rubbing his hair out of his eyes.

'She's out of theatre,' she announced. 'The doctor will be along to see you very soon.'

Chapter Nineteen

Jo lay with her head against Nat's waist. It was hard to know where to lie, where to touch, with the tubes and the bandages and the cages protecting her.

The ward was quiet, except for the steady beeping of the machines. The nurses had been and gone, and were murmuring together quietly at their station beyond the window, behind their desks and computers.

There was the faint, alcoholic smell of hospital hand gel. And there were other people, other beds, each the centre of someone's universe.

Jo watched Nat's heartbeat on the monitor in front of her, her eyes growing blurry. She'd given up trying to think of things to say other than 'I'm sorry.' She'd never been all that good with words, and they failed her now.

It had been twenty three hours, 'No more than two visitors at a time'. They took turns. Tamzin had gone in with Jake. And Alyssa had been escorted by her granny, who had studiously ignored Jo, making it clear just how irrevocably the family had closed ranks against her.

Ed didn't come. Maybe he wasn't allowed to. Krys waited for news at home.

Jo's eyes were heavy. She allowed them to close.

And then, something like a light breeze ruffled her hair, and she struggled back into wakefulness, hearing her name.

'Jo?'

She looked up.

Nat's eyes were flickering open, her hand reaching out for her.

Jo caught it, held it to her cheek and kissed it. She hardly dared to breathe, as she turned, and called, panicking suddenly, for a nurse.

Nat shook her head, disorientated.

'I dreamt that you'd gone away,' she said.

Tears ran down Jo's cheeks, over Nat's fingers.

'I'm *so* sorry!' she whispered.

Behind her, she could hear the hasty footsteps of the nursing staff, coming to check on their patient.

Nat closed her eyes.

'Thank you for coming back to me,' she murmured, as she drifted back into sleep.

Chapter Twenty

July 2015

Sister Ulrika stood at the window of her room and looked down over the colourful sweep of the retreat centre gardens, which were always open to the public from Easter till October.

It had been a strange summer so far. Cloudy a lot of the time, with thunderstorms that rattled through the Yorkshire fells like giants in a tenpin bowling alley, bringing torrential rain and hail that clattered so hard against the stained glass of the chapel, she'd feared it might cave in under the assault and hurl lethal apostolic shards over the celebrants at Mass.

Today, though, it was sunny and warm, and she opened the ancient mullioned window, contentedly breathing in the scent of jasmine, and listening to the gentle buzz of bees as she leaned out, taking her weight on her elbows and smiling up into the sun that warmed her cheeks and eyelids and tempted her to close her eyes and just drift off for a while.

She may have even done so, losing a few minutes, before the faint hum of voices disturbed her reverie, and she looked down to see the small group of teenagers walking through the rose garden with a slightly manic looking curly haired black dog. They were like so many of the young people she saw each summer, dragged there, for the most part, by their parents on drives through the Dales. There were three girls and a long-haired lad who reminded her of pictures she'd seen on T-shirts of a group called... she struggled a moment then remembered the name, quite proud to be 'with it'.... 'The Ramones'.

She recognised them from Jo's emails - Jacob and Tamzin, Alyssa and her best friend, Roxanne, and Dottie, of course, described all too accurately by her name. Jo had joked that she'd had to get a people-carrier to accommodate the expanding family on days out. And Ulrika thought of how Jo had half raised that family with Nat while their father made every excuse he could to stay away.

She wondered how much effort Ed made to see them now. Jo didn't say, still loyal to the man who had been her best friend for almost thirty years. She *did* say that she missed him. And that he'd been saved from jail by Nat's refusal to remember the circumstances of the accident. The lads at work were chauffeuring him until he could get his driver's licence back. And the local divorcees were already circling him, sympathetic, in the main, to someone who, in a moment of madness, may have tried to murder a cheating spouse.

Eagerly, Ulrika scanned beyond the youngsters, over the herb garden, the beech hedge, and down the driveway. She was looking for Jo, whose pain had reminded her so deeply of her own. And she located her, finally, by the gardener's cottage. It seemed strange to see her in a loose, pale lilac T-shirt, cut off white jeans and sandals, when, in her memory, she'd been bundled in thick sweaters, blankets, and during the migraine incident, that threadbare, sage green continental quilt. Ulrika knew that, in her youth, she would have been hopelessly drawn to this tall, blonde, slightly playful looking woman. It was a relief to feel only the slightest pang of wistfulness for that now, experiencing something akin to motherliness and a sense of joy that Jo looked tanned and healthy and happy with her new life - even with her new work, running the cleaning company she'd started in February, that may, someday, earn her enough to buy the 'Jag' she'd always longed for but wasn't really all that bothered about anymore.

By Jo's side, struggling on the sharp rutted incline of the drive, but determined to walk, Ulrika saw the dark haired, beautiful woman who had been both cause and cure for so much of Jo's pain. She noticed that she had chosen to wear red and navy and white, just as she had on the night Jo first met her at the tennis club. And that she had slipped her arm through Jo's, to support herself physically as well as emotionally as she battled up the hill. She saw how painful her progress was, and prayed that time would continue to heal her. She saw how Jo leaned over and kissed her very gently on the cheek, whispering something encouraging to her. She had never doubted the love between them. But she hadn't anticipated anything quite as peaceful as this. It was good to see how well they fitted, at last.

Ulrika felt the breath catch in her throat, as she watched them together, and remembered her own, too brief happiness with Florrie. But then Jo glanced up and spotted her and said something to Natalie who looked up too, bestowing the stunning full-force of her smile. So she pulled herself back into the present and waved down to them, smiling too.

And then, the kids were all jumping up and down and waving and shouting excitedly up to her and Dottie was running round in circles and yapping just because it felt good.

And wondering what cake the kitchens would have prepared today, Ulrika stepped back into the shadow of her room and set off downstairs to greet her guests.

Printed in Great Britain
by Amazon